THE WHOLE STUPID WAY WE ARE

THE WHOLE STUPID WAY WE ARE

N. GRIFFIN

Atheneum Books for Young Readers
NEW YORK LONDON TORONTO SYDNEY NEW DELHI

atheneum
ATHENEUM BOOKS FOR YOUNG READERS
An imprint of Simon & Schuster Children's Publishing Division
1230 Avenue of the Americas, New York, New York 10020

This book is a work of fiction. Any references to historical events, real people, or real places are used fictitiously. Other names, characters, places, and events are products of the author's imagination, and any resemblance to actual events or places or persons, living or dead, is entirely coincidental.

Book design by Sonia Chaghatzbanian
The text for this book is set in ITC Veljovic Std.
Manufactured in the United States of America
First Atheneum Books for Young Readers
paperback edition February 2014
10 9 8 7 6 5 4 3 2 1
The Library of Congress has cataloged the hardcover edition as follows:
Griffin, N.
The whole stupid way we are / N. Griffin.—1st ed.
p. cm.
Summary: During a cold winter in Maine, fifteen-year-old Dinah sets off a heart-wrenching chain of events when she tries to help best friend and fellow misfit Skint deal with problems at home, including a father who is suffering from early onset dementia.
ISBN 978-1-4424-3155-3 (hardcover) — ISBN 978-1-4424-3158-4 (eBook)
[1. Best friends—Fiction. 2. Friendship—Fiction. 3. Family problems—Fiction. 4. Maine—Fiction.] I. Title.
PZ7.G88135934Wh 2013
[Fic]—dc23
2012002595
ISBN 978-1-4424-3156-0 (paperback)

FOR TOAB AND K

THE WHOLE
STUPID WAY WE ARE

ONE

Skint's in the Pit because of Dinah. So she figures she better get cracking and effect his speedy release.

She's lurking in the janitor's closet, waiting for everybody else to leave. From here she has a clear view of the Pit—otherwise known as the Aile Quarry High School detention room—located diagonally across the hallway. The Main Office is just a bit farther along past the lockers. So from here Dinah can keep an eye on things. She can plot. Strategize.

She opens the door a crack and peeks out, even though it's a risk with the hallway full of screaming, just-released kids. She needs the air. Between the reek of the custodian's old mop water and the fact that she is all suited up in her parka and gloves, she's about to suffocate. Carrying her coat isn't an option; it is freezing outside with about a foot and a half of snow on the ground, and she can't count on having time to put on her coat if she winds up having to run.

Let's get a move on, she thinks at her peers as they bang about in their lockers. What's taking them all so long? If she and Skint were free to go, they'd have been out the door before the final bell even stopped ringing. Today is the last day of school before February break and Dinah is so glad for nine days free of this place she could pop.

At last the final bunch of kids bashes its lockers shut and boils out the door. Dinah creeps stealthily forth. She's nearly to the Pit when the hair of the teacher on duty appears in the door window. Whose? It's not gray lunch-lady hair (which is lucky, given their crime), but it's not the thin, damp strands of the dean of discipline, either. Wait. It's better. In fact, it's the best AQHS could offer in this instance. It's the frazzled, dyed locks of Ms. Dugan.

Ms. Dugan is the gym teacher and has known Dinah since Dinah was a tiny kid. Ms. Dugan loves her. Ms. Dugan knows what's what. Ms. Dugan can be counted on. Dinah can taste their freedom already. She slips around the doorjamb, careful to avoid being spotted by the Office.

Ms. Dugan glances up. "Dinah Beach, you old cupcake," she says, and turns back to her newspaper. Skint, the only inmate in the room, snaps to attention from his spot at the far desk by the window. Excellent. Behind him the snowy gray trees at the edge of the playing fields bend and sway.

"Hullo, Ms. Dugan," says Dinah. "I didn't know you had detention duty."

"I don't." Ms. Dugan is fifty with a fast-talking gravel voice, New England flat with a lot of glottal stops. And can she ever tell a story. She looks out at a person from narrowed eyes, slits out her cigarette smoke, and lets a body have it. The cigarette thing bothers Dinah but Ms. Dugan has tried to quit a million times and just can't, even though fitness is practically her middle name. She has a killer bod to show for it, too, which makes her the subject of a lot of non-sports-oriented conversation around AQHS. Some of which is started by Skint.

"I let the kids off track practice today so I figured I better offer to take over detention. Keep the first cancer stick of the afternoon at bay for a while." Ms. Dugan fixes Dinah with a look. "So what brings you here, Beach? Did you want to add a little finishing touch to this?"

She waggles a piece of paper at Dinah. On it, a hastily drawn but very sinister cartoon bird wields a knife and fork in each wing, an unhappy woman speared on the end of each utensil. The bird is recognizable as the execrable Turliff the Turkey, the Aile Quarry High School mascot, and the women as the two lunch ladies who run the school cafeteria. *LET THE TABLES BE TURNED*, thunders Turliff from a speech bubble jagging out from his beak.

"It was all my idea," says Dinah. "Skint shouldn't even be in here. I madc him draw it."

"I wanted to," says Skint from the back of the room. "I was honored."

"I don't even get it," says Ms. Dugan. "What the hell is it supposed to mean?"

"What do you mean, what does it mean?" Skint cries, raking his fingers through his dark hair. "What's not clear about the fundamental hypocrisy it illuminates?" He removes his hands, but his dark hair remains in raked formation, poking out all over.

"What fundamental hypocrisy?"

"Everybody's! The cafeteria's!" Dinah cries. "They have that huge banner of Turliff hanging over the steam table in there and they were serving *turkey tacos* for lunch yesterday! What were we supposed to do?!"

"About what?" asks Ms. Dugan.

"About the cafeteria's promotion of the symbolic cannibalism of its students!" Skint bangs on his desk. "We're holding a mirror up to them! And surprise, surprise, they don't like what they see!"

"Pipe down," says Ms. Dugan. "I don't want the Office in here."

"I don't either," says Dinah.

"Those two ladies don't order the food, you guys," says Ms. Dugan. "They just serve it."

"Well," says Dinah, "someone should be on the job."

Skint's skinny frame slumps over the desk. "Nobody in this town cares about anything but winning sporting events." He stops and sits up straight again. "I mean, I know you work hard coaching, Ms. Dugan—"

Ms. Dugan waves away his apology.

"Nobody pays attention, is what I mean," says Skint. "Nobody *notices*."

"We do," says Dinah.

"Barely," says Skint. "Who's wearing her skirt backwards? Again?"

"That's on purpose, jerk," says Dinah. "The zipper looks ridiculous in the front. And that's some way to talk to someone who is risking punishment by—"

Ms. Dugan raises her hand. "Don't say it. I don't want to know what you're up to. Speaking of punishment, Dinah, why aren't you in here, too? This stunt has you written all over it."

"I know," says Dinah. "But I did my time yesterday. When they caught us. Skint couldn't."

"Why not?"

Skint shrugs. "Appointment."

"Your dad?" asks Ms. Dugan.

Dinah freezes. *Oh, no,* she thinks. Why can't people stop asking Skint about his dad?

"Can we go?" she interrupts. But Skint has already turned away and is looking out the window. "The whole thing was *my* fault, Ms. Dugan."

"I said don't *involve* me, Dinah," says Ms. Dugan. "How'd you get caught, anyway?"

Dinah shrugs. "Skint's drawing style is pretty distinctive. And everybody knows we are always in cahoots." This is true. She and Skint are in the ninth grade. They have known each other since they were tiny, before they were even five. Skint moved away to Kentucky when they were in kindergarten, but he came back again in sixth grade and he and Dinah have been best friends ever since. "We barely got all the posters taped up before they hauled us in and yelled at us and forced us to apologize."

"But you know what the worst of it was?" Skint asks, turning back to the conversation. "It wasn't even what we were saying in the cartoon that made them mad! It was because Dinah snuck into the teachers' lounge and used the copier. The principal said he punished us because we *wasted paper*."

"Well, I've seen better work from you," says Ms. Dugan, squinting at the drawing.

"Ugh!" Skint drops his head into his hands.

Dinah clears her throat and looks steadily at Ms. Dugan, who looks steadily back at her.

"What would you do if it wasn't me in here?" Ms. Dugan asks.

Dinah shakes her head.

"Tell me," says Ms. Dugan.

"You said not to involve you," says Dinah.

"Yeah," says Skint, lifting his head. "We don't want to make you an accessory after the fact."

Or before, thinks Dinah. She has to fish Skint out of detention kind of regularly, and it's nice to have a plan in reserve. He is usually Pitted for skipping or excessive absence. He is very organized, though, and always manages to keep his attendance just above the number of days that would mean repeating a class or a grade or, God help him, cause some guidance counselor to take action and call home.

"Come on," says Ms. Dugan. "You can tell me. I won't take this duty again for months."

Skint meets Dinah's eye and shrugs.

"Fine," says Dinah. "Throw a soda bottle against the lockers. Teacher comes out, I slip in. Then me and Skint out the window."

"Out the *window*?"

"It's just a three-foot drop, Ms. D.," says Skint.

Ms. Dugan puts the drawing down. Then she picks up her newspaper again and snaps it open in front of her face. "Do what you have to," she murmurs, staring intently at an article. "However. If you get caught, I know nothing. I saw nothing. And I do not help you. At all."

But Skint is already up and out of his chair as Dinah skims across the room and grabs his backpack. Skint flings opens the window and Dinah tosses the backpack through and then they hurl themselves up and over the ledge, and *bam*—out they pop onto the snow below.

"Thank you!" Dinah calls back to Ms. Dugan. Skint says nothing, but only because he's glanced back through the window and is distracted by the sight of Ms. Dugan's considerable knockers rearing forth from under the edge of her paper.

"What is the matter with that stupid school?" mutters Dinah as they huff across the frozen field toward the road. "The whole thing with cannibalism is that you're supposed to eat your enemy's heart, not your own, right?"

"If I thought it was a sly commentary on the fetishization of basketball in this town, I'd have been all over it," says Skint. "But no. Just more Aile Quarry witlessness." His voice chitters in the cold and his knuckles are purple. Skint refuses to wear a coat this winter, or even a hat. No mittens, no gloves, no scarf. They irritate him, he says, but that doesn't make sense. This is Maine. It is February and very cold.

"You need a coat," says Dinah.

"You need a brain," says Skint.

"Shut up," says Dinah. "I am stuffed full of brains."

"Tchah," says Skint. "You haven't even cracked the cover of that *Disposable People* book and I gave it to you a week ago. It's important, Dinah! There are more slaves in the world now than there were before the Civil War! And it's our own stupid fault. All people want to do is buy shit. For cheap. And who pays? The workers!"

"I have been busy," says Dinah evasively. "Planning our social lives."

"Inasmuch," Skint mutters. They're on the main road now, passing all the tiny old houses that have been turned into real estate offices and hair cutters and pet grooming businesses. Clumps of their classmates gather in various parking lots along the way, smoking, laughing, kicking sideways at each other's rear ends. All of the kids wear boots and various kinds of jeans. Dinah herself never wears jeans. Pajamas or stripy tights or, if none of her skirts are clean, a pair of her dad's old tweed trousers rolled over at the waist so they stay up. But never jeans. Skint shares none of her views about teen fashion, however, and is himself clad today in a pair of those tight black jeans that make people's legs look like a couple of earwig pincers.

A couple of girls glance at Dinah as she passes. Laley and Sue, who've been in her class since kindergarten.

Sue mutters something to Laley and Laley laughs. Skint eyes Dinah and bashes her shoulder with his. "Remind me what's on the docket, Dinah von Beachface."

Dinah stops short, so Skint, who has continued on, is forced to wheel around and stop, too.

"I hate when you do that," he says. "Drives me up a wall."

"What's on the *docket*?" Dinah cries. "What's the matter with you? How could you forget? Why do you think I went to all that trouble to fish you out of the Pit?"

"Just tell me, dork."

"*Walter*, Skint! Walter is what is on the docket!"

"Walter!" cries Skint, slapping his forehead with his palm. "How could I forget!"

"Exactly," says Dinah. This evening is slated to be the latest installment in what Dinah and Skint call their "Fantastic or Excruciating?" adventures—FoEs, for short. An FoE is an entertainment where you can't tell beforehand whether it will be fabulous and surreal or only just a misery-making fiasco that will make you ache for the performers involved because it is all so awful and the performers are unaware. Or maybe they are aware. And then it is even worse. Dangling in the balance between possible delight and possible agony has become a habit Dinah and Skint can't break, and Dinah spends a lot of time combing the papers and the Internet for promising events for them to attend.

Two weeks ago, for example, they went to an exhibit created by a local biologist that cast visitors in the role of dirt passing through the magnified cloaca of a giant earthworm (Fantastic). The month before that, they saw a group of grim-faced former Girl Scouts, now grown, play popular tunes with spoons on glasses of water (Excruciating). And before that it had been a middle-aged couple who flamenco-danced in full costume, accompanied by their children on too-big instruments (Double Fantastic).

Tonight's FoE, however, is Walter. The show is billed as *Walter the Dancing Donkey*, and Dinah and Skint have been looking forward to it for weeks. It's being held at the St. Francis Church in the town center. HE DANCES! the posters promise, and also music. But Dinah is terrified that, instead of the hoped-for sonatinas on a hurdy-gurdy and medicine-show patter, it'll only be a spirit-crushed donkey made to stand on his hind legs for cash. She can't help it, though, and neither can Skint. They have to go.

"But it doesn't start until seven," says Skint. "So why did you have to spring me? Not that I'm not grateful," he hastens to add.

"Skint! So we can *spy*," says Dinah. "What if the man in charge of Walter is a jerk to him? What if he keeps him in a too-small cage and only lets him out for the performance? What if he doesn't feed him? I want to go over to the church and catch him unawares! See what Walter's life is really like!"

Dinah always frets like this before FoEs. Skint is used to it.

"And what're you going to do if he's a jerk?" he asks. "Punch him?"

"Punching," says Dinah, "would bc a start."

"I think if he's cruel we should just steal Walter and rear him in your home. Think of it: hide-and-seek in the house with a donkey! Beagie would love it."

Dinah's baby brother, Beagie, dearly loves horses, and she imagines he would love an indoor donkey even more. The image of Beagie scampering away from a counting-to-ten donkey makes Dinah almost hope that she will be forced to steal Walter.

"Well, let's go, then," she says.

"I can't," says Skint. "Sorry, Dinah B. I have to go home."

"Skint! We planned!"

"I can't," says Skint again. "Besides, you don't even know if they're over there yet. They may be staying somewhere else."

Good point. "But—"

"Look," says Skint, "if the guy seems like an ass—"

"That's a horrible pun," Dinah interrupts.

"But fully intended," says Skint. "Anyway, if we sense something's up with him during the performance, we can reconnoiter afterwards. Take action. Or you can do it on your own now and report back to me."

"No. I don't want to go by myself. I need an accomplice." Dinah is deflated. "Can you at least hang out a little now?"

"No," says Skint abruptly. "I told you. I have stuff I have to do."

"Like what?"

But Skint doesn't answer her. "I'll meet you there at seven," he says, and slouches off toward home, hands in his pockets, shoulders hunched against the cold, while Dinah stares after him, wishing she could convince him to put on a stupid coat.

TWO

It is a quarter to seven and Dinah and Skint are waiting outside the old stone church. It is freezing out here, ice-crumpled walkways and snow-covered trees. Dinah bounces and rubs her arms. "Why hasn't my dad opened the doors?" Dinah's father is church warden, and part of his job is making sure the building is ready for evening events.

"He'll open them," says Skint, stamping his feet against the cold. "It's early yet. Give the crowd time to gather."

"What if no one else comes?" Dinah worries.

That has been the other concern of theirs, countering their hopes about the show. And given that more than once they have been fully one-half of an audience, or close to it, it's a valid concern. Even the best possible music and a loving donkey caretaker won't help if the hall is empty and the donkey made to feel redundant.

"Well, *we've* come," says Skint, though he does not look optimistic either. Dinah cranes her neck and looks down the street, hoping to see throngs of people picking their way under the lanternlike streetlights that bow their heads over Main Street's curb. It's not like there is anything else to do in Aile Quarry. The nearest movie theater is half an hour away and only has two screens, both of which are always dedicated to showing the class of movie Skint shorthands as "monster love stiletto." And if people have already seen what's on offer there, what's left to do on a Friday night but see Walter?

"But if it turns out to be just us," Skint continues, "we'll really sock it to 'em with the clapping." He breaks off, head cocked to the door. "Listen!" he says. "There's bustling within."

Dinah shakes her head no.

"That's not attendees. It's just Bernadine and the rest of the Girls' Friendly."

The Girls' Friendly Society is kind of a service club at St. Francis, and Bernadine is its leader. Bernadine's old mother, Mrs. Chatham, will be in there, too, fluttering about and unhelpful. Ms. Dugan is also a longstanding member of the Friendly and will be the one doing the brunt of the work, bellying coffee urns and snacks onto the table. Dinah knows this scene well. She has been a member of the Girls' Friendly since she was five. She is its fourth fourth or its fourth fifth, depending on who you ask.

Dinah herself refuses to acknowledge any choice but the latter.

Usually Dinah would be in there as well, folding programs preparatory to passing them out. But this time she is slated for cleanup instead. Skint will clean, too, but he will not be thanked for it. Skint, the fifth fifth of the Girls' Friendly (depending on who you ask), is willing to wear a skirt to appease those who feel strongly about the "girl" part but can do nothing to appease those who might question his very membership. Such people would have staunch and unflagging support from Bernadine.

It was maybe a little bit cheating of Dinah to sign up for cleanup. She cleans the church every Saturday anyway (Skint, too, of course), and she is planning to leave tonight's mess for the morning.

Look at Skint now, stone-cheeked and pale. How can she trick him into wearing her mittens? Dinah has planned about this many times before. But her mittens are pink and he knows her too well. *Please,* she thinks, *just open the doors.*

Whoom.

The church doors are flung wide at last, and yellow light trickles out in a puff of warmth. *Thank you,* thinks Dinah. Not thank you for this, though:

"Dinah Beach!"

A terrible voice.

"Why aren't you helping with setup?" Bernadine is fifty-eight with no-nonsense hair.

"We signed up for cleaning," Dinah reminds her, but Bernadine is already all over the plural.

"It's a big job for JUST ONE PERSON."

"Skint is helping, too," says Dinah grittily.

"As befits a member of the Friendly," Skint agrees, gazing steadily at Bernadine.

Bernadine snarls. Dinah scowls.

They wait.

"We're here for the show, not the Friendly," says Dinah finally. "Can we come the rest of the way in?"

Bernadine steps to one side. "Where's your coat," she mutters, looking over Skint's head. "It's not even twenty degrees."

"I'm fine," Skint tells her, but Bernadine is already turning back to the foyer.

The Girls' Friendly is no hotbed of teen activity, and obviously Bernadine is no barrel of fun, either. So why does Dinah stick with that club?

Guilt is one reason. There used to be more people in the Friendly, more girls Dinah's age. But the Friendly has lost a lot of momentum. People keep growing up and getting bored, or dying. So Dinah stays partly because she'd hate it if Ms. Dugan, for one, believed Dinah thought her so boring that Dinah couldn't bear to spend one measly evening a week with her at the Friendly. Ms. Dugan's a grand gal, and Mrs. Chatham is nice, too. And finding new members has been impossible. When Dinah was in elementary school, Bernadine and Mrs. Chatham were always asking her if she didn't know a girl or two. Dinah never did. Most girls besides Dinah were interested in other things: school, famous people, hair and one another. They were not interested in Dinah, except as occasional gossip fodder, and they were certainly not interested in scrubbing the St. Francis rectory toilets or helping old people address their Christmas cards, which is the kind of thing people do in the Friendly.

But if she's honest, even with more members, Dinah could never stop going to the Friendly. What with one thing and another, her participation in the Friendly has become something of a long-term FoE.

"What do you do in that club anyway?" Skint asked her once on their way home from school almost a year ago.

"Projects for helping." Dinah was crouched beside

him, working a pebble loose from her shoe. "We eat a lot, too."

"So you are in it for the snacks?"

"No, jerk," said Dinah, scowling up at him from her shoe-fixing stoop.

Skint hesitated. "Is it because of your grandma?"

Dinah said nothing. Skint nudged her toe with his.

"Is it some mentoring thing?" he asked. "Do all three of those ladies mentor you?"

"Yes," said Dinah, who often felt mentored to within an inch of her life. "Older members are supposed to mentor the younger ones."

Skint shivered. "Still," he said, "that's good that you do that. My dad used to say everybody should do something to help other people."

Dinah paused at Skint's mention of his dad. "Hey," she said, placing the pebble from her shoe carefully on the toe of his boot. "You should come with me next time."

"Dude, I'm a boy."

"But you are Friendly to Girls," Dinah argued, "and besides, they are always after me to bring in the next generation. Come!"

"Would I have to mentor you?" Skint asked.

"Shut up," says Dinah.

"You shut up," said Skint. "Fine. Count me in. A satisfied stomach and altruism in one fell swoop."

So Skint came. Bernadine did not acknowledge Skint then, nor has she since. Nor does she permit him to speak in the meetings. But he has not been barred outright from coming.

"Why does he want to hang out with a bunch of old ladies, anyway?" Dinah overheard Bernadine shout to Dinah's mother. "With his father needing so—with that whole situation going on, can't his own mother use his help at home?"

"Oh, Bernadine. Why do you think Dinah brings him?"

Now Mrs. Chatham appears behind Bernadine in the foyer and stands helplessly next to the table with a bowl of snack mix in her arms. Her hair is sausaged into its customary curls.

"Lemme," says Skint, and takes the bowl from her hands.

"You are a good child," says Mrs. Chatham, beaming. Bernadine snorts.

"Not really," says Skint. "Just good at snack placement."

Dinah knows Bernadine is extra cranky because of the show itself. ("Animals in church!" Bernadine shouted at the last Girls' Friendly meeting.—"Well, what do you think *people* are? Just with less fur and more prevarication."—"Dinah, you grow more peculiar every year."—"That was Skint, Bernadine!"—But

Bernadine dismissed them: "Good-bye, Girls, I'll see you next week!")

Mr. Beach, Dinah's father, is the one who arranged for the donkey ("What more fitting event for a church called Saint Francis?" he'd cried), but he won't be able to enjoy it. His role at the church tonight is double: He is choirmaster as well as warden and it's essential that his choir rehearse—with only a week left before their Evensong performance and the music so hard, they can't afford to miss a single practice.

Dinah's father hates his choir, but he can't stop trying to improve them.

So Bernadine is not only peeved that Mr. Beach booked the act but also that he is not available to manage the donkey. And forget about the pastor, elderly and kind and in bed nights by eight. Things always fall to Bernadine.

"Can we go in to where the donkey is?" Dinah asks Bernadine. Maybe she can get an eyeful of his living conditions before the show after all. "And have you seen my dad?"

"No and yes," says Bernadine. "But your father is busy. You let him alone." Bernadine gets this way about Mr. Beach. Once, at a bean supper, Dinah saw her trying to cut his meat. "The show is in the basement. You wait until I say you can go down." She strides off, looking for people to boss.

"Grr to Bernadine," says Dinah to Skint. "I'm going to tell everybody about how her toenails have gone black."

"Be fair," says Skint. "You know she paints them that way. Look!" He gestures to the doors. "More people are coming."

Dinah looks round and is cheered. Three more people! One is trying to pour himself coffee, but Bernadine's on the job. ("Intermission only!"—"I'm sorry. Shall I pour it back in?")

"Let's go." Skint tugs her toward the basement steps. The basement is the smaller of the two gathering spaces in the church, but Dinah supposes the show's down there because people worried about the donkey falling through the floor. She is not sure what donkeys weigh, but this church is old and needs a lot of shoring up. The floors in the big room have dips in them that puddle after a rain or a thaw. It's hard to imagine those dips holding up under a donkey.

"Bernadine says not yet," Dinah reminds him. The choir's rehearsal is starting; the unmistakable sounds of Mrs. Wattle's warm-up are coming from within the big room.

Skint doesn't answer.

Dinah looks over her shoulder to where he is looking. *Oh. Ms. Dugan.* Her sweater is particularly fitted. "You look insane," she tells Skint. "You've got an enormous chunk of hair flapping over your temple."

"You look insane," Skint tells Dinah, "because you are." And he propels her toward the steps, where Mrs. Chatham stands primly at the ready.

"Program, Skint, dear?" she asks.

"Thanks," says Skint, and takes two.

"Not *YET*, Mother!" shouts Bernadine. "I said to hold on to the programs until I give the signal!"

"Oh, dear!"

But Dinah seizes Skint by the wrist, and down the steps they go anyway. Dinah stops midway and turns around to face him.

"The donkey!" she cries. "How will he get down these steps!"

"Bulkhead from outside, brain trust. That ramp that leads down."

At the front of the room is the donkey. He is parked no more than three feet from the first row of seats, barrel-chested and still. A rope tethers him to a post set in a concrete block in the middle of the floor, even though he doesn't look like a running-away kind of donkey.

Dinah squeezes Skint's bicep as they sink into their seats.

"Look how he blinks," she whispers. From this close comes a puff of his breath. Dinah is desperate to touch his soft, velvety nose.

Skint nods.

Dinah breathes and breathes. She is sorry for her dad he's not here.

Overhead comes the tramp of many feet. Dinah wheels hopefully round.

Look at her, thinks Skint, *her eyes all shining with hope.* Dinah acts like she's ten. She's a certifiable nut.

If anyone is an asshole to her, he'll beat them until they bleed.

Okay. Maybe not beat.

But he will, at the very least, express himself firmly. Tersely, even. While backing away.

Maybe a sucker punch or two before he runs.

Skint shakes his head no. "It's not audience members," he says. "Only the choir. Won't that sound great once the Wattle gets going. Choir upstairs while the donkey's down—who thought that was a good idea?"

"It's my dad's fault," says Dinah. "He forgot to consult the master schedule."

Kind but disorganized, that is Mr. Beach.

"Here," says Skint. "Have a program."

There are more clompings now as a few people come down the stairs, soft mutterings as they settle. Dinah is pleased that more people have come, even as she scans the stage area for signs of impending awful. "What if it's like that dog show?" she whispers to Skint. Last summer at the state fair she and Skint were seduced by a sign that said DOG SHOW! WITH RIDES! But it turned out to be two hours of dogs limp on leashes, their movements sad and low. The whole time, Dinah cried. An Awful FoE. Excruciating beyond belief.

"Shush," says Skint. "It's starting."

Someone comes out to the front. It isn't the donkey man. It's Bernadine, come to introduce the donkey. "Good evening," she says, hatchet-faced and peevy. "Welcome to Saint Francis. It is my duty to introduce to you—"

"It ought to be her *pleasure*!"

"Shush!"

"—and Walter, his dancing donkey."

Dinah swivels around. The audience, swelled to thirteen people, has smiles on its faces, but they are the kind of smiles people wear when they are ready to make jokes and be clever. And look back there. It's the Vole. Also in ninth grade, part of the cigarette, rear-kicking crowd. What is he doing here? Dinah wouldn't have thought he'd go in for this kind of thing. Those contemptuous eyebrows. That stupid smacking gum. Or it's probably tobacco, knowing the Vole. But their town is so small, and again, what else is there to do when you can't drive? Drink. Smoke. Steal stuff. Disrupt. But it's cold out, and theft takes some planning. Dinah imagines it's easier for the Vole just to go for some heckling.

Beside the Vole sits a small boy, about five years old.

K. T., the Vole's little brother. *Oh,* Dinah thinks. *That must be why he's here. Even the Vole has to babysit sometimes.*

The Vole knuckles K. T. on the head.

Poor K. T. Imagine having such a blarb as a brother.

Oh, Dinah. Skint wishes she would quit glaring around. *Don't attract their attention.*

Skint pokes at Dinah's arm.

"Turn around, idiot."

The donkey man has come out.

He's a tiny man with a sandpaper chin. Gray hair, gray clothes, gray face. Skint stares at him and Dinah's heart is pounding. She can't tell yet whether he is kind or cruel or indifferent.

The room is still.

The man doesn't say anything. He unhooks the donkey's tether, whispers something to him, and pats him, gently, on the cheek. Walter nuzzles the man's hand, then faces front, carefully positioning his feet. The man arranges his own feet and coils the tether loosely in his hand. Dinah stops breathing. The man clears his throat.

He hums.

The music is thin, in a minor key. Dinah's mouth opens a bit. She knows this ilk of music, plaintive and spare, from the singing her dad's granny did when she was alive. Shape note. Buzzy singing, because Granny had adenoids and hummed as much of a song as she sang.

The man takes a step right. The donkey steps away from him, left. The man turns, lightly, a turn to the right, and the donkey turns carefully the opposite way. The man circles around Walter, releasing more rope until there is enough for Walter to circle round, too.

Step left, step right, turn and stop. The man coils the rope as they near one another until the dance brings him close to Walter's head. He lifts the rope from around the donkey's neck and places it around his own, all the while stepping and turning about.

Walter is loose, dancing unled. Dinah loves him so much she can't breathe.

Step back for three. Pause and turn. Stately they dance, and slow.

It's silent in here. Nobody stirs. Only humming, hooves and boots.

This dance is like talking, like being on a porch. Like buzzy singing, like sitting on a lap.

Outside is wind and flailings of snow. In here, the humming grows faster. It leaps and shifts and the dancing shifts, too, the man's feet counterpoint to the donkey's. His steps are faster, light, at first in double time, then even faster than that.

But then the man slows himself down. He drags with

each step. Is he slowing too much? His boots slide a half beat too long. No, not a half, some messier fraction. The man's steps and Walter's no longer overlap. The man drags still more, slows, and finally stops, while Walter circles around to the right.

Their lack of unison makes Dinah uneasy. What happened to the together-dancing? It was so lovely just a minute ago. *Fix it,* she wills Walter and the man. *Do like you did before.*

But they don't. Though the humming slows and slims and the dancing is softer, delicate, the man and Walter are still not doing the same steps. And while the melody shifts back to the thin tune from the start of the dance, even that is not quite the same. Different notes are sounded, or held longer, or skipped.

Then it stops. Everything. Man, humming, feet. And when it does, the donkey is facing the back right-hand corner of the room and the man is facing away from him, to the side. It's awful, wrong-feeling. Ending all separate, not even looking at one another, not even positioned so they could walk in the same direction? The man looks as though he doesn't even remember about the donkey, like they never danced so lovely, like he never sang music for the donkey to hear. Dinah's shoulder blades scrunch with the bleakness of it all. Maybe they made a mistake? But Walter and the man don't look confused, like anything got messed up.

Both of them have finished looks on their faces.

Different ways of feet and buzzy singing. Dinah sinks back in her seat. A wave of missing Granny suffuses her chest, cold and unexpected, thin as a blade and spare.

She waits for the music to start up again. But it doesn't. Nothing more happens but snow.

Three

The audience all are clapping.

"Why do you look like that?" Skint chucks Dinah's arm. "It wasn't like the dogs at all, right?"

"No," says Dinah.

"Quit looking dismal! It was a Fantastic, not an Excruciating, right? Clap!" Skint orders her. "Didn't you think it was beautiful? Didn't you think it was even better than the flamenco dancers' kids?"

"No." Donkey so alone, blinking, forlorn and still. It was not beautiful, even though it was. "I hated it."

"Dinah! He'll hear you! He'll see you not clapping!"

"I don't care. Why did he make it go all separate like that?"

The applause dies down.

"We have introduced ourselves," the gray man says. "The night is cold. Please, get some tea and rejoin us."

Bernadine seethes but there is nothing she can do. People shift and get up, laughing and chatting as they head upstairs.

"Jerks," says Dinah. "All they care about is snacks!"

Skint sighs. He's looking over her head toward the back.

Dinah folds her program into eighths and stuffs it under her seat.

"He should have kept it all like the first part of the dance," she says.

"No," says Skint. He pulls her to her feet. "It was perfect. Come on."

Upstairs the folding tables are open for business with snack mix and coffee and tea. The whole of the donkey audience is clustered round it, with Bernadine shouting people into order. Behind its door the choir is still singing, and over them the burr of Dinah's dad's voice can be heard. Mrs. Wattle's voice blares above it all in her terrible key.

The gray man is there with a cup of tea in one hand and a cup of snack mix in the other. Dinah worries that he won't have time to eat his snack before they have to go back. Never mind that he has to hold both items at once so he doesn't have a hand free to scoop up the snack mix—he can't even chew because he has to talk to the people who are politing up to him.

Skint also has two cups in his hands, one of cocoa and one of the mix. "I'm bummed you didn't like it," he says.

"What are you talking about?" Dinah takes the cocoa cup from Skint.

"The show. The dance." Dinah stares at him. "I *loved* it."

Now Skint is staring at her. She takes a sip of cocoa. It is very delicious.

"You loved it?" he says.

"How could you think I didn't? It was wonderful. Walter is the best donkey in the world. The man is so kind—"

"Maybe because of the part where you said you hated it." Skint flicks her forehead with his finger, then digs through the snack cup for sesame sticks. He crunches. "You know, when you said it loud enough for everybody to hear, including the donkey—"

"Stop! Skint!" Dinah feels awful. She didn't mean hate like *hate*. Oh, she'd better go tell the man—

"Wait," Skint says, grabbing her non-cocoa arm. He's looking over her head toward the gray man. "You can tell him later. He's busy. Plus you look crazed, and he might be scared you're going to tell him off."

Dinah tries to look less wild-eyed.

"What an asshole he is," Skint mutters, still looking.

"What?"

Skint sighs. "Not the man," he says. "Him."

Dinah swivels round. The Vole is doing a rude version of the donkey dance over by the gray man. The gray man looks patient.

"Jerk," she says. Skint holds the snack cup toward her. She takes it and passes back the hot chocolate. "If he laughs during the rest—" The idea of Walter or the man having to dance to laughing—

"We'll jump him," says Skint.

Bernadine bears down on Dinah.

"There'll be a lot of cleaning to do," she says grimly. "These people. Clogging the toilets and throwing dirt all over." Nobody is throwing dirt all over but Bernadine is right about the toilets. Something about choir rehearsal loosens those people up.

"I'm ready," says Dinah.

"You'll need your muscles," says Bernadine. "There will be garbage cans to lift."

"You might want to get a man in for that," says Skint, doubly provocative, but Bernadine is already raving at someone else. Hot cups have been used for juice.

Mr. Beach flings open the door to the room where he is trapped with his choir. "This is a *lament*!" he shouts back into the room. "It is not a *hectic* song! It is not *rageful* in any way!"

"Hello, Dad," says Dinah.

He wheels partway round, distracted and breathing rather hard.

"Hello," he says, eyes still on his choir. "Take a break!" he shouts at them. "But no more than five minutes!"

The choir, subdued, trickles into the foyer. Mr. Beach rakes despairing hands through his hair and realizes at last it is Dinah standing here. "Oh, Dinah, darling, hello. Skint, how are you? How is the show?"

"It's great, Mr. Beach."

"The music was like Great-Granny's," says Dinah, and is filled again with the spare sadness of the man's humming.

"Shape note singing?" says Mr. Beach.

"Yes," says Dinah. "Except with only one voice."

"Lovely," Mr. Beach says. "You'll have to tell me about it later, Dinah. I have miles to go here. Speaking of which"—he turns to Skint—"I know I'm meant to bring the two of you home, but I have to keep these people as long as I can tonight. Do you suppose that your mother could come and pick you and Dinah up, Skint?"

Skint starts.

"Can't we just wait for you?" Dinah cries, glaring at her father. What is the matter with him? She and Skint never ask Ellen to drive them to or from anywhere. Transportation is always left to one or the other of Dinah's parents, or, just as often, to Skint's and Dinah's own feet. And when they hang out, it's at Dinah's. Skint never, but never, has Dinah over to his house. And Dinah does not mind this one bit. Ellen is something of a trial.

"Dinah, it'll be hours! I'll be here until at least eleven."

"So we can just walk home!"

"It's nine degrees out, Dinah!"

That is true. And Skint has no coat. "Let's just call Mom, then. Why should Ellen have to pay for your lack of planning?"

"Don't you get mouthy, Dinah Beach. You're already on thin ice around here, after that detention yesterday."

"Ugh!"

"And if your mother were to pick you up," Mr. Beach continues, "she'd have to rouse Beagie and bring him, too. Besides, I'm sure Ellen won't mind just this once! Will she, Skint?"

Skint shrugs and swills the rest of the cup of cocoa. "Whatever," he says into the cup. "It's fine. I'll call her."

"Nonsense," says Mr. Beach. "I am the one reneging on my responsibilities. I will place the call." He pats his pockets and sighs. "Dinah, I need your cellular telephone. I've lost mine again."

You deserve to lose it for being a beastly non-reader-of-

people's-faces, Dinah thinks. But, trapped between her father's determination and Skint's forced acquiescence, she starts to tug her phone out of her skirt pocket.

But Skint shakes his head. "Don't bother," he says. "I'll call her."

"Please give her my apologies, Skint. And my thanks!" cries Mr. Beach as Skint heads outside. The cell reception is awful in here.

"What do you mean, can I come get you?" says Ellen.

"What I mean is, would it be possible, in any way, for you to insert yourself behind the wheel of the family car and—"

"And do what with your father, exactly?"

"Perhaps Dad, too, could be inserted into the vehicle and—"

"Don't be ridiculous."

Skint is silent. There's a hangnail on the side of his thumb and he picks at it.

"Does that really make sense to you?" asks Ellen. "Bringing your father for a spin with your flaky girlfriend—"

"She's not my girlfriend."

"—so she can babble at him and stare at him and go gossiping all around town?"

"Mom, I am the only person Dinah gossips to."

"She has that mother, Skint."

"It's a four-minute car ride, Mom. No one is going to talk or say anything."

"You don't know that."

Skint pulls the hangnail the rest of the way off. It bleeds, so he curls his thumb under his other fingers and rubs the blood against his palm.

"You'll have to find some other way," says Ellen.

"Mom—"

"No," says Ellen. "No. I'm a wreck. I'm a *wreck*. That bank appointment is on Monday, Skint. Two days. What if you father can't even sign that stupid form? What if the bank says he's incompetent? We lose all access to those funds if that happens, Skint. They'll refuse to fork over that money!"

"Mom."

"Is that what you want, Skint? Have you thought through what that would mean?"

Shut up.

"Haven't you been listening to me? Do you want people in our business again? Do you want your dad to be put into—" Ellen's voice catches. Skint presses his nail into the cut on his thumb. "I can't handle the risk, having that girl in the car with him," says Ellen. "I can't."

Be steady. Be calm.

"I can't leave him to work and I can't stay home without that money," says Ellen. "So, no, Skint. No."

"I don't know what else to do, Mom," says Skint, as evenly as he can. "Mr. Beach can't drive us and he will freak out if Dinah has to walk home late with it so cold out."

Silence.

"Mom. Please. It'll look weirder if you don't." He folds his fingers around his thumb again. "They'll wonder why you won't come."

"Let them wonder."

More silence.

Then: "Fine," Ellen says at last. "But you better—"

"I will," says Skint. "I will."

His mother's voice is ragged. "I just want the whole bank thing to be done."

"It will be," says Skint. "Soon." Then: "We'll be done here at nine," he says, and hangs up.

Fuck the fucking bank. The bank is not half of what Skint is worried about.

No. Stop. Don't think about it. Go.

FOUR

Dinah hurries over to meet Skint as he comes back in.

"I'm sorry!" she cries. "I should have told my dad to give the choir a break and run us home in between. The choir would probably thank us—they could seize the moment to make good their escape."

"No big deal." Skint shoves his hands in his pockets as they move toward Mr. Beach, who raises his eyebrows hopefully as they approach.

"She'll be here," Skint tells him.

"Marvelously kind of her," says Mr. Beach. "Be sure to say thank you, Dinah."

"I'm not five," Dinah says irritably.

Mrs. Chatham carefully flickers the lights to signal the end of the break.

"Let's go," says Skint. Dinah follows him down the steps, turning back to give her father one last glare.

She will just have to make the car ride entertaining, is all. She had better start thinking of funny things to say.

Something of her earlier sadness licks at her as they take their seats. Despite his denseness, Dinah is glad for her father that he missed the donkey dance. It would have depressed him, too.

Though actually. Actually. He'd have probably been fine. He'd have admired their commitment to the music, or the dance, or to expressing a difficult theme. He'd have somehow made it all to do with God, probably. He does that all the time. Look at the way he is about that choir.

The rest of the show is hurdy-gurdy music, wheezing and zesty and as bizarre as they had hoped for, not at all like the dance in tone. Dinah claps very hard at the end. Skint whistles out the sides of his mouth and adults turn disdainfully toward him.

"He *means* it," Dinah tells them but Skint nudges her quiet.

"I have to congratulate them," Dinah says, determined to make amends for being rude by mistake before. She would also like to hug Walter. But she is too late for any of it; the man and Walter scuttle out while everyone is clapping.

Rats! What can she do? She can't bear the thought of them leaving thinking she hated them and their work.

She will write them a letter. No, more. She will make them a parcel of treats, a box of things nice for a donkey. "Sugar cubes," she mutters. "Maybe a carrot."

Skint knows what she is thinking.

"Act your age, please, infant. We haven't left anyone a parcel of treats in years."

"Nobody's too old to leave a parcel of treats." Dinah punches Skint briefly. "I'd like to see you say no if I left you a Skint-based one." (Bike stuff. Snack chips. Loud, tectonic music.)

"If it were cash-based, then sure." He returns the punch on her shoulder. "Otherwise I'd think you were a crazy person."

Grr to Skint in his no-fun aspect.

It's a few minutes before nine. They head outside to wait for Ellen.

"What do you want to do tomorrow?" Dinah asks. "Saturday! First day of vacation!"

Skint shrugs irritably, glancing down the road. "Bank heist?" he says. "Steal chickens? Tether up your brother and teach him that dance?"

"Better to tether you."

"Sounds kind of dirty."

"Shut up. After the cleaning we can decide."

The choir is still at it in the church, the music wailing on.

It is shivery cold, colder than before, even, and still snowing lightly as well, but Skint didn't want to wait inside and Dinah is less worried about Mr. No Coat now since they will be in a car in a minute. Though who knows, with Ellen. Maybe they'll wind up having to call Dinah's mother anyway, if Ellen bails on the job. Dinah is half hoping she does. Not just for Skint but because her own mother was all too glad to be rid of them this evening, with Beagie asleep and Dinah watching donkeys, Mr. Beach out dealing with his singers. Tchah to Mrs. Beach's Alone Night!

Though Dinah doesn't really want to call her mother. Mrs. Beach is already not overfond of Ellen Gilbert. Plus, poor sleeping Beagie. Still, Dinah's stomach is tight the way it always is when she anticipates Ellen, who is herself not overfond of Dinah.

Thump clatter crash—the Vole punches down the steps behind them. "Rotmouth, Flake," he greets them. He smacks Skint in the chest as he flies by and jumps the remaining four steps to the ground.

"I've told you I won't a thousand times, dude," says Skint as the Vole runs toward a waiting car. "Quit trying to get with me."

"Fucking freaks!" echoes back toward the church

before the car door opens and the Vole folds himself into its backseat.

"Self-naming," says Skint as the car drives away. He glances at Dinah. "Strangely honest, and certainly apt."

"How could he call Walter and the man that?" Dinah scowls.

Skint stares at her. Then he eases back and smiles.

"You are the weirdest person on Earth." He rubs his forehead against her temple, like a baby deer.

"Jerkie," says Dinah, and pats him on the head.

The door opens behind them. K. T., the Vole's little brother, steps carefully onto the stoop.

"Hi, K. T.," says Skint. "Are you looking for your brother?"

"How do you know my name?" There is a ring of chapped skin around K. T.'s mouth and his lips are very red.

"You are famous," Skint says and smiles at him. K. T. smiles shyly back.

"I'm not looking for my brother. He's going to his friend's house. My dad's inside."

"Is he in the choir?" asks Dinah.

"Yes," says K. T.

Poor K. T. It will be a long wait.

"Do you have anything to play with?" Dinah asks.

"Yes." K. T. nods. "I brought some little guys." He

opens his hands and shows them two tiny plastic figures.

"Oh, good."

"You should wait inside where it's warm," says Skint. "You aren't wearing your coat."

K. T. looks down at his stomach. "My coat is inside," he says. "You don't have your coat on either, though."

"But I am old and wizened, K. T., and impervious to the elements."

"Do you want us to go inside with you?" Dinah asks. "We could fix you a cup of cocoa."

"No, thank you," says K. T. "I can go in by myself. I just wanted to look out here. I never saw church outside at nighttime before."

He steps backward back into the foyer and closes the door.

"How does the same family produce both a Vole and a sweet kid like him?" Skint wonders.

"I know," says Dinah.

"Likely the niceness of the one is due to the assholery of the other. K. T. squashed to the point of docility under the cruel knuckle of the Vole."

"Stop," says Dinah. "I think K. T. just got all of the nice genes."

Skint rolls a sardonic eye at her and snorts, then falls silent.

They wait. Skint says nothing and rocks back and forth on his heels.

* * *

There's the car. Ellen has shown up after all. Dinah dreads getting in. Skint exhales through his teeth beside her.

Mr. Gilbert is there too, in the front seat next to his wife. Dinah is surprised. She assumed Ellen would be alone. She saw Skint's dad more often when he used to come to the St. Francis Adult Day Services Center, which Dinah's mother runs. But he stopped coming ages ago. He was bored there, Ellen told Mrs. Beach. He felt cooped up, wanted to do his own thing. And since Skint obviously doesn't want them to hang out at his house, it's rare that Dinah even sees his dad.

Dinah glances up at Skint. His face doesn't look like anything.

"If this were a science fiction film," she offers, "those would be analogs, not your parents, and we would be flying to the mothership for an intergalactic adventure." Dinah is ready with a uniform design and technological superpowers for them both, but Skint is already heading down the steps.

"Let's go."

Dinah follows more slowly.

Maybe she should have said that they looked nice, his parents, like maybe they had been out to a supper. From up on the church porch, couldn't you imagine that was possible?

Or maybe not something romantic. Mr. Gilbert is

seventeen years older than Skint's mother. Maybe something old-fashioned, like a gentleman out with his ward? Ugh. That sounds kind of skeevy, actually, and besides, Dinah's whole point is to distract him from his parents. *Think,* she tells herself. *Be fun for the car ride.*

On the whole, it would be much better to be confronting an Analog Ellen.

The falling snow is illuminated in the headlights, the music from the radio tinny. Skint's mother doesn't say hello when Skint opens the door, or even take a moment to look askance at Dinah's stripy skirt. She's facing forward, ready to go.

Skint glances in at his mother, then at his dad.

"Hi, Dad," he says. "Shouldn't you buckle up?"

Mr. Gilbert doesn't answer. Dinah hesitates, holding the door. Skint's father is startling in his thinness, skin petal-fine over his skull. His bones are like a bird's.

"Dad," Skint repeats. "Your seat belt."

"Your seat belt, Thomas," Skint's mother echoes. "He wants you to fasten your seat belt."

Mr. Gilbert starts.

"He's fine, Skint," says Ellen shortly. "It's a three-minute ride. Just get in. Get in, Dinah. Let's go."

They get in. Skint, scarlet-cheeked, looks straight ahead as they drive and thumps his thighs in time to the music. Dinah twists her fingers into interesting shapes and looks at the back of Mr. Gilbert's head. Silver hairs slicked down, Mr. Gilbert is silent, unmoving.

"How are you, Mr. Gilbert?" she asks.

"I wonder about it," says Mr. Gilbert. His voice is thin as a reed. "I wonder if it's true to who we really are."

Dinah hesitates. "What do you wonder about?" she asks.

Mr. Gilbert says nothing.

Skint stops drumming and looks at her.

"Sorry," says Dinah. "I thought he was talking to me."

Skint furrows his brow. He looks at his dad.

"Dad?" he says.

"It's turning a blind eye," Mr. Gilbert says. "Unethical in the extreme."

"A blind eye to what?" Dinah asks. "What did somebody do, Mr. Gilbert?"

"Dinah," says Ellen irritatedly.

What? Wouldn't it be rude of her to just assume that Mr. Gilbert isn't making sense? Dinah turns to Skint but he is looking at Ellen, reflected in the rearview mirror. Ellen is using the mirror to look sharply at Dinah. Then she narrows her eyes at Skint.

Mr. Gilbert bows his head. He does not speak again.

Skint glances at Dinah for a moment, then shifts his gaze to the window. He beats his thighs double time.

Say something to make it better, Dinah orders herself. But she can't think what. She racks her brains the whole way home but the rest of the ride is silent except for Skint's drumming on his thighs, faster and faster and faster.

FIVE

Dinah missed Skint unbearably after he moved away when they were small, and was overjoyed at his unexpected return in sixth grade. He was so skinny when he came back, though. Bleak-eyed and old. His breath was terrible, too. Dinah wondered if he ever ate or brushed his teeth. Didn't anybody make him?

"Have some toaster cake," she said one day soon after his return, splitting her own in two, but he shook his head no. "How about a mint?" she offered, tackling the other problem.

"Okay," he said and took the mint. He didn't look any more cheerful, though. What else could she do?

She stood up and brushed off her hands. She rested the fingertips of her left hand on her left thumbtip, and Handcreature, thus formed, peered at Skint with beaky interest.

"Do you still like rock candy?" Dinah asked Skint. "Does your dad still keep bags of it in his pockets?"

Skint's face went in.

Handcreature drew back.

Dinah cursed herself; she was dumb, dumb, dumb! Why did she have to mention Mr. Gilbert? He was the whole reason the Gilberts were back in Maine in the first place, and it was not for anything nice or because they missed it here so much, but because Mr. Gilbert was not well. "Beginnings of dementia," said Mrs. Beach. "Early onset; tragic."

Dinah knew what dementia was: sadness and forgetting and a long time of worsening. Skint's dad might just be starting, but it was awful to think about. Awful for Skint and awful for Mr. Gilbert, growing strange and far away. Dinah's chest went bleak to think of it. No wonder Skint was so solemn the whole time. So could she please quit making things worse? Could she please quit mentioning his dad?

"The Vole picks his nose and collects the boogers on a piece of paper in his desk," she said to distract him.

"Who is the Vole?"

"Oh," said Dinah. "Avery Vaar. There's a picture of a vole in the science book and it looks so much like him you'd be shocked. I only really call him that in my head, though."

"Shoot," said Skint. "He does look exactly like a vole. That is sick, by the way, the thing about the boogers." He shook his head.

Handcreature did, too. She wiggled toward Skint and nipped at his neck.

"Quit it," said Skint, squeezing his chin to his neck against Handcreature's pecking. But he was smiling. See? Not to worry. Dinah was good at distracting people and cheering them up. Look how she could always get her dad laughing at dinner. Look how well she could entertain her mom. Not even jokes or funny routines, most of the time. Mostly just telling about her mistakes.

Outings, she thought firmly, *and good ideas to think about. Pretending, talismans, things to do with trees.*

"Do you ever go to the Center where your mom works?" Skint asked her after school.

"No," said Dinah. "I hate it."

"You do? Why?"

"I just do, is all. Let's go down to the bridge."

"Are they mean there?"

"No," said Dinah. "Let's skip stones."

"My dad might go there. Some days if my mom is working."

Dinah stopped. "I only hate it because my mother's there all the time," she said quickly. "And she is always more bossy to me there."

"Oh," said Skint. "Not because it sucks?"

"No," said Dinah. "Other people like it a lot."

No way would she say how some of the people at the center—the most ill, the thinnest under their blankets—were so sad-eyed and lonely-boned they made her want to cry, made her want to hit someone, made her too unhappy to even breathe.

A couple of weeks later the class showcased its science projects. Skint was the third to present.

"Come on, Skint," said the teacher, calling him to the front of the class. "Your report was great! Come up and give us the highlights."

Skint shrugged and waved his hand at the wall where his owl poster was hung. The owl loomed over a table upon which Skint had arranged a set of tiny smooth stones. Taped to the wall beside Skint's owl was Dinah's own project, a grisly poster of the human skeleton, blood in the bones and marrow.

"Owls have large wings," said Skint, "and hollow bones. That's what makes them able to fly, even though they're so big. They eat stones like these to help them digest."

What was the matter with the teacher? When Skint talked, her eyes widened and her head snapped back a little. She smiled extra big but when she spoke again, her words were chumped up, as if she were holding her breath.

"Amazing!" she cried. But when Skint was done she didn't make him open the floor for questions like she had with the others, and let him go back to his seat.

Skint let out air in a sigh. Immediately Laley and Sue fanned away from him, faces twisted and heads turned to the side. The three of them looked like a letter *W*, with Skint the poking-up part in the middle.

The Vole, two kids away from Skint, flapped his hand in front of his nose.

"Pyew," he said. "Old new boy stinks."

Jerk!

"Avery! Stop that."

Skint's face looked like nothing.

But it was true. The smell was not like a dirty kid smell, but a smell like old eggs and sick. It was coming from high up on Skint. It was coming from his mouth.

Dinah was four desks away but even she could smell it. How had his breath gotten even worse? What could be wrong to make that smell? Skint and toaster cakes and eyes black as ice.

A stir of yucks and exhaled breaths, curled up noses

and fanning hands, swept through the other kids. The teacher tried to quell them.

"Kids. Kids!"

Dinah's chest churned. She leaned forward, around Laley, and tried to catch Skint's eye, but he didn't see her. His eyes were like nothing.

Out on the playground Dinah eyed Skint.

His jaw. Was that a swelling part? Why hadn't she noticed before?

"Skint?" she asked. "Is something wrong in your mouth?"

Skint looked shocked. Then he looked angry. His knuckles were purple and dry.

The playground was bordered on three sides with forest. The evergreens, with their snow-clumped branches, were like kings in ermine-trimmed robes. The other kids shrieked beneath them.

"I'm sorry," said Dinah. Skint looked angry enough to do punching. But she couldn't help herself. His jaw looked wrong, distended. "Does it hurt?"

She lifted her mitten to his cheek.

Skint reared back his head, unspeaking. Dinah paused, her hand still; Skint's eyes on her face.

He opened his mouth.

Oh, no; no; oh, no, please, no.

One of Skint's molars was crumbled and gray, the

flesh around it shredded with rot. The stink was awful.

Dinah's mittened fingers touched his chin and her eyes filled up with tears.

"It must hurt a lot." Her own jaw throbbed, and she put her other hand on top of it.

Skint shrugged.

"What are they doing about it?" Dinah asked.

Skint shrugged again.

"Does your mom know?"

Skint still didn't say anything. Dinah's chest seized; how could his mom not know?

"Don't worry," she said. Her brain churned. Oh, why wasn't she a magical dentist with unhurting powers? "I'll help you. I'll help. My mom'll know what to do. I'll help. Don't worry. I'll help."

"Your mom?" he asked.

"Yes," said Dinah. "I'll ask her today."

Skint hesitated.

"Don't worry," said Dinah. "I won't say anything bad."

"Okay," said Skint slowly. "If you think she'll know what to do."

"She's good with this kind of thing," said Dinah. "I'll talk to her today."

"At the Center?"

"Probably when she gets home," said Dinah, mindful of not delving into things that made him think of his dad. "Don't worry. She'll know what to do."

"Okay," said Skint. "Okay. It's only because my mom is busy," he added suddenly.

A boy named Harlan, the Vole's particular friend, ran past. "Rotmouth and the Flake!" he cried.

"It's the title of a manga he likes, I think," Dinah said hurriedly, watching Skint's face.

"Not one I've ever seen," said Skint, "and I'm kind of a connoisseur." He flicked her forehead with his finger. "You weirdo."

Handcreature snatched his finger and refused to let go.

I will punch anyone who is mean to Skint, Dinah vowed. She'd like to, anyway, and so many of them deserved it.

The treetops bent toward them under the weight of the snow.

"Open wider. Wider, I said!"

Dinah and Skint were alone in the cubby room the next day. They were skipping gym.

Skint moaned and waved his hands about.

"What?" Dinah stepped back.

Skint closed his mouth and massaged his jaw.

"That's as wide as I can do," he said.

"Well, we need room for you to bite on this." Dinah flourished a wad of brown paper towel, filched from the girls' room at lunch. It was damp and smelled like turpentine. Dinah had soaked it in bourbon brought from home.

More like stolen than brought, she supposed, but not really stolen; it couldn't be stolen if it was for helping. Although her mother didn't exactly know she'd taken it.

She popped the paper towel into Skint's mouth.

"It's what's good for a tooth," she explained. "My mother says. Bite down. Hold it. Hold it! Like that."

"Alcohol?" said Skint thickly around the awful-smelling wad. His eyes were watering. "I'll smell like a drunk! I'll get suspended!"

"No, you won't!" cried Dinah. "Because of Part Two of my plan! We flush the paper towel, and then you rinse, and then after that we do cloves."

"Cloves?"

"Yes," said Dinah, and opened her palm. Three brown, screw-shaped buds rolled across it. It was oil of cloves that was supposed to be good for teeth, according to Mrs. Beach. But there wasn't any of that in the pantry. Dinah hoped that chomping on these would work just as well. Wouldn't the oil get squeezed out as he chewed?

She rubbed the buds and held them up for Skint to sniff. They smelled lovely, like Christmas, like incense in church.

"You'll bite down on these," she told him, "with your other teeth. It helps the pain, and also then you won't smell like liquor." The cloves would also help with the overall mouth stink, Dinah hoped, but she didn't say that part out loud. The kids would call him Spice Mouth now, or maybe even Lovely Breath.

Dinah scanned Skint's brow.

"What did your mom say when you told her about me?" he asked thickly around the wad.

"I was wily," said Dinah. "I didn't name names. I told her I was writing a story with a character with a toothache. I didn't give you away."

Skint's face fell.

"What?" Dinah asked anxiously. "Does the bourbon taste awful?"

"No," said Skint. His eyes were bleak again.

"Behold," said Dinah frantically, flinging her arms about. "Waves of unhurting beam from my mighty hands! Flee, pain, from this tortured head!" She flung and made magical vanishing noises until Skint's eyes crinkled up smiling.

"Dope," he said. "Freak. Weirdo."

Plan from there on out: Keep up with the bourbon. At the same time, play. Point out how good Skint is at drawing as well as science.

After a few days Dinah decided to lay off with the cloves. The buds were so pointy and hard and she couldn't bear the thought of them poking into Skint's flesh. But now there was no cover for the bourbon stink, and that's what tore it. In no time the plan was discovered.

Skint, bourbon, teacher, yelling.

"Consequences!" said the teacher, and also the principal. Skint was suspended.

"I'm sorry!" Sobbing Dinah. "Please let me confess!"

"I'll hate you if you do. Don't be dumb. Shut up. You tried."

But Dinah was sick with failure. What kind of friend was she? What kind of moron helper? Skint already with hurting teeth, already with his dad. She'd only made things a thousand times worse.

Be better. Be better! Work and work and be the best friend in the world. Make it so he never has to think about a single sad thing, not his dad or his teeth or anything bad. Make him happy and glad and happy and glad, every day, all the days, the rest of his life.

Suspension wasn't the only consequence for Skint. A social worker showed up at his house. Ellen was white and tight and boiling with anger. Nothing happened after that visit, though, so Skint guessed the social worker decided he was being well cared for after all. He didn't tell Dinah about it. He didn't tell a soul. And he never told about how he got the bourbon.

Six

Walter's performance ended hours ago, but Dinah is still up and in the kitchen when Mr. Beach finally comes in from his choir rehearsal.

"I am very glad it is vacation next week," he says, slumping into a chair. Mr. Beach is the music teacher at a middle school in the next town over, so he has the nine days home as well. "It will be a challenging week of rehearsals and I am not sure I could tolerate a lot of children on top of it all."

"I am glad, too," says Dinah.

"It is too bad you hate that school so much," says her father.

"I don't care that I do," says Dinah.

"This is a difficult town," says her father, "in which to grow up unusual." He rubs his eyes in their sockets. "The donkey was wonderful?" he asks.

"Better than wonderful," says Dinah. "Perfect."

"I am jealous, of course. One could not say that anything about my own evening was perfect." He leans back in his chair. "The dancing?" he asks. "Also perfection?"

"Yes." Dinah fixes him with a look. "As was the music."

"Yes, yes, I think you mentioned that," says Mr. Beach hurriedly. "I'm awfully hungry; I wonder if there's any—" He makes as if to peer round the kitchen, but Dinah traps him with her gaze.

"Wouldn't you like to hear a bit?"

"No, no, that's quite all right—"

"It was like this." Dinah stands up and aligns her feet like hooves.

"No need, darling! No need at all! I caught a little snippet of it during—"

"LA LA LA—"

"Your brother is sleeping!"

Dinah switches to whisper-singing. *"La la la!"*

Her father sucks in his cheeks and gasps like a fish. Dinah's singing voice is not terrible, but that is only because the word "terrible" is not large enough to describe the awful toneless blartiness she emits. Mr.

Beach's eyes roll and he sinks from his chair to the floor, twitching. Dinah stands over him, triumphant.

His hair is thinning, she notices as he writhes, but not a lot, and none of it yet gray.

Dinah leaves off singing.

"You should dye your hair when the time comes," she tells him.

Her father untwists his limbs.

"I'll keep it in mind, old thing." He glances up at her warily. "Am I safe?"

Dinah steps to one side. Mr. Beach unfolds himself and creaks back up into his chair.

"I thought you said he hummed like shape note," says Mr. Beach. "Though, indeed, perhaps that's what you were trying—"

Dinah makes as if to punch him in the shoulder.

"That was Elvis, what I was singing."

She punches him a very tiny punch. The gray man did sing shape note, but Mr. Beach doesn't need to hear that right now. Neither does she.

Dinah is in the woods and the gray man is there, too. Walter is beside him, feet lined up neatly in the snow. Tether held, he and the gray man face front. Do they see her? Dinah thinks so, but then she thinks not. Silver coat and whiskers, they are still-faced, quiet; snow falling down.

Are the three of them on the road or in the woods? Too much snow falling and she can't look down. Only at Walter, only at the man. Nothing to tell her. Only snow.

Dinah wakes, uneasy, and wonders if Skint is sleeping or awake.

SEVEN

Skint half sits, half stands at the breakfast table the next morning, one elbow on its surface and his palm across his mouth. He has the table to himself in the mornings because he gets up so early, with or without the benefit of having slept. But with sleep or no, Skint always forces himself to wait until at least five o'clock to get out of bed, so it counts as morning and not the middle of the night. Then he gets up and sits down to the paper (the physical paper, never online) with the fierceness of a militant, fists and stomach clenched, sick at the smell of the ink. He reads every word, from the global headlines on the front page straight through the national news and the county reports to the quarter columns given to local events. He saves the editorial page for last.

The Gilberts' kitchen is very cold this post-Walter early morning, but Skint is fired up with reading the paper and doesn't feel the chill. The news is stomach-turning; Burmese monks seized, killed, maimed. How can people be—

"Did you make the coffee, Skint?"

Skint starts. What's she doing up? It's not even half past six.

"Did you?" Ellen reaches behind her and pulls his dad ahead of her into the kitchen. She is still in her robe but his dad's faded plaid shirt is tucked neatly into his pants, his damp hair streaked with combing. Skint flushes. His hand wavers over the edge of the paper; should he put it away?

"No. Sorry." He clears his throat. "Hello, Dad."

"No," sighs Ellen. "That would be too much to hope for. Sit," she says to Mr. Gilbert, and he does, taking a spot at Skint's elbow.

"It would have been undrinkable by the time you usually get up," says Skint. His mother looks tired but not angry; Skint doesn't think so, anyway. His dad's face is still lined with sleep, bristled with silver whiskers. Skint lowers his rear the rest of the way down until it rests on the edge of his chair. "Hi, Dad," he says again. "You're up early."

Mr. Gilbert glances at the paper on the table and furrows his brow. Then his gaze is caught by Skint's cereal spoon and he picks it up, looking carefully into its bowl.

"Say hello when someone says hello," Ellen tells him.

"Distortion," says Mr. Gilbert, moving his head about as he considers his reflection in the spoon. "Distortion and reversal. Good Lord. Look."

Skint leans over but the spoon goes lax in Mr. Gilbert's hand. Mr. Gilbert stares out the window, eyes dim and hollow. Outside the tree branches are coated in ice and snow, silver over bone.

One Saturday, years before they moved back from Kentucky, when Skint was in the first or second grade, he sat at the kitchen table just like now, with a bowl of cereal in front of him, feet hooked around the rungs of his chair. His mom was at the table, too, while his dad stood leaning against the window frame, looking out into the neighbor's yard.

"When is that guy going to do something with that thing?" Mr. Gilbert said, nodding out the window. "Why take a gorgeous antique truck like that and park it out back, practically in the woods, and then let it rust and rot? If that were ours, Skinty, you can bet that you and I would be out there every weekend, restoring the heck out of it. Would you look at those running boards?"

"I could stand on those and hold on while you drive," Skint agreed, slipping off his chair to join his dad at the window.

"Exactly," said his dad. "We'd get a dog, too, to ride along in the passenger seat."

"With his head hanging out the window," said Skint.

"Yep," said his dad. "Wearing a neckerchief."

They beamed at one another.

"Pathetic." Ellen shook her head. "Not your plan. I mean having a truck like that in the yard."

Skint's father laughed. "Right? He's displaying that metal carcass like it's his high-school wrestling award. God. He comes off like that old guy at the mini-mart who stands around making passes at all the teenage girls."

"Look who's talking. You're the one with the trophy wife." Ellen grinned. "Seriously, Thomas, if you were the one with that truck, you'd make it amazing. You wouldn't heap it in the yard and hope it made everyone think you had a big organ."

"Dinah's dad had a big organ," said Skint. "Remember? Back in Maine? But I don't think he was a show-off about it."

Skint's parents wheeled around to look at him. Skint swallowed and his throat felt as though his cereal were stuck in it sideways.

"He did," he said feebly. "I remember. In the church."

Skint's parents looked at each other and laughed and laughed.

"Oh, Skint," said his dad, grabbing Skint up and kissing him. "You are a treasure and a dear and I love you unspeakably. Get dressed. If we can't have that truck, then we must stir up some other kind of adventure. Hurry! To the Museum of Natural History we go! There's an interactive exhibit called *Dinos That Soar*, and those mechanical pterodactyls are not going to fly themselves."

"The snow woke us up," says Ellen now. "Falling off the roof."

"What for a world," Mr. Gilbert murmurs, "that has such—"

Ellen puts a bowl of Cheerios down in front of her husband. "Eat."

Skint clears his throat. "Has such what, Dad?"

The trees outside are still.

"Thomas!"

Mr. Gilbert starts. His gaze falls on Skint, and he grins, slowly, beaming as if with remembered delight. Skint's heart pounds, but Mr. Gilbert's eyebrows fall, as they always do, from delighted arcs back into furrowed, puzzled lines.

Quit it, Skint tells his chest. *Just quit it.*

"Hello, Dad," he says. "I was just saying hello." The pounding lessens but his cheeks flame.

Mr. Gilbert stares at Skint, head cocked as if trying to catch the edge of a tune playing in some other room. There isn't any tune, though, only the sound of coffee dripping, and now, outside, some wind.

He drops his gaze.

"What for a world," he says, "that has such people in it?"

Ellen sits down and takes the spoon from Mr. Gilbert and puts it in his bowl. "I said, eat."

"What's that from, Dad?" Near quote, maybe; something about it's wrong.

"Dream of man?" Mr. Gilbert wonders. "Or dream of Atman?"

What is that, "dream of Atman"?

Ellen takes a sip of coffee.

"Hello, there," says Mr. Gilbert to his wife. "And who might you be?"

"Just some broad you picked up on the street," she says. Skint shoots her a look. "Oh, Skint, stop. It's not like he's going to remember who I am if I tell him, anyway."

Shut up. "You don't know that."

"Don't be irritating, Skint."

Don't be an ass, then.

Skint crunkles up the corner of the paper and clears his throat. *Do not antagonize her. Do not let her get shirtier.*

"Dad?" he says, waving his fingers slightly toward the open page. "Mr. Tedges has the editorial today."

"In exile?" cries Mr. Gilbert. "In hiding? Did they run my byline?"

Skint's heart pounds again.

"Jesus God," says Ellen.

"No." Skint swallows. "I don't think so."

Mr. Gilbert stares out the window and his face grows grave. "What for a world," he says. "Dream of man or—"

"For God's sake," says Ellen. "Eat!"

But Mr. Gilbert is still, caught by the trees.

"Gus Tedges," Ellen mutters into her coffee, "is a work-shirking ass."

"Dad is perceptive about tone of voice," Skint says to his mother, forcing his own to be light.

"Skint, if he had two memory cells left to speak of, your father would say the same thing. He practically had to run the paper alone that last year."

Mr. Gilbert's gaze breaks and he looks at Skint with concern. "Is your father ill?" he asks.

Skint swallows. Mr. Gilbert's face softens.

"I'm so sorry," says Mr. Gilbert. "How long since he passed?"

Skint folds up the paper and wedges it under his chair, taking care not to bump his father's unshod feet.

"I am wiped," says Ellen. She frowns. "Put that paper away where it belongs."

"Dad?" says Skint. Mr. Gilbert looks puzzledly at the spoon in his hand. "I'm going to go out in a minute, Dad."

"Wait a sec." Ellen puts down her cup. "Hold up there, kid. You are not going out. I am going out. You need to watch your father."

Skint's stomach twists.

"You have to go out, this early?" he asks. "I'm cleaning, remember? I do it every week. We have to have it done before nine. I reminded you several times."

"You did no such thing," says Ellen.

"I did," says Skint. *Be very calm and very measured.* "Yesterday when you were making the bed, and the day before that when you came home from the store. I did."

"Cleaning," says Ellen.

"Yes," says Skint.

"For the Girls' Friendly."

"Yes."

"No," says Ellen. "I was up too late with one of your damn uncles on the phone and now I am up too early with your father. I need a walk to clear my head, and then I need to go back to sleep. You're staying here."

"I can't," says Skint, irked to hear his voice gone high. He wishes that Ellen would let his dad go to Mrs. Beach's Center so she could have breaks when she needs them, but she won't. She hasn't brought him there for more than two years. ("You want them to take him, Skint? You want them to see how bad it is now and tell us we have to put him in a home?")

"I made a promise," says Skint. "I'll be back in less than two hours and then you can go out or take a nap or whatever, for as long as you want."

"Oh, I'm sure it's much more important you keep your promise," says Ellen. "I'm sure your stripy girlfriend can't possibly clean that church alone for one week."

Mr. Gilbert's brows are drawn in.

"I can tell them," he says urgently. "I can tell them to have it ready to go as soon as you give the word."

"Thanks, Dad," says Skint.

"Thanks a bundle, Thomas."

Skint flinches. "Mom."

"Girls' Friendly," she says. "You are the most—"

Skint's phone goes off, crarking like a crow. He glances at the number. Dinah. He lets it go.

"That your stripy girlfriend?" Ellen asks.

"No, it's a telephone."

"Funny, Skint."

"Dad?" says Skint, ignoring Ellen, but Mr. Gilbert is silent, staring at the trees. His eyes are dark. Skint's heart skips, and his cheeks grow warm.

"You say hello," Ellen warns Mr. Gilbert, "when someone says hello." She turns back to Skint. "If she's not a girlfriend, Skint, then why are you so red?"

"What for a world—" says Mr. Gilbert.

"Out last night," says Ellen. "*And* I had to come get you. *With* your father! You had better make sure that girl doesn't—"

Skint's bones tighten. "I said, I'll make sure. I always make sure—"

"And now you think you can go out again this morning? As well? While I have to start the day with no sleep and a life-size dress-up doll, followed up with a chaser of adult diapers? Ridiculous. Ridiculous."

Dad does not wear diapers and is not deaf. Shut up. Bitch.

"Nonetheless," Skint says, "nonetheless, I will, in fact, be ridiculously going out to ridiculously clean that church to a level of ridiculousness that the king of ridiculous himself would approve, and then I will be home and you can sleep or leave for the rest—"

"I said no!"

Ellen's cup bangs onto the table.

Mr. Gilbert jumps and Skint's blood pounds in reverse, searing in toward his chest with each beat until his ribs are so tight he could burst.

His father's startled gaze moves from the trees to Skint. He beams as if with remembered delight.

"Son," he says.

"Dad," says Skint, and his chest explodes.

Ellen stands up, fast, between them.

"Go," says Ellen. "Fine. Get out of here. Go!"

Mr. Gilbert's smile fades and he stares at Ellen, head cocked as if trying to remember a song.

Go? Go? Skint can't go.

"Hello," says Mr. Gilbert to his wife. "And who might you—"

Skint grabs his phone and the paper and he's out of there, he's down the hall and in his room.

Dinah, he thinks. He'll call Dinah.

"Jesus Christ!" Ellen is shouting. "Can you please just fucking eat!"

EIGHT

Dinah's on her bed, hunched over her crochet hook. She is making herself a hat, stripy like the skirts she wears but in a set of colors she hasn't put together before. Skint makes fun of her all the time for crocheting. He says she's like a cross between a second grader and an old lady, and the weirdest parts of each. Well, let him say that. Who cares. Dinah loves to crochet. It's peaceful, cheering and productive all at once. Skint is just mad because of that time she made him slipper booties.

Beside her on the bed is the copy of *Disposable People: New Slavery in the Global Economy* that Skint gave her last week. Dinah knows she should read it, probably right now, instead of selfishly crocheting herself a hat. But she can't bring herself to, not just yet. She has to gear herself up. It is awful to think about, the stuff in that book. She can't think about it every minute, the way Skint can. When she reads that stuff, her stomach hurts so badly she can't think. So she has to take breaks. It makes her feel guilty, Skint doesn't take breaks. Ever. It is hard, sometimes, having a best friend who is so aware of everything the whole time. It can make a person feel like she isn't entirely adequate.

Ugh. The last bunch of crochet stitches are all messed up. She's going to have to rip out the whole section. But the Beaches' home phone rings and it's Skint, so luckily Dinah is forced to put down her crocheting.

"Twelve years imprisoned, some of these monks have been! Bones broken, tied with cables, made to stand in tubs of shit." Skint's voice is something threaded through a piston. "What is *wrong* with people? How can people get to the point where they let themselves do that to another person?"

Dinah does not pay attention to the bones gone jagged beneath her skin or the knifing in her knees. She leans on the hall table and clutches the phone and twists her ankles around each other as Skint talks. She imagines him hot-eyed and pacing, or sitting thin-shouldered with cereal in his spoon, and she racks and racks her brain.

"Dinah? Are you there? Are you listening? Don't you get it? These people! They are *human*. Every single one of them is somebody's Beagie!"

Dinah does get it and feels sick about the monks but it is Skint she is worried about right now, because he feels so bad all the time, reading all those stories and remembering every word.

"We'll save them," she promises. "We can do letter writing."

"Letter writing!" Skint shouts. "Dinah, they are dying! You wouldn't believe what they do to them—"

"You told me," Dinah says hurriedly, not wanting him to have to tell it again.

"I *spared* you most of it!" says Skint. "I spared you the worst!"

"Come over," says Dinah. "Come *over*. I was calling you before to come over for breakfast before cleaning."

There is a pause.

"No," says Skint. "We have to go clean in about two seconds. Besides, I'm still getting ready."

"I'll come there, then," says Dinah. "I'll come get you. I'll come right now."

"Whatever," says Skint, still irritable. "Fine. I'll meet you at the end of the driveway. Bye."

Dinah relaxes a tiny bit. Six minutes it'll take her to get there. Enough time to think of a way to help him think unmonkish thoughts.

What would really work would be for everybody to be lovely to each other, all the time, but Dinah can't think of a way to get people to agree to that one.

She'll bring him a rock cake. He loves those, and she just made some the other day.

Mrs. Beach stops by the phone table, Beagie's plush pony in her hand. "You look bilious," she says. "What's wrong?"

"The world. People. Doing awful things—torturing—"

"Oh, Dinah! Stop *thinking* so much. Think how lucky you are, how beautiful it is outside."

It is beautiful outside. The snow is thin on the branches, velvet over stone.

"What does that have to do with anything? How does me looking outside help people who are dying and need help?"

"Oh, Dinah," her mother says again. "Why do you let Skint tell you those things? You're never yourself after."

Dinah's brows draw together in a scowl. Her mother makes no sense, ever, not for a minute.

"I *am* myself," she says. "This, here, is myself."

"This is you *cranky*. You are not cranky by nature, Dinah! Exasperating, but generally cheerful, when you are not furious."

"I am sorry I am not my usual dippy self for you, Mrs. Beach."

Her mother sighs and makes like to smooth Dinah's

hair but Dinah rears her head out of the way. Her stomach is killing her.

Isn't she supposed to do caring? Isn't she supposed to feel awful when something is awful? Why does her mother want her to stop?

NINE

Dinah hurries down her driveway and past the Harps' house next door with its little fenced-in field, past all the other houses on her street, too, until she reaches a stand of white pines that loom ancient and needle-sleeved overhead. The road forks at these pines and its right tine is Skint's street. While most of the houses near Dinah's are little and old and hug close to the road, the ones on Skint's street are mostly split-levels or one-story ranches, dark and low with long driveways winding their way up to garages. The whole area up here used to be a farm, but it's been gone for forty years or more and the fields that haven't had houses built on them are grown over now with thin paper birches and new evergreens.

Just ahead, Skint is coming down his driveway to meet Dinah in their usual spot by his mailbox. After last night, Dinah is especially glad he never has her meet him in his house. She has no interest in another encounter with Ellen.

"Let's go," Skint says as soon as their paths intersect, and together they continue down the road. There's a shortcut ahead that loops them around to the bridge over the river not too far from the town center. From there the church is just a few minutes' walk. So is the high school, for that matter.

Dinah puts a rock cake in Skint's unmittened hand. "Here."

"Thank you."

Skint has a squiggle between his brows and does not look like he is thinking about cookies. But he gives it a couple of approving hefts. "Dense," he says.

Dinah beams and nods. That's the way they like them.

"Me and Beagie made them," she says. She eyes his coatless torso. "Jog!" she orders. "We're nearly late!"

They are not even close to late, but Dinah's ruse works: Skint bites off half his cookie and grabs her arm and they're off.

Hurrying, trotting, practically running—despite the ice patches and snow, Skint and Dinah move along at quite a clip. Too hot for Dinah in her extra-puffy coat but good for skinny Skint and his skinny cold bones.

Mr. Beach offered to drive them ("I have a meeting with the man who's fixing the church roof"), but Dinah told him no. Mr. Beach's meeting wasn't for another hour and she wanted to go to Skint right away. Besides, they had to get a move on if they were to finish cleaning the church before the weekly AA meeting got started in there at nine. Skint would be happy if they biked but Dinah won't, not in winter. Too many ice clumps waiting to grab your wheel and make you fall.

"It was nice to see your dad last night," Dinah dares to say.

Skint glances at her sharply, eyes narrowed.

"What about him?" he asks.

Dumb, dumb, dumb, Dinah thinks. Can she please quit mentioning his dad?

"Nothing," she says. "He's nice, is all. Too many raisins in the rock cake?" she ends hastily.

Skint snorts. "No," he says at last. "It's good. Come on."

Just before they reach the bridge is the Rural Routes' house. It's as old as Dinah's and sits gray and still under the trees. The Rural Routes themselves are on their porch. They are people, not roads. Two people, old;

unfathomably old. Skint and Dinah call them after their mailbox, which has only RURAL ROUTE 1 stenciled on it and no name, just a faded E on the front.

The woman Rural Route is thin and wears tablecloth-looking dresses, thick-soled shoes, and a knitted hat pulled over her ears. The man Rural Route's pants are buckled high over his pelvis and skim the tops of brogans that look heavy as stones.

After school, every day, even when it's snowing, they are on their porch when Dinah and Skint go by. The woman sits and the man stands, though the porch holds a second chair. *What a lot of work for such an old skeleton,* Dinah thinks. Does the man stand up at the time of their coming, or is he all the time standing? Do the Rural Routes have a name for her and Skint, too?

Every day there is waving, Skint and Dinah at the Rural Routes and the Rural Routes back at them. One tired hand up from each Rural Route; one hand up, still, arm bent at the elbow. Skint and Dinah wave back the same way. No words or helloing, though Dinah always smiles. She's not sure whether the Rural Routes do. Their little house is far enough from the road that she can't see their faces.

But look: The Rural Routes are out this morning, even though it's early and gray, with Skint and Dinah jogging and it not a school day.

Two old hands up, arms bent at the elbow.

Skint's and Dinah's hands up in response as they jog past.

"What keeps them on the porch, do you think?" Dinah puffs as they run. She is boiling. Maybe Skint has the right idea after all.

"Better than most places—why not?" Skint puffs back, but that isn't what Dinah means. She means their skinniness, their arms, so porous and light. She means she keeps expecting them to float off the porch and up through the trees.

"Those shoes," she mutters darkly. "They must pin them down. Good thing, or they'd clonk their heads on the branches."

Hurry, hurry, hurry.

TEN

Years ago, the whole Girls' Friendly cleaned the church together, but it's been a one-person job for some time now. Dinah took it on about four years ago and Skint joined her when he took up with the Friendly, too. The two of them split the ten-dollar per week salary. Even though Dinah has not attended services or Sunday School at St. Francis since kindergarten, nobody has ever said she shouldn't be allowed in the Friendly because of this, or oughtn't to be let to clean. Probably because the Friendly is so low on members, and anyway, who would want to clean the church besides her?

Or maybe it's that they feel that at least they've got her in the church at all, whatever her reasons.

Now the nave of the church smells of old candles and stone and the fetid air of Dinah's vacuuming. But at least she and Skint are done in here and are ready to tackle the detritus of last night. Skint heads into the bathroom off the church foyer.

"Ah, my nemesis," he mutters to the contents of the bowl. "We meet again." He whacks away with his plunger. "Jesus!" he cries. "It's like they save it up for rehearsal nights!"

"Well, they are singing Thomas Tomkins. It is very dolorous and stressful." Dinah stuffs old cups and plates into her garbage bag.

"Your dad should switch to show tunes, then," says Skint, bashing away. "Every week I'm an hour with this plunger, breaking up choir-loosened poo."

"That is not a very socialized thing to say."

"If you can't take the conversation of a church sexpot, Dinah B—"

"*Sexton—*"

"—let alone the nature of the work, then I don't know if you're the girl for this job."

"Grr." But at least he is not thinking about monks.

Dinah is exhausted. Sad-mad Skint, monks and all that running. She wouldn't mind lying down on the couch in the big room for a nap. But that couch smells awful and there is that meeting at nine, and plus, she promised Bernadine. And a promise about cleaning is also a promise to Dinah's father, because, along with maintaining the integrity of the building, the cleanliness of the church is within the purview of the warden. Doubly beholden, then, is Dinah. Oh, well. At least it is vacation week. There will be plenty of time for sleeping.

"What the hell!" Skint's voice is far away.

"What?" says Dinah, looking up from her garbage. Where is he?

"Over here." The toilet conquered, Skint is outside the door to the food pantry, leaning over a box of food left as a donation.

Oh, no. The food pantry. The St. Francis Food Pantry is not something that is going to distract Skint from thinking about monks.

Though the Pantry is technically another warden domain, Bernadine's the one who runs it, and Dinah and Skint hate everything about the way she does the job. There's a pile of cod that's been in the freezer for over three years now, for example, and Bernadine refuses to throw it away, even though it's gone gray and furry with age. And she's always putting the Pantry mop back in the closet before it's dry so it gets full of mildew and stinks the place up. Worst of all, from Skint's point of view, at least, she arranges the cans on the shelves by height and color rather than by food type.

But at the moment, it isn't Bernadine and her ways that are bothering Skint.

"Look!" he cries, shaking a can in Dinah's direction. "Creamed corn? Nobody eats creamed corn! Nobody eats 'salted mushroom stems,' either," he continues, flashing her another can, "or 'pearl onions in faux butter sauce.' What is wrong with people? If you're hungry, you want food, not cans of crazy crap. People in this town donate garbage!"

Skint flings down the can and lurches into the Pantry with the box. Dinah follows him, pulling the garbage behind her. Entering the Pantry is unavoidable; they need the sink in there to fill the bucket for mopping.

Skint runs hot water into the bucket. "People only donate what they wouldn't eat themselves."

"I like creamed corn."

"Not pureed, you don't." Skint shuts off the faucet. "You might as well eat the contents of someone else's stomach."

"Ugh." Dinah takes up a broom. "Not everybody does that, though, with donations. I brought those sardines in our box last month."

Dinah adores sardines and had had her eye on that particular can of them for some time. They were part of a Christmas basket full of fancy things someone had sent the Beaches, the can of sardines even labeled in Italian. Her father had had his eye on them, too. Both of them love the salt and calcium crunch of the bones.

"I will disown you if you eat those without me," Mr. Beach threatened her.

"I won't," Dinah promised. And she didn't. Peeved at his unenthusiastic reaction to her Christmas gift (a CD of New England string quartets performed and arranged by Tommy Tune and the Boston Pops), Dinah gave the sardines away to the Pantry instead.

"Giving away those sardines only made *you* feel good, Dinah," says Skint.

It certainly did make her feel good, but not in the way Skint means. "Anybody would be happy to get sardines," says Dinah. "You are just picking on me because you can't yell at the other can-bringers for being stingy."

Skint sets the bucket on the floor. "You're right," he says. "Besides. Who'm I to talk? I have brought and done nothing for anyone. I am a whole lot of talk about the base nature of man but do jack-all to elevate our status."

Dinah thwaps him with the handle of her broom.

"Your plunging," she tells him. "That is your donation."

"Stool loosening for Jesus," Skint agrees. "Me and your dad both."

A small head pokes round the door of the pantry.

"Hello," it says.

"Hello," says Dinah.

"Hello," says Skint.

The owner of the head moves into the doorway. It's

K. T., in his too-big winter coat with the pirate skull on the back, hands tucked into his pockets.

"Could I come in?" he asks.

"Sure," says Dinah. "It's nice to see you again." *Let's hope the Vole isn't here, too.*

K. T. steps carefully over the threshold.

"What are you guys doing?"

"Cleaning," says Skint.

"What are you cleaning?"

"Everything," says Skint. "The whole church."

"Oh." K. T. squeezes a tiny blue Super Ball in his palm. His eyes take in the shelves. "You have a very big amount of cans," he says.

"We do, indeed," says Skint, glancing around. "God. The floor in here is disgusting." He leans the mop against the counter and grabs another broom and starts sweeping.

"What's the matter?" K. T. asks Skint.

"People are messy," Dinah explains. "It's okay. K. T., who is taking care of you right now?"

K. T. thinks. Then: "You?" he guesses, holding his Super Ball up to one eye. His other eye is on Skint, who sweeps the floor with hard, irritated strokes.

"Well, yes, I guess I am, right now here in the food pantry. But I mean, who brought you here to the church?"

"My dad brought me." *Good. Not the Vole.* "He has a meeting."

"I bet it's with *my* dad," says Dinah. K. T.'s father is a builder and must have something to do with the roof.

"Beets in with potato sticks," Skint mutters, sweeping and glaring up at the shelves. "That woman. Does your father know you're in here, K. T.?"

"I'm not sure." K. T. holds his Super Ball up so Skint can see it. "I just got this," he says. "At the mini-mart."

"Very cool, K. T. Great color." Skint turns to Dinah, bashing his broom upright against the Pantry sink beside the mop. "I am sick of this, Dinah. I am sick of everything. I am sick to death of Bernadine and her messes and her talking over me and her crazy-ass theories about this Pantry and everything else. Enough!" He points at the freezer across the room. "I'm defrosting that freezer. And I'm getting rid of that god-awful ancient cod for once and for all."

"Skint!"

"What? We're supposed to clean, aren't we? It's our sworn responsibility. So we'll clean everything. Including the freezer."

"Well—" Dinah hesitates. It would be awfully satisfying to get rid of that cod.

"Indeed." Skint stalks over to the deep freezer and flings it open.

He stands stock-still.

"Holy shit," he says.

"You say a lot of bad words," says K. T.

"He does," says Dinah. "Skint, stop saying bad words."

"That bitch."

"Skint!"

"Dinah, please come here."

K. T. sails his ball slowly through the air. "C'mere," he murmurs, "c'mere, c'mere."

Dinah steps over to the freezer and peeks in. "What?" she asks. She sees nothing untoward; the freezer is chock-full, as always, and bordered with its usual cuff of ice.

"Look closely," says Skint. "Compare the contents as you see them now to the contents as we have previously noted them."

Dinah looks again. "Oh," she says. "No cod."

"Exactly!"

"What are you on about? Aren't you glad she got rid of it? Or are you just mad because you can't thwart her by throwing it away yourself?"

"Shut up, please, Dinah, and think. The cod is no longer in the freezer, but could you please note what is here in its stead?"

Dinah peers back into the freezer. Instead of flat, plastic-wrapped parcels of fish, the freezer is filled with large, round, netted shapes.

She looks at Skint questioningly. "Turkeys?"

"Exactly!" Skint shouts again.

Dinah stares at him. "What's the big deal?"

"Don't you get it?" Skint cries plaintively. "Jesus Christ!"

"Hey," says K. T.

"Is this Turliff-related?" Dinah asks. "Because I don't think it matters if people eat turkey *outside* of school—"

"No!" Skint says. "Think, Dinah! Two dozen oven-ready turkeys? Hannaford labels?" He stabs at one of the turkeys with his forefinger. "Dated *last December*?"

Dated last December?

"Oh. Oh!"

"Yes!" cries Skint. "That troll never gave them away! And not only that—"

Dinah gasps and nods. In her mind's eye, she remembers Mrs. Samatar carrying a parcel out of the pantry. A curiously flat one, not at all humped-up like a turkey.

"She gave people that horrible, spoiled cod in their Christmas parcels!" she cries. "Instead of the turkeys!"

"Exactly!"

"What's a parcel?" asks K. T. He holds up his ball. "This guy is a bird. A person. A birdperson."

"Oh, but it's too horrible, Skint! Even for Bernadine."

"Oh, you're right," says Skint. "What are we thinking? It's not assholery—it is our very own Christmas miracle! An avian version of the loaves and fishes with a net deficit of fish! *Jesus has acted amongst the freezer parcels, right here in Aile Quarry!*"

"But why would she do that?"

"Because she is a hateful, god-awful woman," says

Skint. "You know how she's always going on about the poor not doing enough for themselves. Jesus! I have *had* it with her bullshit."

"We have to report her immediately!" Dinah cries.

K. T. is resting with the back of his head on the counter, balancing his ball between lip and nose like a squat little moustache. "Who are you guys mad at?" he asks. His talking disrupts his ball and it rolls off and drops to the floor. He scrambles after it.

"Nobody, K. T.," says Dinah hurriedly as Skint says, "Beelzebub's best minion."

"Oh," says K. T., straightening up. He points to a can on the bottom shelf. "What's that stuff?"

"Ranger hash."

"Could I please have it?"

"Sure." Skint tosses it to K. T. "Consider it yours."

"To keep?" asks K. T., catching it against his chest.

"Certainly," says Skint.

"Thank you," says K. T. He smiles at Skint, who smiles back.

"Skint," says Dinah, "you can't do that. The Inventory!" Bernadine has lists and charts all over, cross-referenced and dated.

"Who cares about the Inventory at this point, Dinah! If there's any justice on the planet at all she'll be out on her ear and the Inventory torn to shreds."

K. T. picks up his Super Ball and holds the can up in

front of his face. He carefully sets the ball on top. "My birdperson just landed on this building."

"That's neat, K. T.," says Dinah. "Skint, even so, you can't just take the stuff in here and give it away. People really need that food."

"Oh, you're right," says Skint. "What am I thinking? Giving food away in a *food pantry*?"

"Skint!"

"What?" says Skint. "I'm agreeing with you! Hoarding is clearly the rule of thumb here at Saint Francis! Hang on to donations until Bernadine decides a body is fit to have them. That's the way God would want it, right?" Skint slams the lid of the freezer shut.

"I'm going to eat this stuff later for snack," says K. T., indicating his can.

"Great," says Skint. "Here, I'll get you a can opener."

"Skint, you are twisting my words. You know I hate what Bernadine did, too!"

"All I am saying is that withholding food would be in keeping with the ethics of this whole Food Pantry operation." He stops and looks at her. "Bernadine's part of it, I mean, of course."

"Tchah." Skint knows as well as Dinah does who is the bottom line of the Food Pantry. Mr. Beach, church warden, that's who. Skint may be feeling suddenly solicitous about her father and Dinah's position, but Dinah is not. For once Mr. Beach is going to have to do something about that beastly Bernadine. "*That's* the solution, Skint. This is my dad's mess! He should be the one to clean it up!" Dinah wields her broom like a saber. "You can bet that I will be having a word with good old Mr. Beach," she says.

"Swell," says Skint. "Then you and I can both have one with Bernadine."

"Why? Let my dad deal with her! He can *fire* her."

"This guy is a space guy," K. T. says, and loops his ball through the air.

"I thought he was a birdperson," says Skint.

"What?" says K. T. He spacemans his ball through the air. "Mneep, mneep."

"You just want a showdown, Skint. You just want to yell at Bernadine because you hate her."

Skint looks at her. "And you don't?"

"Of course I do!"

"Well, then!" Skint takes down Bernadine's section of red cans and starts slinging them about into new groups. "Who organizes a pantry by aesthetics?" he cries. He looks over his shoulder at K. T. "That hash tastes like barf, K. T., but if you want to chow down—"

"Skint!"

K. T. has set down the can and is resting his cheek on the counter, marching his Super Ball along its surface. "This guy just landed," he murmurs. "He's looking around the planet."

"Here," says Skint. "Let's tuck that can in your pocket

so you can have it for later." He fits the hash into the pocket of K. T.'s coat. Then he sticks the can opener in as well. "You might as well take that, too," he says.

"Skint! Come on," says Dinah. "Quit goading me."

"I'm not goading you!" Skint wheels back to the cans and heaves diced beets over near whole and tomato paste next to crushed.

"Goats are nice," says K. T. He bounces his ball gently in front of his nose.

Dinah and Skint exchange glances.

"They are," says Dinah. "K. T., if you are bored, you can be the one to work the mop if you want."

"No, thank you," says K. T., his eyes on his ball. "I just want to play in here a minute."

"Okay," says Dinah. She bundles the fingertips of her left hand and Handcreature pecks at Skint's head, hard.

"Don't be an ass," says Skint, bopping Handcreature away with his hand, but she rears back up and fixes him with a glare.

"Don't you call people"—Dinah glances at K. T.—"things to do with a rear end! Especially when there is a small person here!" Dinah is relentless. Handcreature stabs at Skint's knuckles in time with each word.

"Assiness is not to do with a rear! It means like a donkey!"

"Fine, then! I'm proud to be like Walter!"

"Excuse me," says K. T.

"Quit it!" Skint begs, flapping his elbows at Handcreature, but she bites at his fingers all the more. Then Skint feigns left and grabs Handcreature tight in his hand.

"HA!" roars Skint.

"HEY!" roars Dinah.

"Excuse me!" K. T. shouts between them.

Dinah and Skint jump. Handcreature ceases her furious struggles.

"Sorry, K. T."

"Sorry."

"You shouldn't hit him!" K. T. cries.

"It wasn't really hitting," says Skint.

"More like poking," Dinah agrees. "I'm sorry, K. T. We were only playing."

"He might hit you back sometime."

Dinah starts. Her eyes meet Skint's over K. T.'s head.

"I would never, K. T." says Skint, looking into the little boy's face. "Never, okay?"

K. T. furrows his brow.

"He wouldn't," says Dinah. "Really, honey, he wouldn't." *Oh, K. T.*

"Is that what happens at your house, K. T.?" asks Skint gently.

K. T. picks at the plastic seam of his ball and doesn't answer.

What do we do? Dinah thinks. *What do we do?*

Skint releases Handcreature and puts his hand on K. T.'s head.

K. T. looks up at him. "What I was wondering is, what is 'goating'?" he asks.

"It's turning someone into a goat," says Skint. "Giving them horns and hooves."

"You can't turn people into animals," says K. T.

"No need to," says Skint automatically. "We already are."

"What?" K. T. asks. His eye is caught by a box of Pop-Tarts Skint has positioned halfway between the breakfast and snack items. "Could I please have one of those?"

"Sure," says Skint.

"Skint!"

K. T. drops his ball. "My space guy!" he cries, and looks for it this way and that. He spots it and stoops to pick it up. "Whoo, whoo," he sings, and sails the ball about the room.

Dinah hides the Pop-Tarts box under her coat.

"Oh, for fuck's sake!" Skint says.

Dinah's stomach roils and she gouges at the floor with her broom. "Stop swearing with K. T. in here. And don't be so *mad* the whole time!"

"Why shouldn't I be? Aren't you supposed to be mad when someone's an ass? And small-minded? And unkind?"

Of course yes, but Dinah is too worked up to think what else to say.

A piercing squeal sounds from the foyer.

Skint looks questioningly at Dinah. "Beagie?" he asks.

"Beagie," she confirms.

"What's a Beagie?" asks K. T.

"A bipedal puppy, functionally," says Skint as Dinah answers, "My brother," and punches Skint in the bicep.

"What's 'bipedal'?" asks K. T. "I like how you use other kinds of words."

"Dinah!" That is her dad calling.

Hating Skint, Bernadine and the rest of the world, Dinah thrusts the dustpan at Skint without a word and leaves, with plans to train Beagie up against him.

ELEVEN

In the middle of the big room, Mr. Beach clutches Beagan, who beams when he sees Dinah and tries to leap out of his father's arms.

"Yeeee!" Beagie cries.

"Yeee!" Dinah cries back.

"Stop encouraging him, Dinah!" Her dad looks grim. "My God, the squealing we've had all morning."

His words enrage Dinah, and, to judge from his ensuing howls, they enrage Beagie as well.

It's true Beagie screeches all the time, but he is only thirteen months old and can't help it if he can't talk much yet. He's doing his best. Dinah never minds his yowling attempts at speech but other people do. Their mother, for instance. Mrs. Beach says she won't take Beagie in to the Center for visits anymore until he's got some more words to replace the screeches. Dinah thinks that's nuts. How will Beagie ever learn to talk if they stop him from having people to practice on? Even though Dinah avoids the Center herself, from all accounts, the people there love her brother. Besides, many of them are sort of deaf.

Dinah reaches for the baby.

"No," says her dad firmly, holding him away. Beagie flaps his arms with rage. "We have to go, right now. I can't bear to have to pry him off you. I just wanted to remind you two to remember to turn up the heat." He winces as Beagie seizes his hair.

Dinah beams approvingly at her brother. "That's what you get, Mr. Beach," she says, "for always sticking up for Bernadine! Wait till you hear what she's done this time!"

"What's the matter with you? What on earth are you talking about?"

"Bernadine is what I am talking about! Bernadine the . . . the Christmas Fiend!" she sputters. "You want to know what she gave the people who came to the pantry at Christmas? That three-year-old cod, is what! That grayed-out, rotted-out, freezer-burned cod!"

Mr. Beach eyes widen. "What?" he asks.

"Yes! And guess what? The Christmas turkeys are still in the freezer!"

"Dinah, are you sure about this?"

"Yes!" says Dinah. "She's hoarding the turkeys like a miser hoards gold! And here's you, always defending her the whole time, you old Mr. Beach."

Mr. Beach's brow is furrowed. "You're positive? Not just assuming?"

"Yes! We just were . . . cleaning out the freezer and we saw! And the meat parcels were *flat* at Christmas. Have a look for yourself." Dinah stamps. "*Do* something!"

"Hush," says Mr. Beach, his brow furrowed. "I have to think."

"What's there to think about? Fire her!"

"Stop talking like you're waving a pitchfork, for heaven's sake. I said I need to think about it. Thank you for letting me know." Mr. Beach shifts Beagie to his other arm. "Come along, Beagie, we need to get home."

"What!" Dinah explodes. "You aren't even going to go in there and see?"

"Calm down, Dinah. I believe you."

"Calm down?!"

"Yes," says her dad, and levers Beagie down toward her. "Kiss your brother good-bye."

"How can you?" Dinah kisses Beagie distractedly but rears back in revulsion as her father presents his own cheek. "How can you just let her do like that and then just keep going along, tra-la?"

Her father withdraws his cheek. "Don't be unfair. You know how much she cares for you and how much she does for this church. For people all over this town, for that matter, volunteering here, at the hospital, all over. You can't not take the whole picture into account and I for one refuse to be hasty, even to satisfy my own ghastly firstborn. Come on, Beagan, darling." Mr. Beach unpeels Beagie's fingers from his eyebrows. "Time to go and feed you. Good-bye, Dinah," he says and carries the baby out the door. Dinah glares. She does not say good-bye back.

Calling Beagie "darling"—who cares if Mr. Beach is sweet with endearments when at his core he is a Bernadine-be-evil enabler who ignores his duties as warden? Her father is as awful as Bernadine.

Skint is scrubbing down the counters when Dinah returns to the food pantry. The reorganization of the canned goods is nearly complete, each item arranged on the counter by meal or snack type, and alphabetized. K. T. is tossing his ball up and trying to catching it one-handed, over and over again. Sometimes he is successful.

"Well?" Skint, still scrubbing, his back to Dinah. "What's the verdict?"

"Nothing," says Dinah. "No verdict. He says I am

unfair and that Bernadine does a lot for the church."

"Oh," says Skint. Then: "Oh."

"He's a wuss!" cries Dinah. "He wouldn't—" She breaks off, staring at K. T. With one hand he tosses and catches his ball, it is true. But with the other, he delivers a rectangular pastry to his mouth at regular intervals.

"Skint!"

"What?" Skint takes in Dinah's furious face and the torn foil wrapper that she has snatched up from the counter, which contains the mate to the Pop-Tart in K. T.'s hand.

"Oh, come on!" Skint says.

"What's the matter?" K. T. asks, his face anxious.

"Nothing, K. T." It is not K. T.'s fault. He deserves to enjoy his Pop-Tart and Dinah does not want to wreck it for him. "I am . . . I'm only surprised that Skint and I still have so much more cleaning to do."

"I don't like cleaning," says K. T. and takes another bite.

"Oh, I am with you there, my man," says Skint.

"Tchah," says Dinah. Skint's statement is belied by the sparkle of the counters.

K. T. bounces his ball against the cabinets and Dinah takes advantage of his not paying attention to glower some more at Skint. Mindful of K. T., she keeps her voice at a furious whisper. "For the last time, giving away the food in here to just any old body does not punish Bernadine! It punishes the people who come here needing food! It punishes the wrong people!"

"I don't think the people who come here would mind that I gave K. T. a Pop-Tart," Skint replies in his normal voice.

"How do you know? Maybe someone is hoping for them specially," Dinah says. "Besides, what if K. T.'s mother doesn't believe in sugar or something?"

"Sugar exists, man," says Skint. "I have seen its evil ways."

"My mom believes in sugar," says K. T. unexpectedly. "She has some. We bake with it. Today we are, even! I have my visit with her. I get to stay overnight and we are going to make cake."

"There," says Skint.

"We made a house out of cookies at Christmas. I like baking," K. T. confides.

"Me, too," says Skint.

Dinah fumes. K. T. turns his attention back to his ball.

"What if my dad asks me about those Pop-Tarts?" says Dinah. "What if there's some big Inventory check after all this goes down?"

"I'm not trying to get anyone in trouble, Dinah," says Skint, squeezing out his sponge. "Besides Bernadine, of course. And I really don't imagine your dad is on the job at the level of the Pop-Tart."

"What's that supposed to mean!" The urge to punch

Skint in the sternum is overwhelming. But K. T. is staring at her with eyes big as dishes. He wipes his nose on the shoulder of his coat.

"You guys fight all the time," he says.

Skint's chest rises and falls but he forces a smile at K. T. "We don't really," he says. "Not really. Are you too hot in that coat, K. T.?"

"Yes," says K. T. "But I'm not allowed to take it off because of if it gets lost."

"I'll hold it for you," Dinah offers but K. T. shakes his head no.

"I can't. I lost it for a little while last night and my dad was mad."

"Oh. Okay." Dinah and Skint look at one another. Dinah hugs K. T.'s shoulders and fumbles with the Pop-Tart box.

Skint squeezes out the mop and begins on the floor.

"Maybe my dad will reconsider," says Dinah hopelessly.

"Right," snorts Skint. "Maybe he'll kick her ass from here until next Tuesday."

Dinah slumps over her broom.

The door to the pantry swings open. A tall man in a windbreaker stands in its frame. It's Mr. Vaar, K. T.'s dad.

"K. T." Mr. Vaar nods to Dinah and Skint, who nod back. "K. T., what are you doing in here? Where did I tell you to wait for me?"

"Hunh?" says K. T. He loops his Super Ball over the countertop in long, slow arcs. "My space guy has balloon boots on. He does big bounces to go where he needs to."

"How fitting," says Mr. Vaar. "A fellow space cadet for you." He gives a short laugh and winks at Dinah and Skint, who look coldly back at him.

"K. T.," says Mr. Vaar again.

K. T. wafts his ball over the countertop.

"K. T.!"

"Dude?" Skint says to K. T. "Your dad is talking to you."

"Hunh?" K. T. looks up. "This guy can fly," he tells Skint.

"Cool," says Skint. "Better than space boots if there are parts of the planet he can't stand on."

"Someone's going to get a space boot in the ass if he doesn't start paying attention." Mr. Vaar emits another laugh and looks knowingly again at Dinah and Skint.

Dinah hates him. Skint's face is implacable as he turns back to K. T.

"K. T.?" he says.

K. T. turns around. He sees his dad and smiles. "See my space guy, Dad?"

"I see two. I also see that you disobeyed me."

K. T.'s smile fades.

"I see that you chose to come in here and play some little game rather than do as you were told."

K. T.'s cheeks grow red.

"Where did I tell you to wait?"

"In the foyer," he mumbles.

"In the foyer. Is this the foyer?"

K. T. stares up at him.

"Is it, K. T.?"

"No." K. T. shakes his head. He blinks.

"No," says Mr. Vaar.

K. T. blinks some more. Dinah moves toward him but Mr. Vaar puts up a hand to stop her. "I'm talking to him," he tells her. "Don't you start with the crying, K. T. When I'm doing things here, your job is to do what you're told. Last night I could hardly concentrate on my singing with you running all over the place. I can't do my best when I have to worry about you getting in everybody's way."

"He wasn't in our way, Mr. Vaar. He was just visiting," says Skint. "He was helping us."

"I wasn't helping!" K. T. cries, surprised, his cheeks and eyes red. "I was playing space guy!"

Mr. Vaar yanks at K. T.'s arm. "Get over here," he barks. K. T. stumbles and drops his Pop-Tart, which shatters on the floor.

"Hey!" says Skint. He pushes himself off the counter.

Mr. Vaar cuts a look at him. "It never occurred to you to find out where he was supposed to be?"

"We knew you were here," says Skint. "Fixing the roof."

"So you thought you'd just hang on to him where I couldn't find him?" Mr. Vaar glances at the Pop-Tart on the floor. "And feed him a crap snack without getting permission?"

K. T. looks down at the Pop-Tart with chumped-up cheeks.

"I don't think a Pop-Tart is so bad, sir," says Skint.

"I don't feed him sugar. It makes him spacier than he already is."

Punching.

"K. T.?" says Skint. "We enjoyed having you."

"We enjoyed having you very much," Dinah says earnestly. "You are great at thinking up playing."

"Did you hear a word I said?" says Mr. Vaar, leaning toward Skint. "No idiot kid is going to undermine what I do with my son."

Skint looks at him steadily. "Even if what's done with him is idiotic?" he asks.

Mr. Vaar narrows his eyes. "You want to talk like that to me again?"

Skint says nothing. Mr. Vaar stares at him some more.

Then he snorts. "Skinny little shit," he says. "Come on, K. T. We're leaving. Right now."

"Good-bye, honey," says Dinah, her stomach and fists knotted. K. T. is blinking and winking and red. She moves to hug him good-bye but Mr. Vaar grabs his arm by the elbow and pulls him toward the door. K. T.'s ball slips out of his hand and bounces across the floor.

"My space guy!" cries K. T.

"Maybe that'll help you remember to stay where I tell you. You stay away from kids like him," says his dad, nodding toward Skint. "And you," he looks at Skint, "stay away from my son."

He hustles the little boy out.

The church door slams shut with a bang. Through the pantry window, Skint and Dinah watch Mr. Vaar pull K. T. across the parking lot, K. T.'s legs scissoring too quickly as he tries to keep up. K. T.'s dad thrusts him into the car. They drive away.

"I hate him!" Dinah picks up K. T.'s Pop-Tart pieces and holds them in her palm. His Super Ball is wedged underneath the baseboard.

"Who wouldn't."

"How can a jerk like that have such a wonderful kid?"

"I don't know." Skint shakes his head. Then: "What the hell! A kid like K. T. should be protected, not name-called and yelled at. What is wrong with that guy?"

"I couldn't think what to say," Dinah says helplessly. "I was all riled and I couldn't think what to say! You were great, though."

"Oh, I was phenomenal," says Skint. "Especially that part at the end where I couldn't think how to respond. I made a huge difference."

"At least you talked back to him. That was good. Though you probably shouldn't have."

Skint snorts. "If I didn't say anything, wouldn't that make K. T. believe we agree with his dad? That we think it's okay for him to be treated like that? That we think his dad is right to be such a tool?" Skint turns and grabs the boxes of breakfast foods with names beginning with *A* and shoves them, hard, onto a shelf. "What is wrong with people? Why have kids if all you're going to do is bash at them and needle them and make fun? Add the Vole in the mix, and there's a recipe for a great little life." Skint sorts and stacks and shoves. "I am beyond sick of human assiness."

Dinah cannot bear it. Imagine Beagie stuck in a house like the Vaar house, with two testosterone jerks at the helm. "At least his mom sounds nice. It sounds like he likes his mom."

"Who cares? They're divorced and he lives with Mr. Charmface there." Skint slaps at the labels on the cans. "The A foods are done, here's B's and C's. No fucking D's."

"Yes, D's. Those Dairy Dream bars."

"I was counting those as a snack." But he slams them into place.

Stormy-eyed Skint, mouth lines tight. Dinah's brain is churning like sixty. Phone call to Mr. Vaar, pretending to be the police? Poison pen letters to scare him?

"We could send K. T. a parcel of treats," she offers at last. "Cookies, games, some books."

Skint looks at her.

"Sure," he says. "That'll turn things around. Dorketta."

He lifts her coat from the countertop and takes the leftover Pop-Tart from the foil.

"We are not truly nice people," he says, giving her half. "If we were, we would feel bad for the Vole, too, and want to make him a parcel of treats as well. And yet, I only wish him ill."

"He would just beat us up with the parcel."

"Not if we tied it up with a pretty yellow bow, just so."

"The only thing I will tie up with a bow for him is punches."

"That's a parcel I can get behind. I'm telling you," Skint says, chewing. "When we start our new planet, we're stealing all the kids who are stuck with people like that and taking them with us."

"Yes," Dinah agrees. She crumbles her half of the Pop-Tart. "Only not the Vole. He can stay stuck."

"Fine," says Skint. "He'll miss me, though. Coveting my manly form the way he does." He slumps. "Jesus Christ. I don't know what we can do."

TWELVE

"Sardines on toast is a marvelous thing, Beagan Beach," says Mr. Beach as he totes his son across the parking lot. It's windy out here, with enormous clouds scuttling across the sky, but Beagan isn't paying attention to them.

He has just discovered something so wonderful he almost can't breathe.

When he moves his foot, like this, the sunshine ripples across the front of his father's shirt and the icy surface of the ground.

See—there:

ripple ripple sun

Beagie can make the sunshine dance. His feet are magic.

Oh, he better tell his dad. Beagie squirms and bounces but before he can squawk at his father, it happens again: He wiggles his feet and there goes that sun.

Beagan crows with joy. He forgets about his dad. He waves his foot to make the sun dance and laughs and laughs when it does.

"What's so funny, sweetheart?"

Beagie screeches and laughs and points.

"Yes, that's your foot," his father agrees. "And what a fine one it is."

That's not it at all. But Beagie can't make his father understand, no matter how much he yells and points. His dad only opens the car door and lowers Beagan into his car seat.

Beagie weeps with rage. He kicks his feet as hard as he can but this time the sun doesn't dance or help him. He's captive under all these straps with a father who has no idea that Beagie, out of this car seat, is the boss of the sun.

THIRTEEN

What a long Saturday it's been already, with cleaning and Bernadine and K. T. and everything else. Dinah sits in the window seat in her living room, her forehead pressed against the glass. Snowing again out there, the yard and woods already blanketed blue. It'll be a chilly walk to the Girls' Friendly meeting later. Over in the Harps' yard next door stands their horse, perfectly still, his neck bowed and his mane speckled with white. Beagie loves that horse, but he is napping. Dinah is in here alone.

"Dinah." Mr. Beach stands in the doorway. Dinah's

stomach jumps. "A can of hash is missing from the food pantry, as well as a box of Pop-Tarts."

What? Dinah sits up straight. Mr. Beach *is* on the job at the level of the Pop-Tart!

"Do you know anything about it?" asks Mr. Beach.

"What makes you think they're missing?"

"Because Bernadine just phoned. She's upset."

"Because you fired her?"

"No, Dinah, because food is missing!"

"When will you fire her, then?"

"Dinah Christine." Mr. Beach is grim. Dinah is skating on very thin ice. She subsides back against the window.

Ghastly Bernadine. Even when you tell on her and reorganize her cans, she comes out on top. Skint shouldn't have alphabetized. Too easy to check against the Inventory.

"Well, Dinah?"

"K. T. Vaar visited us while his dad was with you," Dinah says at last. "He was hungry. So I . . . gave him a snack."

"You gave him *hash*, Dinah?" says her dad.

Dinah shrugs and turns back to the window. "He wanted it."

"You are the oddest child." Mr. Beach beetles his brows. "And you know better. That food is the property of the people who need it."

Really? Like the turkeys? But she knows her father will explode if she says it out loud and all at once she's exhausted, too brain-weary and thrown by the half-sort-of-lie she told to cover for Skint to figure out how to take up the whole turkey thing again. Too much already today and Dinah is old-feeling and cold to the bone.

"Well, Dinah?"

"I'll buy more hash," says Dinah. Dinah the cheater, cheater, hard-topic shirker. "I'll replace the Pop-Tarts as well. Only, I don't have any money. But if you advance me some, I'll babysit it off."

"Fine," says her dad. "And you better apologize to Bernadine. Don't be so hasty all the time, Dinah." Her father waits for a minute, but she says nothing, and he leaves the room.

Apologize? *Apologize?*

The window glass is cool. *That horse must be cold. Someone please give him a blanket.*

Five-year-old Dinah holds her great-grandma's hand in front of her nose. Granny's fingernails peek over the tops of her fingers like brims of hats. Dinah plays that the fingers are people. Behind her and over her head is Granny's singing that sounds like buzzing.

"Lay up nearer, brother, nearer . . ."

Big-knuckled Granny does buzzy singing all the time, shape note songs from her big blue book. Walking outside, sitting in the window seat, during Friendly meetings too.

The singing breaks off.

"Come on up my lap," Granny says to Dinah. "Come up and help me remember this song." And she pulls Dinah up onto her thighs and starts singing again above her head.

I am going, brother, going,
But my hope in God is strong.
I am willing, brother, knowing
That he doeth nothing wrong.

Dinah knows most of the words, but when she tries to sing like Granny, it comes out more like honking.

"That's fine, little goose. That's just how this song should sound," Granny says and they keep singing. When Dinah forgets the words she leans back against Granny and breathes in the smell of Granny's pear-scented talc and hums along instead.

FOURTEEN

There's a half-eaten bag of chips on the coffee table and Skint decides they'll do for a late lunch before the Friendly meeting.

"Chew!" Ellen's voice comes from the kitchen. "For God's sake, take smaller bites."

Skint's father doesn't answer.

Across from where Skint sits with his chips on the couch is the little table his mother uses for holiday displays. Valentine's Day has come and gone, but she hasn't yet changed the arrangement. A box of candy. Two red carnations. A plush toy, two frogs intertwined, that she brought home from the drugstore. The boy frog is bigger than the girl and his foreleg is slung around her shoulders. The girl frog snuggles up into his armpit and her eyes are in the shape of hearts. HOP SPRINGS ETERNAL! her T-shirt exclaims. WANNA COME OVER TO MY PAD? his T-shirt says back. I'M IN YOUR CORNER FOREVER!

The longing and wish in the hand that picked out those frogs is enough to kill Skint, slay him, mow him down dead. His head is in his hands.

His dad coughs and stops. He coughs again, louder. It sounds like he's hacking up a lung.

"That's what I'm talking about! You have to fucking chew!"

His dad coughs one more time, and stops.

The hair on the back of Skint's neck stands on end, his hand stilled inside the bag. He is tight, taut. He wishes he were less rational because he would really love to put someone through a wall right now.

Skint gets up because he has to go in there, has to check, just in case.

His dad is at the table, eyes full of tears. Skint glances sharply at Ellen. She is red, tense.

"Go," Skint tells her. "Go."

"You do it," she hisses at him. "You do the coaxing all day, every day—twenty minutes with the cereal and fifteen with the pants and another twenty to get him to remember how to sign his own name. You try to explain to him what we have to do at that bank on Monday. You do it."

"I do. I do do it."

"Oh, I know. You're a bastion of patience. A regular saint of a kid."

Skint crouches at his father's feet. He puts his arms around his father's knees.

"Dad," he whispers. "Dad."

Ellen gets up and leaves.

"Who will help them?" His father sobs. "Who will help those people? No water, shelter, not enough food. Empty promises. No hope."

Later, his dad asleep on the couch and his mother in her room, Skint grabs his bike and goes. He stands on the pedals and rockets down the dirt road between the trees. It's icy and full of stones but that's the way he likes it—every moment a decision, any fraction of a steer the possibility of broken bones or blood or death. Impossible to be anywhere but in this particular second, in this particular plan to not crash.

Careen—rocket—dirt—stone. Tree to tree to tree to tree. No need to think about the fabric of the whole; no need to think about anything but taut body, breathe, and lean.

Too soon Skint comes out onto the paved road, one maintained more thoroughly by the town plows and also by the heat of exhaust from the cars on its surface. No perils here, only salt and wet dirt splashing onto the legs of his jeans. Past the post office, the mini-mart and the start of the long curving road up to the high school; past the stores and houses, more and more of them, crowding up to the edge of the road.

"Effing people," Skint mutters to himself. *All of these houses and all of them crowded full of us. Why do people keep making more? All we do is kill each other, rape; cut each other for blood and make each other's life a hell.*

Dinah's scowling face and her tangle of dark hair; Dinah, furious and punching.

Okay.

One good one.

Doesn't outweigh the ass stupidity of the whole.

House, house, house.

Pole, pole, pole.

Another small square house and a little boy standing at the curb in front of it.

"Hi!" cries the boy, and Skint is well past before he realizes it was K.T. The little guy is probably waiting for his mom to pick him up.

He turns around to wave back, but K. T. is looking at the ground now and doesn't see that he has been acknowledged.

FIFTEEN

Dinah and Skint bash their way through the snow, down the shortcut path in the woods between Skint's house and town. They're on the way to the Girls' Friendly meeting. It's late afternoon but already dark out. The Friendly always meets on Saturday and today is the day they will vote on projects for the spring. Neither Dinah nor Skint feels like it's a normal Girls' Friendly day, not after the turkey debacle (their second in as many days, if you count Turliff) and nothing being changed and now they are going to have to see Bernadine herself in person. But they can't not go to the meeting. Heck, maybe Mr. Beach did do something without telling them and Bernadine's spirit will be quashed. Maybe she will welcome Skint warmly and beg him for his thoughts.

Sure, Dinah. And maybe she will greet them in a suit made of owls, too.

Theoretically, Dinah and Skint likc to walk and rarely accept the offer of a ride. Dinah, particularly, has always loved stalking about in the snow with her boots. But it's different now, with Skint and this no-coat thing. She better start asking her mother to drive them more often, even though Mrs. Beach hates the production of organizing Beagie into the car when she is only going to have to bundle him right back out again.

But for now they are walking. The snowy dirt path finally turns onto the paved road, and their boots clunk onto its surface. Past the Rural Routes' house; the Rural Routes themselves are not out this late in the day, of course. No lights on, either, but a plume of smoke, spare and gray, curls out the chimney.

"That smoke plume looks like words, doesn't it?" Dinah says. "Like it could be the Rural Routes' singing, floating out of the house and up."

Skint glances at her, hands in his pockets, uncoated shoulders hunched. His skin is stiff-looking, cold and smooth as granite.

"It's a pretty thin smoke plume," he says.

"Yes," says Dinah patiently. "That's why I think it

looks like their singing would look, thin-voiced and kind of nasal."

"That's stupid."

What?

"It is," Skint says, hunching his shoulders. "It's such a thin curl of smoke. Doesn't that worry you?"

What does he mean, worry her? "Do you mean they might not have the flue open enough?"

"I mean it's cold and that doesn't seem like smoke from a fire big enough to warm a house."

"They probably have the heat on, too, dork."

Skint shakes his head. "I bet they don't. No lights on. Them so thin."

What's he on about? "You're thin, too. What does that have to do with smoke being singing?"

"Jesus," says Skint. "Don't you see? Maybe they can't afford to pay their electric bill. Maybe they can't afford enough heat. It's hard for me to get behind some stupid singing idea when they might be actually cold in there."

Stupid? Dinah stomps ahead. But the wind blows snow from the branches onto her head, and she stops stomping and turns around. Whether or not Skint is a jerk, it is cold to the bone out here, and Skint's voice is as stiff as his cheeks.

"Speaking of cold," she says, "if you are worried about people being cold, why won't you wear a coat?

Why are you treating yourself like a side of beef the whole time?"

"I am like a side of beef. So are you. What's flesh but meat?"

"Well, you are mean meat."

They walk. Dinah thinks of the Rural Routes, thin, waving from the porch. That knit cap on the lady Rural Route's head. Maybe it isn't the lady Rural Route's particular aesthetic, as Dinah has always assumed. Maybe it really is freezing in there.

Dinah and her smoke singing. Her willful positivity drives Skint insane sometimes. And that damned skirt she has on and those silly striped leggings. For the first time Dinah's clothes irritate him beyond belief.

"You can't run around acting like things aren't real, Dinah," he says. "Like people aren't real. Making up stuff so you don't see what's real. For fuck's sake, that's childish and absurd."

Look at her face. Why does he do this? Why does he want her to feel so terrible? He's an asshole. Dinah is the kindest person he knows.

"What's your problem? Say something."

Dinah looks miserable. Bleak-eyed and sad. What the fuck has he done?

"Dinah. I'm sorry. I'm being a shit."

"No, you aren't. I mean, yes, you are, but you are right. I've been a jerk. It's worse because I always think I'm nice. Even though I talk about punching people all the time, I secretly think I am pretty good."

"Dinah. You are. You're the best. My favorite."

"Don't say that. It's not good for me."

"Dinah, it only just hit me, too. That their house is too dark and they are twig thin." Skint is the selfish one. The Rural Routes are so skinny and old and always alone; why has he never thought about if they are okay? "I'm an asshole to throw it on you."

"Me, too, though," Dinah says miserably. "I am also an asshole."

Even though he is being so mean, Dinah is full of shame, hot streaks of it piercing her insides. Skint is right about her. How can she not have been thinking about the Rural Routes? What if they are cold in there? Why hasn't she helped? Be honest, awful girl; be honest.

Part of it must be how she dreads being around old people, but it's right, what Skint said, about her making the RRs not real. The truth is that they have always seemed imaginary to Dinah, a thin-boned pair, like people in a dream, untalking and light as clouds. *Oh, Dinah. How dare you pretend they are not real?*

The Rural Routes solid up in her mind with the thought, and Dinah's spine slopes into the lady Rural Route's stoop. Sharp stream of spinehurt and Dinah's neck hairs rise. *Stop stop stop.*

But she can't. That thin and that old with only shoes to pin them down.

Candy, maybe; they could send them some chocolates. A lot of old people have sweet teeth. She remembers from Great-Granny, who ate loads of sweets, even though she wasn't supposed to.

No.

Don't think about all that right now.

Her mother says it a lot about old people having sweet teeth, too. She confiscates care packages of candy and cookies from them at the Center, because if she doesn't, they eat it all in a go. She saves it for them instead and doles it out, one piece at a time.

"Dinah, stop!" Skint bumps her with his hip. "You are the anti-asshole."

"Bluck. That is a disgusting thing to picture."

"Honestly, Dinah B. I'm sorry."

"It doesn't matter. Let's talk about the meeting."

"Okay," says Skint. "But I am. I'm sorry. I am such a jerk."

"No," says Dinah. "You aren't."

Dinah tucks her hand under his arm. Cold Skint, cold Rural Routes. She better get her act together.

They walk on.

"Dinah?"

It is good they always have hot bevs at the Girls' Friendly meetings.

"Dinah!"

Ten more minutes, though. His toes must be ice.

"For God's sake! Dinah!"

"Yes?"

"Oh, my God."

"What?"

"If you could pay attention for more than five seconds at a time, please—"

"I am paying attention!" Look at those cheeks. Dinah unwinds the scarf from her neck. It is one of her crocheted creations and awfully bright.

"What was I saying, then?"

"My name!" says Dinah, waving her scarf. She flaps it at him menacingly. He skitters his torso to one side, but Dinah is faster. She snaps it up over his head and wraps his head up as smooth as a balloon.

"Much better," she says, satisfied. "Now no one has to look at your mean head."

Skint squawks and flails. Dinah uncovers his eyes and he looks at her steadily.

"Hello," she says and squashes the scarf down

around his neck. "There," she says. "A goiter."

Skint growls and rears his chin up over the wool.

"Dinah. Shut up. Please. Just listen a second."

"All right."

"We have thinking to do."

Handcreature pokes up her head inquiringly.

Skint pats her firmly.

"No," he says. "This is a mouth-talking topic."

Handcreature sulks back down.

"We haven't talked about quitting the Friendly, after what we found out today about Bernadine."

Dinah starts. But she says only, "That is true."

"Why haven't we talked about quitting the Friendly?"

The back of Dinah's neck pricks and grows hot. They haven't talked about quitting the Friendly because she has always strenuously deflected Skint from the idea any time she has sensed him creep up on it in all previous instances of their being peeved with Bernadine. Dinah knows she's a hypocrite, a jerk and a wuss. But even now with all this new material for outrage, when she thinks of what will happen if she quits, she could barf.

It's not just the guilt of depleting a too-small membership. If Dinah leaves, the Friendly will fold. There'll be no girl-aged Girls left at all. And without a girl to mentor, they won't be allowed to keep their charter and there would be no more meetings for people to go to. Dinah can't bear the thought of people—Mrs. Chatham, for one, or even people Dinah hates—home by themselves all the time, home all alone with cups of tea and no people, with nothing to do and no one to talk to, all because Dinah left and killed the Friendly. Trouble and shouting are all kinds of good, but misery and isolation are not things Dinah can inflict on anyone. Unless maybe they were murderers or something. And no one actually died from that cod.

"Because," Dinah says.

"Well, maybe tonight we should."

What? Her stomach is killing her.

"How can you quit something you aren't officially a part of?" she asks, stalling for time.

"Shut up," says Skint. "You know what I mean. I think tonight is the night. The timing is perfect. And the Friendly is betwixt and between projects, so it's a good time for a shake-up."

Dinah is silent.

"Come on!" says Skint. "If we keep participating, we're tacitly approving what Bernadine does. That means we are complicit! If we aren't stopping her, we're aiding her! Inaction is passive action! Why have we kept doing that?"

"Because!" Dinah wraps her arms around her stomach and racks her brains. How can she get him off this? "Change from within! That's what you always say the whole time. If we quit, how will it ever be different?"

"Well, our staying has done jack," Skint points out. "We have done jack. Our appeals to higher authority have gone unheeded and all our oblique hinting has done nothing. All our ideas have been thwarted."

It's true. Skint's vote isn't allowed to count, of course, and Bernadine keeps a pretty tight hold on the discourse anyhow. Plus Bernadine's mother always has to take Bernadine's side, so even if Ms. Dugan votes with Dinah, it's not enough to get anything done.

"Well, that is because we have been wusses," says Dinah.

"Exactly."

"We should do more."

"Now you're talking."

"We should do something control-wresting."

"Like what?"

Dinah thinks. "A coup?"

"What?"

"Yes," says Dinah. "A coup. I think that is better than quitting."

"I am completely up for a coup! Usurp the power!" Skint rubs his hands together, for which Dinah is glad because it warms him and also he is off the quitting topic, but now she has to think of what she means by a coup.

"Maybe we could try to get them to do a different kind of project," she says. "Instead of the ones Bernadine proposed." Bernadine wants them to do a can drive for disaster relief overseas, and she also wants them to schedule regular visits to the Center.

"What'll that accomplish?"

"It would show her we have some muscle! We can think of an idea quick right now that would make her look bad if she doesn't agree."

"That doesn't sound like much of a coup. And I really have no problem helping with the disaster relief idea. I think it's a good thing to do." Skint kicks at a stone. "Though I could do without visiting the Center."

Dinah feels exactly the same way, but nonetheless she is surprised. "Does that make us jerks?" she asks. "After what we were just saying about the Rural Routes?"

"That is different," says Skint. "That is not the same as a field trip to the Center to make God's eyes out of Popsicle sticks."

"I don't want them to think I don't want to help the elderly, though."

"Well, you don't. You hate being around old people. You get all skittery."

"I do not," says Dinah, and considers bringing up the Rural Routes to support her case, but technically speaking, she is not exactly around the Rural Routes. She is more like at a respectable distance from them. So she says nothing.

It's not that being near old people makes Dinah

skittery, exactly. It's seeing what getting old does to them that makes her miserable. Being with old people makes Dinah's stomach sore, even though her mother's whole job is to do with old people, and Dinah used to visit the Center a lot herself when she was small. It's that getting old is such a terrible way for things to work. All that aching and sitting, unhappy. Bones that hurt and glasses. Great-Granny asleep for so long in her chair with one slipper on, the other foot in a woolen sock.

Who ever thought that was a good way to make human beings? No. Dinah can't bear it. She can't. And she won't. She has a plan. Well, more of a resolve. She calls it Backwards Aging. She is willing to go up to fifteen—Skint is already there, and has always looked much older to boot—but starting after that she's going backward back down to one. Why grow up and be an adult when it only means you're that much closer to dying, to breaking down and being gone? Forget it. She won't. She refuses to grow all the way up.

For his part, Skint thinks the time between being a teenager and being dead sounds a whole lot better than either one, but he says he is willing to go along with Backwards Aging for Dinah's sake. To keep her company.

"Plus," says Skint now. He stops, then continues. "From my point of view," he says, "visiting the Center is redundant."

"You're right," Dinah agrees. "Everybody is always going there. All those trips from the elementary school. My mom's whole job. *Beagie* even visits as a project."

Skint glances at her. "I mean my house is its own geriatric ward."

Jerk. Jerk! Think, Dinah! What else can you talk about?

"Let's invite the Rural Routes to do Backwards Aging with us!" she cries. "We could have them do it in increments of five."

Skint could put her through a wall.

Calm down, calm down. You love this about her, remember? Calm down.

No. Fuck calming down. Fuck all manner of bullshit and prevarication. If he goes along with that he will explode.

"The hell with it," says Skint tightly. "The hell with it, Dinah! Forget just switching up the projects. Let's burst this shit open."

"What do you mean?" Dinah takes away her hand.

"Forget all this dancing and pussyfooting and willful not-doing. Just tell everyone what Bernadine did!"

"In the *meeting*?"

"Yes!" says Skint. "Name her perfidy! Out loud to the group!"

The trees on the sides of the road are heaped with

snow, their peaky heads leaning in as if listening.

Dinah is silent. Publicly calling Bernadine out seems somehow more cowardly, not less. Shouldn't they at least take her aside? Dinah's stomach twists up even to imagine it.

"Come on!" says Skint, reading her face. "Don't you want it to stop? Do you want the same shit to go down with the hams come Easter?"

"No," says Dinah. "No."

Yelling at Bernadine might feel very splendid in that moment, but afterward . . . her dad, Ms. Dugan, everybody angry? Bernadine empurpled or deflated and sad? What if everything snowballs and Bernadine is made to give up the whole church?

Mr. Beach. He should have done something about Bernadine ages ago. He should be dealing with this very thing, right now. He is cowardly and weak and now look what's happening.

"Say something," says Skint.

"Is it mean of us?"

"So what? You reap what you sow!"

Dinah is silent, thinking, thinking. Bernadine living all alone with her mother. Dinah's own stupid dumb father.

"For God's sake, Dinah! Why do you think the world keeps on sucking? This is why! People are too weak! We have to take a stand!"

"I know," says Dinah.

"But what?"

"Nothing."

"What?"

Dinah is quiet.

"You love this stuff!" says Skint. "You are always the one who wants to do shouting."

"I know," says Dinah. She wishes she were home right now. "I do usually like to shout."

"So you'll do it? Or at least join in when I do?"

Dinah pauses. She wants so badly for Skint to be happy. Plus he is right. You should speak up. Stand up for your principles even when it's hard. She can't not do that, not if he's willing to be so brave. Not if she is ready to shout at her own father for not doing the same thing.

"All right," says Dinah. "I'm in."

Skint cuffs her on the arm.

"Great," he says. "We'll seize an opening."

After several hectic minutes of planning, they are silent for the last bit of the walk.

As they near the church steps, Dinah breaks the silence.

"I do love the Rural Routes," she says. "I do love them."

Skint feels awful again. He knows she loves them. Why does he get so mad? "I do, too," he says, and does deer head-butting. He would like to point out that, in addition to the Rural Routes, the way Dinah loved her own great-granny is further proof of her non-assholery in regards to the elderly. But he would never do that, never wake up that grief for her. Never.

"Do I really love them, though?" he wonders. "It's not as if I really know them."

"We've waved to them for years."

"Yeah," says Skint. "But I've never even called out hello, much less gone up on the porch and asked them how they are, or offered to pick up something for them."

Dinah nods. "Me either," she says.

"I love some idea of them," says Skint. "I have no clue who they really are. What kind of love is that?"

Dinah squeezes his arm. "We will say hello out loud next time," she says. "And maybe bring them something nice."

Skint smiles at her and holds the door.

He has got to get it together with his temper.

SIXTEEN

Ms. Dugan mans the tea station in the kitchen, cigarette dangling unlit in the corner of her mouth. Behind her is one of the bulletin boards where people tack notices about church doings. "Woman's Auxiliary Meeting!" announces one. "Evensong!" cries another. "Saint Francis Episcopal Choir performs a selection of music by Thomas Tomkins. William Beach, director." The poster of Walter is still up there, too.

"Well, well, well," says Ms. Dugan around her cigarette. "If it isn't my favorite couple of so-and-sos."

"How goes it, Ms. D.," says Skint, hitching his gaze upward to a more appropriate place.

Ms. Dugan shrugs and winks at them. The wink is barely perceptible, what with the way Ms. Dugan's eyelids droop so far down they threaten to take over her irises. Not because Ms. Dugan has her gaze fixed downward on an inappropriate spot but because that is the kind of eyelids she has. Ms. Dugan's mother had the same kind, only even more so. Once, during a field trip to the Center when Dinah was seven, the senior Mrs. Dugan beckoned her over with a finger and handed her a roll of tape.

"Tape my lids up for me, toots," she said. "Stick 'em right to my brows."

Horrifying. Both the taping and the way she looked after.

"Come on, doll," Ms. Dugan says now to Skint. "Grab a cup of tea and warm the hell up."

Dinah starts pouring.

"MS. DUGAN." Bernadine. "COME HELP ME MOVE THIS WHITEBOARD."

"Whiteboard." Ms. Dugan mutters, dragging pointlessly on the cigarette. "You'd think we were the goddamn CIA around here, the way Chatham tracks the twists and turns of our game plan. I'm going in there, kids, and I don't know if I'm coming out."

She grins at them and moves toward Bernadine.

Dinah turns around so Skint can get into her backpack.

"Ha-*ha*! Little does she know!" Skint mutters under the cover of Ms. Dugan and Bernadine wrestling the whiteboard into submission. "Operation Take-Her-Down about to commence!"

"Shh!" Dinah hisses as Skint unzips her pack and fumbles within. "Do you want to give us away?"

Though she can't help but think it would be kind of great if he gave them away and his plan were cut off at the knees.

"Oh, stop," Skint scoffs as she turns back around. "They're making too much banging to hear us."

"You know she has bionic ears."

Skint rolls his eyes at her. He shakes out the sarong he's just fished out of the backpack and ties it snugly around his hips. Pink and printed with umbrellas and mai tais, it slits right up the thigh and shows a daring amount of Skint's jeaned leg. The sarong is an old one of Mrs. Beach's. Skint wears it to the Friendly every week.

"ALL MEMBERS OF THE GIRLS' FRIENDLY PLEASE ASSEMBLE IN THE ALCOVE."

Dinah and Skint look at each other and nod. Dinah doesn't want him to think she will wuss out, so she makes like to do power fists with him. But he rears back and looks at her warningly. "Who's giving us away now?" he whispers. He is right. This is no time for a public mark of solidarity. They head into the meeting room.

"This meeting of the Girls' Friendly Society, Saint Francis Church chapter, shall commence," says Bernadine once everyone has settled into folding chairs. "All present say aye!"

"Aye!"

Ms. Dugan winks at Dinah and rolls her eyes.

Bernadine stands up at the whiteboard and uncaps a dry-erase marker. "Four members present and accounted for; note that please in the minutes, Mother."

Dinah glares at Mrs. Chatham and holds up her hand, all fingers outstretched. Mrs. Chatham becomes very busy with her notebook, eyes firm on the page, but two red spots bloom on her cheeks.

"Item one," says Bernadine, and writes *1. CLOTHING* on the whiteboard. She glances at Skint. "All donations of winter clothing collected by the membership have been sorted and sent to the appropriate organizations. Leftover items can be found in the box at the back of this room and are free for the taking." She clears her throat. "Coats and the like."

She turns and writes *2. THANKS.* "Item two. The membership thanks Alma Chatham for the fine muffins she has provided for tonight's refreshments. Get that down in the minutes, please, Mother."

Thanks to . . . , Mrs. Chatham writes. Her brow wrinkles. . . . *me,* she finishes uncertainly.

"Muffins!" How did Dinah miss them? She'd love a muffin.

"*ORDER*."

"Behind you, toots." Ms. Dugan nods at the snack basket.

Bernadine writes the third agenda item—*APPROVAL*—on the whiteboard and Dinah grabs two muffins under the cover of her turned back. She tosses one down the table to Skint and assumes an expression of intense attention-paying as Bernadine wheels back around.

"Next order of business," Bernadine says, poised with her marker. "Approval of proposed upcoming projects—"

Skint clears his throat and Dinah looks at him, alarmed. Already? What? He is waggling his brows at her over his muffin. Does he want to start the shouting right now? But wasn't he going to shout first?

"—of the Girls' Friendly, followed by development of organizational structures to support same, namely and to wit—"

What should she do? Maybe he thinks she should start now because, as a girl, she is allowed to speak. But if she tries to interrupt Bernadine—to dress her down, no less—Bernadine will be furious and the shouting will be about that and not turkeys. What is Dinah supposed to do?

"—to raise funds to donate to the World Food Programme to help aid the people of—"

She better do something or else Skint'll be angry

and they'll be at the part of the meeting where they are having to say aye and before you know it Bernadine will be bossing them around and Dinah will have lost Skint's chance forever.

"Aye!" Dinah shouts.

The others, including Bernadine, stare at her.

"Sorry," says Dinah. "I thought we were voting."

At least there is a little break in the action so she has some time to think. Skint is looking questioningly at her over the teacup clutched in his hand and she would like to look questioningly at him right back, but exchanging looks would be unwise with Bernadine staring at her like this.

Bernadine squints at Dinah and harrumphs. "Well," she says. "We may as well vote. All those in favor say aye."

"Aye!" Dinah votes again, extra enthusiastically to make up for her coming treachery.

"Aye," say the others.

"Motion passes four to zero. Note that please, Mother. Mother!"

Mrs. Chatham looks up from the *Five* she has written in her careful hand and blushes under Bernadine's glare. She looks sideways at Dinah, but Dinah, her stomach tight, looks steadfastly the opposite way.

Mrs. Chatham crosses out her *five* for a *four*, and Bernadine moves on.

"Proposal number two, namely and to wit a regular schedule of visits to the elderly and infirm who make use of the Saint Francis Adult Day Services Center—"

Dinah's stomach is killing her. Is Skint wimping out? Is she? Oh, she hates every part of this. Why can't she be home, just playing with Beagie? Playing and hugging him and teaching him about words. Why does she have to be thinking about turkeys and people? Turkeys and people and lines at the food pantry. The lines here at Christmas with snow falling outside. Mrs. Rijekac waiting and wiping her glasses, Mr. King's hand against the wall as he removed his boots, his shoes underneath shined and lovely.

Shined-up shoes and brogans to hold a Rural Route down. Thin plume of smoke too delicate for warming.

"Bernadine?"

"All those in—*what*, Dinah? Stop interrupting!"

"I'm sorry. I . . . I thought we were going to discuss. Before we vote."

"You were awfully quick to vote a moment ago, Dinah."

"I know. Sorry! But I have something to ask before we vote this time."

"What is it, Dinah. Be quick."

Skint is looking at her over his teacup again.

"Well, I have been thinking. About another proposal for us. Instead of the Center-visiting one."

"Another proposal! Late stages for that, Dinah!

Proposals were due last week for consideration by the membership."

Yes, well, last week Dinah didn't know what all was going to happen on the way here and she bets Bernadine would rather hear her idea than the other item on Skint's docket, namely and to wit, shouting.

"Yes," Dinah says, "I know. I'm sorry. But I didn't have my idea yet last week."

Ms. Dugan stubs out her unsmoked cigarette.

"Let her speak, Bernadine."

Snort, snort, puff. "Well?"

"I was thinking." Dinah plays with the handle of her cup. "The food pantry is a big job. For just one person. And you already do so much."

Bernadine's eyes narrow. So do Skint's.

"So what I was thinking was that we—the Friendly—could run it together. Sort of as . . . sort of as a collective. To help. Because the job is big."

"Is it."

"There's a lot of people that need help. . . ." Dinah trails off a bit. *Would you look at all those eyes.* Ms. Dugan's are questioning, Mrs. Chatham's worried. Dinah doesn't dare look at Skint's.

"Your solicitousness is kind, I am sure," says Bernadine. "But I think it's unnecessary. The job is not too big for me. I think it would be a waste of the group's time and energy, especially with other worthy projects that need our attention. Such as the proposed work at the Center."

"Um," says Dinah. She might barf. Skint and his phone calls and we never do jack. "I mean more, though. I think the food pantry should . . . should *expand*. I mean *we* should expand it. Us. The Friendly."

Up on the porch. Ring the bell. *Hello, elderly RRs, can I help you in some way?*

"I was thinking of kind of a delivery service." The idea uncurls itself, slowly, as Dinah speaks it aloud. "We could bring food. Right to people. Who can't get here. Who don't have cars." Or who Bernadine doesn't like. "Or who live far. Or maybe who don't even know about it. Or feel shy about coming."

Fatten them up, warm them up, everybody included and getting lovely things. Bernadine no longer the boss of distributing and nobody given anything inedible or unspeakable, or nothing at all.

And she'll make Mr. Beach talk to Bernadine, alone, and she and Skint can make sure about the food.

Dinah risks a glance at Skint. He is beaming.

See, he told her she was the nice one. All he wanted to do was beat the shit out of Bernadine.

Ms. Dugan looks proud of her, Mrs. Chatham pinkly interested. Bernadine notes this with alarm.

"We are a small church, Dinah! How much do you think we have to give away? And besides, you aren't old enough to drive and neither is Sk—Mother doesn't drive either. That means the load would fall to Ms. Dugan and me, and frankly, I do not see how that makes my job smaller, as it were."

Dinah shakes her head. Her idea is blooming.

"No, Bernadine! Not just you! Or even just us. I mean the Friendly would be in charge, but everybody helps. The whole church. We could figure out who could drive where and when and also have projects for everybody to help in some kind of way so no one feels jerky about being helped or smug because they did the helping, because everybody could be both. Like you need food but you can offer, I don't know, singing lessons."

That last part was kind of stupid but Dinah knows what she means.

"Sounds jazzy, Dinah B.," says Ms. Dugan. "I don't know, Bernadine, I like it."

Oh, Ms. Dugan!

Bernadine's eyes narrow. "Do you."

"We could make a schedule!" Dinah cries. "A rota of duties!" *A brilliant touch,* she congratulates herself. Bernadine loves a rota of duties. "We could make an announcement in church—"

Bernadine cuts her off. "Oh, really? You'd deign to come to church, Dinah Beach?"

Dinah's face begins to twist into a scowl, but she catches it and hastily reschools her features.

"I see what this is really about, Dinah." Bernadine's voice is steely.

Ms. Dugan looks at her quizzically.

"You don't want to hang around in the Center. You're a teenager," says Bernadine, "and being around your mother would *cramp your style*."

What is she talking about? But Dinah can't pay attention to Bernadine's outdated lingo when she is so happy about her own idea, and so relieved to be spared having to openly take on Bernadine's food pantry exclusions.

"What does that mean, dear? 'Cramp her style'?"

"It means she wants independence from her mother, Mother!"

What? Hey! "I do not!"

Wait a minute.

"Well, I guess I do, but that's not why I want us to do this."

"Oh, no?"

"No!"

"Then why? Are you telling me you don't want to help the elderly?"

"No!"

"Bernadine, I don't think that's what she's saying."

"Really, Ms. Dugan! Then what is she saying, since you seem to understand her so well?"

"Bernadine—"

"It's only that everybody already helps at the Center," Dinah cuts in, aware that she is telling only a partial truth, which is next door to a technical truth, but there is only so much she can take on at once. "In school and things," she continues. "Kids go there all the time. Brownies, Sunday school, everybody does that for a service project."

"And well they should! Have you thought about what it feels like to be old, Dinah? And alone?"

Mrs. Chatham pinkens again.

"I volunteer at the Center myself," says Bernadine, "and with the elderly at the hospital, too. And sometimes those visits are the one thing—" Her voice is shaking.

"But the people at the Center are visited to within an inch of their lives!" cries Dinah.

"Dinah Beach! I cannot believe that a daughter of your mother would be so uncaring—"

"Uncaring?" Skint. His voice is incredulous.

"Yes! I mean, ORDER! You will not speak out of turn, Dinah!"

"That was Skint, Bernadine!"

"Never mind!" Bernadine is nearly gnashing her teeth. "So do you want to curtail our efforts for disaster relief, too? You want to divert the money we raise to this . . . this unnecessary taxi service?"

Skint clears his throat. "That's not what she said."

Be quiet, Skint!

"Order!" shouts Bernadine hoarsely. "So it's just the Pantry, then! You don't approve of how I run it? Is that it?"

Saying *no* would go beyond partial or technical truth straight to lie, and not the helpful kind of lie. How did this get so hotted up? Skint is breathing hard over there and Dinah doesn't know what to say.

"Oh, ho! That *is* it!"

"Now, dear—" Mrs. Chatham murmurs.

"Am I not organized enough? The cans not consistently arranged by contents within meal type? Or is it something else you don't find to your liking?"

"Oh, good Cod!" says Skint.

The silence is total.

Bernadine draws in her breath.

"What did you say?"

Skint's gaze is imperturbable, Ms. Dugan's questioning, Mrs. Chatham's fluttering and worried.

"Oh, Skint, how funny—I thought you said 'Cod'!" Mrs. Chatham quivers, eager to dispel the tension even if she doesn't understand its cause.

Silence.

"Bernadine?" Mrs. Chatham looks at Bernadine's folded-in lips and red, red cheeks, then at Ms. Dugan, who is looking at Bernadine, too.

Dinah might barf.

Mrs. Chatham appeals to Skint.

"Skint, dear? What's the matter? Did I say something?"

"At least let's be consistent," says Skint. "At least make it clear that, either home or away, needful people shall not be fed by the Girls' Friendly."

"Order!"

"Neither dollars nor canned goods nor Christmas turkey—"

"ORDER!"

"Better that some food should rot than be eaten by the wrong people—"

"That is enough!"

"—or that rotten food be eaten by the ones you think right."

Ms. Dugan is still looking at Bernadine, with surprise now, and something like shock.

Bernadine presses her fists against the table and leans onto them.

"Our families worked when they came over here," she hisses at Skint, beyond fury. "They *worked*."

"So you think if someone's out of work they should be punished until they are employed? Or until they get a visa?"

"Nonmembers are required to be silent!"

"Even in the face of bullsh—"

"THAT IS ENOUGH, DINAH!"

"Bernadine, that was *Skint*!"

"Those people can go down to Lewiston. The church in Lewiston is larger than we are—"

"We don't live in Lewiston!" Skint shouts and Dinah can't help herself, can't sit by and let Skint be the only one to speak, Skint being brave after a year of Bernadine meanness, of watching unkindness and not speaking up. She shouts too.

"We live *here*! And so do all the people who came here at Christmas!"

"Leaving aside that you are not even really a member of this church yourself, Dinah Beach—"

"Oh, come now, sweetheart! Dinah is a wonderful member of our church—"

"Mother!" Bernadine's voice shakes with rage. "Dinah, you do not go to church and have not graced a Sunday school class with your presence since you were five—"

"So what? I clean!"

"—so who are you to say who belongs here?"

"Well, who are you to say?" Dinah yells back recklessly. "I thought nobody was supposed to say! I thought that was the point! Anybody can come and help and be here. Otherwise there isn't a point!"

"God is the point!"

"I thought you were supposed to be helping!" *Hypocrites! Hypocrites! You pretend there is a God and it doesn't even make you kind.*

"How dare you," says Bernadine. "How *dare* you?"

"Twenty-four turkeys in the freezer before Christmas," Skint says softly, looking Bernadine in the eye. "Twenty-three turkeys still in the freezer after. I counted. I counted. Who got the one turkey, I wonder?"

Silence.

Dinah and Bernadine breathing and stormy-eyed; Skint calm, almost pleasant.

"Anyone who is not a member of the Girls' Friendly Society," Bernadine says at last, "may leave this room. Immediately."

Skint gets up.

So does Dinah.

"Dinah Beach!"

"The piece of Cod," says Skint, "that passeth all understanding."

"Dinah!"

"Bernadine, THAT WAS SKINT!" Dinah slams the door open and she and Skint slam out, Skint's sarong whirling around his hips in an angry tangle. The door crashes shut behind them.

"Sweet Jesus Christ," says Ms. Dugan.

The agenda for the meeting is on the whiteboard over Bernadine's head. *CLOTHING,* it says. *THANKS. APPROVAL.*

"Sweet Jesus, be merciful," says Ms. Dugan. "Bernadine, Bernadine." She stands up and reaches for her coat.

Bernadine is hunched of shoulder, chin jammed onto fists. "Storming out like that," she says. "Not even wearing a coat. He'll catch his death." Her eyes are dark. She puts her head in her hands.

SEVENTEEN

What the heck happened in there? Dinah was angry and so was Bernadine. Skint, of course, as well. But why did Dinah join in? She should have calmed things. But she couldn't. She couldn't.

Nothing Dinah said was wrong. Then why does she feel so bad?

Unfair fighting. You shouldn't yell like that. You shouldn't wait and then burst around with the reasons you are mad. Is that why she feels so awful?

There's more to it than that but Dinah can't sort it out. Her mind is a tangly rage jangle of thin trails of smoke like singing and ankles in heavy shoes, images of Bernadine alone in the foyer of the empty church.

Skint is stalking forward so quickly she has to run to keep up.

"Skint. Skint!"

"Fuck it. *Fuck* it." *That bitch. That bitch. Focus, kid. Think. Calm down.*

Fuck it fuck it fuck it.

"I didn't know what you wanted me to do!"

Years *of that shit.*

"I thought you were going to start the shouting!"

Fuck it fuck it fuck it.

"Skint, please!"

"I can't really think right now, Dinah."

"Are you mad because I did a new idea instead?"

"What?"

"A new idea. Instead of what we planned."

"Oh. No. Your idea was great."

They are at his house.

"Skint?"

No light on.

"Skint!"

"I'll call you later," Skint tells her. "Good-bye, Dinah B."

Dinah stays still outside Skint's house. She feels like nothing, hollowed out and cold. Snowflakes fall on her hair and face, but they are old ones, falling from the evergreens, jarred loose by the wind.

Out of the Friendly, out of the Friendly. That day she and Granny joined when Dinah was five. Granny in her plastic glasses. Dinah's forearms on Granny's big soft thighs, buzzy singing overhead.

She storms into her own house, trailing coat and mittens behind her.

"Dinah Beach! Get back here right now!"

Dinah does not get back there right now. She slams upstairs to her room, slams her door open then shut, winces as Beagie howls, and sits on her bed, chest heaving.

"Get back down there and pick up your coat!" Mrs. Beach shouts up the stairs.

Dinah doesn't answer.

"What's the matter?"

"Nothing!" Dinah stands and storms out of her room and down the stairs. She grabs up her coat and hangs it up very hard. "There! Happy?"

"What's the *matter*, Dinah!"

Mitten, mitten, boot.

"I'm out of the Friendly!"

"Kicked out or by choice?" asks her mother.

"Who cares!"

Her coat falls back onto the floor as Dinah flings her boots down and slams back up to her room.

She lies down on the floor, knees tented, her neck mashed against the baseboard. It's uncomfortable but also good.

How did it all get so crazy? This morning: normal Saturday (if you ignore the turkey debacle), looking ahead to the Friendly, games in the kitchen with Beagie. This evening: upended, anger waiting for her in the kitchen. Skint out of the Friendly and also so is she.

What will her father say? He is not going to be pleased. What will happen with Bernadine? Will Dinah be fired as sexton?

Beagie will still love her, but he'll be the only one.

EIGHTEEN

It's later that night, close to midnight. Skint rubs the side of his hand, sore and scraped raw. He's in his living room, phone in his hand. He wants to call Dinah, but it's too late. He doesn't bother to turn on the light.

In the corner by the kitchen door is a spoon, lying as if flung, as it was when he came in from the Friendly this evening. In the same positions, too, are an upturned bowl on the floor of the kitchen and chunks of cereal congealed on the tiles.

Think about Dinah, or snow. Trees with whitened branches. Do not think about any other thing. Not now, not ever. Not the fact that, rationally speaking, there is no point to all of this, the biological accident of human beings. No explanation, no help, no justification good enough; no real reason for any single one of us to be around.

NINETEEN

Dinah calls Skint early the next morning.

"Hello?" His voice is tight.

"It's only me."

"Are your parents up?"

"Yes," says Dinah. "Beagie woke everybody up singing."

"Have you talked to them yet?"

"No," says Dinah. "I told my mother I was out of the Friendly when I came home last night but not about why. I skipped dinner. I am hiding, kind of."

Skint exhales.

"You are glad," Dinah accuses him. Then: "Are you glad?"

"Maybe. In the main," says Skint. "Though I wouldn't say my heart is especially glad at this particular moment." He pauses. "So nobody called or anything? This morning?"

"Not that I know of. I thought maybe someone did last night, but no one came up to yell at me, so probably not." Dinah lies back against the wall and rests one ankle on her opposite knee and plays with a strip of rubber peeling up from the sole of her shoe. "I'm afraid to go downstairs, though," she confesses.

"I'm afraid to leave the house," says Skint.

Dinah rears herself up.

"Why?" she says. "You sound all skittery. Are you okay?"

"I'm fine," says Skint. "I'm fine."

"Don't be scared my dad will blame you, Skint. He already thinks I'm the dumb one."

"Smart man," says Skint.

"Jerk," says Dinah, and falls silent. "My idea," she says sadly and squooshes down against the wall again. "I liked my idea."

"It was a great idea, Dinah B. In fact, I'm still going to do it. Or a part of it. Something for the Rural Routes."

"You are?"

"Yeah. I'm going to make them a parcel. Like you always want to do."

"Me, too, then! Me, too, please."

Skint doesn't say anything.

"What? Do you not want me to do it with you? Is it because I was thoughtless about them yesterday? Are you mad at me still?"

"No, dorkface. Shut up." He's quiet. Then: "Of course we can do it together. We'll put in food, maybe a blanket."

"I have a hat I'm almost finished crocheting," says Dinah. "I can make another one and we can give them those."

"You and the crocheting," says Skint. "Please tell me it's not some kind of crazy old-timey bonnet."

"Shut up," says Dinah. "It is more like a beanie. It is right up the lady Rural Route's alley. And I'll make the man a balaclava helmet."

"Great," says Skint flatly.

"We should include cookies in the parcel, too. As well as healthful things. It'd be terrible to get a parcel with only healthful things."

"What?" says Skint. "Your voice sounds a little compromised."

Dinah rears herself up to straighten out her neck. "Come over," she says. "Right now. It's Sunday, so they'll be off at church soon and we can use the kitchen. We'll bake for the Rural Routes."

Another pause.

"Is everything okay?" Dinah asks. "Was there something bad in the news?"

"Everything's fine," says Skint. "Shut up."

"You shut up. Come over, then."

"Fine," says Skint. "I will. Why shouldn't I."

"No reason at all," says Dinah. "I keep telling you, my dad isn't going to blame you."

They ring off.

Yeep and yuck. Better go down. She'll have to sooner or later.

TWENTY

"I paved the way for us to make cookies, but only by shouting for permission from upstairs," says Dinah when she opens the front door for Skint a few minutes later. "I haven't been brave enough to go in there yet." She nods toward the kitchen.

Skint looks awful. His eyes have circles under them and crusty things in the corners. She bets he hasn't slept.

"I'm just being dumb," she says, taking his wrist. "Come on. Come eat breakfast foods with me." And she leads him into the kitchen.

Dinah's father is stretched out on the kitchen floor with his hands over his eyes.

"There is no hope," he is saying hollowly to Dinah's mother as they enter. "Every time I give the sopranos their starting note, Mrs. Wattle shakes her head and gives them another one that isn't even in the same key and they follow her because she terrifies them with that scowl. And Ken Vaar can't keep his hands off the thermostat because he feels there is a precise and narrow temperature band his vocal cords need in order to achieve the emotive depths for which he believes himself famous. The altos can't carry a tune between them. And the basses! So loud they could signal the distant shores. We are an accidentally atonal collection of foghorns with a lunatic screamy woman leading us into the cliffs."

"Awful," says Mrs. Beach, clutching a straining Beagie in her arms.

"Good morning, Dad." *Bareface it,* thinks Dinah. *Test the waters with normalcy.* "I'll help. I'll come sing. Extra loud, to drown them all out."

"If you ever," says Mr. Beach, peeking at her through his fingers.

"In fact," Dinah continues, "I could start right now."

"Please don't," says Skint. Dinah fixes him with a look as beaky as an irritated egret's and gazes down at her father on the floor.

"Say hello to Skint, Dad."

Mr. Beach drops his hands from his face. "Someone's in the kitchen with Dinah?"

"Grr," says Dinah, with slitty eyes.

"Dinah Beach and Skint Gilbert," says Mr. Beach, staring up at them, "if either of you ever repeats a word of what I have said on this kitchen floor, I will creep into your rooms in the night and steal your most-loved things and then jump on them."

"If you do that," says Dinah, "I will call the police and have you brought up on burglary charges and then I will laugh when they put you in jail."

Skint stirs.

"Good morning, Skint," says Mr. Beach at last. "It's nice to see you."

"It is," says Dinah's mother. "Hello, Skint."

"Good morning," says Skint, and pats Beagie on the head. Dinah's mother is very haggard-looking this morning, and there are splotches on her front from where Beagie must have barfed.

"You smell awful, Mrs. Beach," says Dinah.

Her mother's cheeks grow scarlet. "You *are* awful, Dinah."

"Dinah Beach!" Her father scowls and hauls himself creakily to his feet. "Give me the baby, Penny."

"I'm sorry," says Dinah quickly. Better not to rack up debits in her character account before she even finds out if her parents have heard anything about the Friendly.

She does not have to wait long. Mr. Beach sinks back into his seat with Beagie in his arms and looks firmly at Dinah and Skint.

"I hear some hell was raised last night."

Skint starts.

Dinah glances at him. What is up with him this morning? He is wound tighter than a top. He's still worrying about if her parents hate him, the dork. Can't he see how kindly her dad's gaze falls on him the whole time? If anyone should be worried, it's Dinah.

"Did Bernadine tell you?"

"No," says Mrs. Beach. "Denise Dugan called just before you stormed in."

"Just now?" asks Skint. "She called just now?"

"No," says Mrs. Beach. "I meant just before Dinah stormed in last night."

Skint exhales a fraction.

"It was my fault," Dinah says firmly. "I was mouthy. But I don't regret it!"

Dinah's dad looks stern. "Were you rude, Dinah Beach?"

"It was *my* fault," says Skint. "I escalated things. I interrupted and talked out of turn."

"Honestly, Skint," says Mrs. Beach. "You are a saint."

Dinah and Skint look at her, astonished.

"I mean it! I would have snapped ages ago!" cries Mrs. Beach. "Not to insult your girlfriend, Bill," she says, smirking at Mr. Beach, "but Skint, I don't how you ever put up with all of Bernadine's nonsense about you helping out in that club. Have a biscuit." Mrs. Beach passes the basket, but Skint shakes his head.

"I'm fine, thank you," he says.

"Well, I, for one, think they need to feel your absence a bit," Mrs. Beach continues. "See what you kids have done for them. You, Skint, in the face of all that loopy persecution. And you too, Dinah. I'm glad you're standing firm. I support you both completely."

Dinah and Skint stare at one another. What the heck? This is nothing like what Dinah expected here in the kitchen this morning. Ms. Dugan mustn't have said much at all, then, when she called, other than that the meeting was heated and that Dinah and Skint quit. The Beaches must think the whole thing came about because Skint and Dinah were fed up over the silencing of Skint.

"It's your battle to pick," Mr. Beach agrees. "It's sad, but I'm sure you thought through what it would mean to you to leave the group."

"*My* battle?" *That's a fine cop-out!* Little does he know that it was her dad's battle that they fought for him! "Don't you even care? Don't you want to hear how it all happened?"

"No," says her father. "Unless you think I need to."

Of course she thinks he needs to! What kind of answer is that? But Dinah is thrown by this turn of events and doesn't quite know what to say. How come Ms. Dugan didn't spill the whole of the beans? She must be protecting Bernadine, too. They're all cowards! Mr. Beach *ought* to have to think about the whole food pantry awfulness and be made to feel guilty for not doing anything when he found out the first time, for just sitting around and letting things happen. Him and his "darling"s and his "it's your battle to pick"s! It's his fault they're out of the Friendly!

Scowling, Dinah meets Skint's gaze. He looks wary but also puzzled. And her ghastly parents' attention has already shifted.

"As I was saying before your choir diatribe," says Mrs. Beach, handing Beagie's bowl of cereal to Mr. Beach, "poor old Mr. Ennethwaite didn't know what to do with her, Bill. He hadn't any idea how to take care of her at all. Poultices, can you imagine, some recipe from a hundred years ago—"

Should Dinah say something? She looks again at Skint, who looks back at her blankly.

"—and what she needed was a catheter, of course."

"Poor man," says Mr. Beach.

"Poor woman, too." Mrs. Beach sighs. "Anyway. They got her to the hospital around three this morning, Gail said. Let's hope it turns out well." She turns to Skint. "How is your dad doing?"

"Don't forget we're making cookies," Dinah intercepts, but not quickly enough.

"We miss him at the Center," her mother continues. "He was always such a gentleman."

"He's okay," says Skint.

"Is he? How is his language?"

Dinah gives her mother the evil eye. "We need to get started, Mrs. Beach. When are you leaving?"

"I always mean to call your mother," says Mrs. Beach. "I should drop in sometime—"

"He's fine," says Skint shortly. "Mrs. Beach, should Beagie be so close to the oven?"

Beagie has escaped his father's arms and is squatting in front of the glass oven door, greeting his own reflection like a lost and treasured friend.

"Oh, Beagie-onimus," cries Mrs. Beach. "It's cooled down from the biscuits, but still! Bill," she says scoldingly. She scoops the baby up and he roars with frustration, kicking until she sets him to stand on her sheepish husband's lap.

"Have a biscuit, Beagie," says Dinah. But Beagie bashes the biscuit out of her hand and begins to sing instead as his father wrestles him into a holdable position.

"Buh, buh, buh!"

"He's certainly his father's son," Mrs. Beach sighs.

"His sister's brother," Dinah mutters.

"More like his great-grandmother's great-grandson, with that nasally little tone, isn't that right?" says Mr. Beach to the baby. "You're a Patty Beagan descendant, aren't you, Beagie Bee?"

"Oh," says Skint. "I always wondered why someone would name a kid Beagan Beach."

"Why *wouldn't* someone name a kid Beagan Beach?" Dinah and her father cry in unison.

"No reason," says Skint hastily.

Beagie gently clocks his plush horse with a spoon, and Skint stares at Dinah's dad staring at Beagie.

The phone rings. Skint jumps. Mr. Beach picks it up.

"Hello?" he says, taking Beagie and the phone out of the room. Dinah strains her ears toward them, hoping the caller is Bernadine. "Oh, hello, Reverend," says Mr. Beach before he is out of earshot. *Rats.*

Skint grabs her wrist. "We have to go buy ingredients," he says. "Let's get *going*."

"All *right*," says Dinah. He's all pressure-steamed again and ready to blow. This is not going to be much fun. "Calm the heck down! All we need is chocolate chips. We have everything else already. Let me get my coat and mittens."

"You'll find your mittens on the floor where you flung them last night," says Mrs. Beach. "Since we do not have maid service here."

Mr. Beach is in the doorway.

"That was Reverend Michaels," he says.

Skint lets go of Dinah's arm.

Beagie, under his father's arm, sticks out his feet and wiggles them as hard as he can. The sunlight fades from the room, and Beagie crows with delight as the kitchen grows dim.

"Look at you, Beagie." Dinah smiles. "You have magic feet, don't you? You're making that sunshine disappear!" Beagie beams and babbles with joy.

Mr. Beach shifts the baby's weight to his hip. "The reverend thought he saw someone enter the church by the side door late last night," he continues, "and the jamb on it is broken this morning. A strip of wood off the side where the lock holds."

"Whoa," says Dinah.

"Oh, no," says Mrs. Beach. "The same kids again, do you think, Bill?" A group of senior boys did the same thing a year or so ago and drank beer in the vestry.

"No, I don't. Most of those kids aren't around anymore; you know Ted and Jarvis are in the army, and the Corwin boy is away at college. No bottles this time either. And the reverend says he doesn't think it was a burglary of any kind, either—nothing inside seems to have been taken."

"Maybe it was someone trying to get in out of the cold," says Mrs. Beach.

"Tchah," says Dinah darkly. "It was shenanigans. And I bet I can guess whose." Or draw up a short list, anyway, topped with the Vole and his sidekick, Harlan. It's exactly the sort of thing they and their ilk would do, derivative and destructive at the same time. Dinah tries to look meaningly at Skint, but he is listening to her father and she can't catch his eye.

"Perhaps," says Mr. Beach. "Anyway, I'm going to go over right now. Get this sorted before services."

"Poor Reverend Michaels," says Mrs. Beach.

"Yes," says Dinah. Reverend Michaels is a nice man with thick glasses, cloudy-pated and slow of movement. "Why do people have to scare him? Can't they bust into a barn or something if they have the urge to bust into someplace?"

"Was he frightened, Bill?"

"More rattled than frightened," says Mr. Beach, setting Beagie on the floor. "I'll be back."

"Come on, Dinah," says Skint, punching her elbow. "We should go, too."

"Wait," says Dinah. Her parents begin to plan about the timing and making of an artichoke dip for a potluck tonight with their book club, and under the cover of their words Dinah whispers, "I should quick talk to my dad. He's going to have to deal with the Pantry thing sometime!"

"Dude, one thing at a time. Come *on*. You can get him when he gets home."

But it'll be tomorrow, most likely, what with all this potlucking. Dinah hates waiting.

Still, Skint is right. They should get a move on, if they are going to get the baking done before church is over. Then they can do the fun part, the parcel-making and leaving and all of that. Besides, her dad really should get over to St. Francis.

"We should give Reverend Michaels some of the cookies too," Dinah says, remembering.

"Fine," says Skint. "But let's go."

"Have a good morning, kids." Mr. Beach kisses Beagie and hands him over to his wife as he leaves the room. "I won't see you until later. More Evensong rehearsal after church."

"Come!" says Skint, a hand in the small of Dinah's back. He propels her toward the door.

"I want this kitchen spick-and-span when you're done with those cookies," says Mrs. Beach. "I need to come home from church with a whisk in my hand, practically, in order to get everything ready for this potluck. Nobody ever brings a main course! Good old Penny, they think! She'll bring something!" Mrs. Beach disappears into the hallway, muttering darkly to herself.

"Let me look at our cans first, Skint," Dinah says, resisting his propulsion. "I want to make sure we have lots of nice ones for the Rural Routes so we can do the parcel right after. Otherwise I can get some more when I buy the chips."

Skint groans in irritation. "I have a ton of cans for them at my house," he says.

"Really?" There is never any food at Skint's.

"Yes," says Skint. "Let's just use those. We'll stop at my house and get them on the way to delivering the parcel."

"No!" Dinah squawks. "I want to do the parcel up all nice, not just slap a bunch of stuff together any which way."

Skint groans some more. "Fine," he says finally. "You go get the chocolate chips, then, and I will go home and get my cans, and then we'll meet back here. *Come on!*"

"Fine," says Dinah. "Bossy!" She grabs a tote and they head for the door.

"Where is your coat, Skint?" says Mrs. Beach, poking her head back in the kitchen, with Beagie's head bobbing inquiringly below. "It's cold out there!"

"Don't like coats, Mrs. Beach."

"Skint, you need a coat. Take one of Mr. Beach's."

"No, thank you, Mrs. Beach. I'm fine," says Skint and hustles Dinah bodily out the door.

They take the reverse route to town this time. It's faster for Dinah to get to the store that way. No Rural Routes are out today; their house is empty and dark. Nonetheless, Dinah calls out, "Just wait!" as they dash by. Then she stops short and wheels around.

"Skint!"

"What?" His eyes are wide. "What?"

"I never thanked the donkey man!"

Skint exhales.

"I think he'll live, Dinah B. Come on. Let's go."

He pushes her lightly toward the bridge and town, and turns up the shortcut path to his street.

TWENTY-ONE

"Why do they call it 'creaming' the butter?" Skint flicks the recipe card with his hand. "Butter doesn't turn into cream; cream turns into butter."

Dinah snatches the card from his hand.

"We have made cookies one million times," she says. "You know what they mean. Give me the spoon." She whacks away at the butter and sugar in the bowl. "Is it because of the Friendly that you are all keyed-up and cranky?"

"For God's sake, Dinah, let's shut up about the Friendly."

"Fine." Whack whack whack with the spoon. "Be useful, at least, then. Put in the eggs."

Skint cracks them against the side of the bowl. "Watch us poison the Rural Routes with salmonella," he says grimly.

Dinah stops stirring. "You are making this about as much fun as a root canal."

"Sorry," says Skint. "Hooray, cookies."

Dinah looks at him beakily. But she takes up the spoon again and stirs. "Where did you put your cans? I want to see what you brought."

"I left them on your porch," says Skint, nodding at the door.

"Why?"

"To save us a schlep. Why bring them in when they're only going out again?"

"But we have to arrange it nicely!"

"We will," sighs Skint. "Later. But it's all top-notch chow, believe me."

"Let me see!" Dinah makes as if to head out the door to the box but Skint grabs the hem of her sweater.

"Later," he says. "We have cookies to finish first."

Dinah allows herself to be pulled back to the table and its bowl.

"I have to put at least a couple of our cans in, too, though," she says. "Otherwise I'm not contributing anything."

"All the ingredients for these cookies are from you, dork." Skint pulls the bowl over to himself and gives the mixture a stir or two before adding oats. "And you're contributing the sweat of your brow as well."

"Ugh," says Dinah, imagining droplets.

Skint's phone goes off. He glances at the name on the screen and makes a face. Ellen.

"Hello," he says. "Why? Where's yours? What? I'm just asking. Fine. I'm at Dinah's." He pauses. "It's no big deal," he says. "They're not here." He hangs up. "My mom," he says to Dinah. "She can't find her house key, so she's coming here to get mine."

"She and your dad are out?"

"Yes. At one of my uncles'." Ellen has a lot of brothers, all of them younger than she is and always having trouble with their jobs and apartments and breaking up with their girlfriends. Ellen spends a lot of time bashing them into shape.

"Lucky for her you have an extra key." Dinah should know. She has lost more of the Beach house keys than she cares to admit.

How could Ellen lose her key? Skint wonders. And just that one, with the others still firm on the ring?

His dad. It must be. Thinking the keys are his. Thinking he's going to work, a late night, the paper going to press.

His father's hand, thin as a leaf, holding a key in its palm. *Like jewelweed,* Skint can imagine his dad thinking, *like the wing of a winter bird. Oh, let's toss it, let it fly. Watch it float away on the wind.*

Dinah takes up a measuring cup and fills it carefully with flour. "When do you suppose Bernadine will report us to my dad?" she asks.

"Jesus Christ but can you talk about anything but the Friendly!" Skint takes the flour from her and dumps it in the bowl. "Who cares? What did we do that's so bad? Make a proposal to give people stuff they need? Speak up in the face of injustice?"

Dinah slumps over the table, chin in her hand.

Skint pours some chocolate chips into his palm and tosses them into his mouth.

"Right?" he says. "Right?"

"Quit stealing the chocolate chips."

Skint eyes her steadily and pours himself another handful. "You were all intent on telling your dad yourself not an hour ago." He puts three chips in Dinah's non-chin-holding hand. "Which is it? You want him to know or don't you?"

Dinah considers the chips. "I want something to happen, is what."

"Well, if that something is more recriminations and action and everything changing, forget it. People love the status quo." He adds nutmeg to the dough. Also cloves and a plop of cinnamon. "This," he says, holding the bowl firmly, spoon poised, "is how you stir a batch of cookie dough. Take note of my manly technique." Whack, whack, whack.

"I'm agog," says Dinah. "Your forearms are terrifying in their might. So what do you think about the church bust-in?" she asks. "I can just see the Vole clobbering up there in the night, smacking around and bashing stuff. Trust him to not even have enough imagination to think of a new crime. Trust him just to copy last year's." The Vole cuffed and led into the station house to be booked on charges—oh, it is a wonderful image. "Don't you think so? Doesn't it all just smack of Voleishness?" Poor K. T., though. Own brother to a felon.

Skint shrugs irritably. "How do I know?"

"Who else would do it? Harlan, maybe. But he wouldn't act alone."

"Who are you, the new chief inspector? Who cares."

"You," says Dinah, "are impossible today."

"Let's just get a move on," Skint says impatiently. "We need milk for brushing the tops, please."

"Bossy." But Dinah gets up and goes to the fridge.

"Let's get these mothers onto the cookie sheets and into the oven before the flesh-and-bone kind of mothers start infesting the place," says Skint just as someone knocks on the kitchen door. "Too late." He sighs and opens it. "Speak of the devil."

Ellen enters in a rush of cold air.

"Me? Am I the devil?" she asks. "Oh," she says, catching sight of Dinah. She looks back at Skint.

"She lives here," says Skint.

"Funny," says Ellen.

"Hello," says Dinah.

"Hello," says Ellen. "Parents not home? It's just the two of you?"

Skint's grip on the spoon tightens. *Ugh!* Dinah has always suspected that Ellen thinks she and Skint are a secret couple and she's sure Ellen believes Skint came over here so he and Dinah could make out. *Oh, please,* thinks Dinah. *Just get the key and leave.*

"They're at church," Dinah says. "With my brother."

"Oh," says Ellen and glances at Dinah's hair and skirt.

What's wrong with her hair and skirt? Maybe the hair is a little messy, but the skirt is just a skirt, with regular old pajama pants on underneath.

"Is everything okay with Uncle Joe? Did you guys already go over there?" asks Skint.

"We tried." Ellen turns to look back out the open door. "Things were a little protracted at home this morning. When you weren't there. Sorry we missed you. I guess you must have cleared out pretty early."

"What do you mean?" Skint asks lightly. "What happened?"

Ellen looks at him sharply. "Nothing," she says. "The usual complexities."

"Where's Dad?"

"In the car." Ellen glances out the still-open door.

Dinah sets down the container of milk and tries to catch Skint's eye. His face looks like nothing. "We're making cookies," she says inanely.

"I'll go out and h—say hello," says Skint.

"Don't bother," says Ellen. "Just let me have your key."

"Okay," says Skint. "But I just want to say hi to Dad first."

Oh, blarp, don't leave me in here alone with Ellen.

"Were you planning to be here much longer?" Ellen asks Skint. "When are you coming home?"

"We can finish quickly—" Dinah begins, but Skint is already saying "I'm going to be out all day."

"Really," says Ellen.

"Yes," said Skint. "I thought you'd be at Joe's."

"Sorry to disappoint you," says Ellen.

Dinah detests her.

"It's no disappointment," says Skint. "I'm glad to see you, actually. We should talk. You can fill me in on last night."

Ellen's eyes narrow.

"It looked like you had a pretty active time," says Skint, his voice light. "I'm interested to hear about it."

"This isn't anything that would make for interesting conversation with your friend, Skint," says Ellen.

"You're right," says Skint. "I guess you should head

out, then. We'll bring you each a cookie when they're done. And then we can talk." He looks at Ellen. "I did the dishes before I left this morning. That cereal bowl. The spoon. The ones you left from last night."

Ellen face goes blank.

"I scrubbed the floor as well."

A figure appears framed in the doorway behind Skint's mother. "I'm thinking about it," it says. "I'm trying to weigh the consequences."

Ellen starts. It's Mr. Gilbert.

"Hello, Mr. Gilbert," says Dinah.

Mr. Gilbert does not answer her, but steps into the kitchen and stands motionless, his arms dangling at his sides.

"Come on, Thomas," says Ellen quickly, taking his arm. "We're going!"

Mr. Gilbert is thinner than Dinah remembers, and smaller, somehow, as well. It strikes her that, aside from the ride home from the church the other night, it has been a long time since she has seen him in person, and even longer since she's seen him standing up rather than sitting in his chair, framed by the kitchen window, with Dinah outside at the mailbox waiting for Skint.

"How are you, Mr. Gilbert?" she asks. He stands like a Center person, frail-boned and a prominent skull. Dinah hesitates, then makes as if to stand. "Shall I take your coat?" she asks.

"No," says Ellen. "We're leaving. Skint, the key!"

Skint hands it over. "Bye, Mom. Bye, Dad." Mr. Gilbert raises a hesitant hand and unzips his coat.

"I said we aren't staying, Thomas!"

"Mom," says Skint.

Ellen rezips Mr. Gilbert's coat firmly. "Jesus," she mutters.

"We're in someone else's house," says Skint, his voice light, and Ellen glances at Dinah as Mr. Gilbert reaches up again to unzip his coat once more. But he stops partway, his hand dropping down.

Didn't Mr. Gilbert used to be tall? He looks the same as when they were small, but also not, like his body is a slim, bent copy of itself.

He raises one hand to his chest, then lowers it again; stands motionless, gaping at the kitchen as though it were a spaceship.

Dinah slides her eyes to Skint, but he is looking, implacably, at Ellen. Dinah stands the rest of the way up. "Mr. Gilbert?" she says hesitantly.

He starts at the sound of her voice, then glances down at his coat. With uncertain hands he tries to tug it off, but because of the half-zipped front, it gets stuck partway down his arms.

"Could I help you?" she says, even as Skint himself says, "Dad, can I fix your coat?" and stands the wooden spoon up in the cookie dough. He pushes past Ellen to his father and eases the jacket back up over his father's shoulders.

Mr. Gilbert's eyes grow dark, set deep in his skull, brows drawn sharp over top.

"Young lady?" he says to Dinah. "Young lady? Can you tell me, is this my home?"

Mr. Gilbert. So calm and quick at the playground when they were small, tall with bags of rock candy and all the time speaking with large words. "Dinah the cat, the Wonderland cat," he used to call her, and gave her and Skint extra-high pushes on the swings.

"No, it isn't," says Ellen shortly.

"Tone of voice," Skint says casually.

Ellen gives him another look.

"Come on," she says to Mr. Gilbert. "We're going."

Mr. Gilbert, re-coated, turns to his wife.

"And you, young woman?" he says. "Who might you be?"

Oh, Mr. Gilbert.

It's too sad, too much, too sad. Sadder and worse than the last time she saw him; sadder—worse. Dinah wishes she could put her arm around Mr. Gilbert's shoulders, rest her cheek in his sparse gray hair; she wishes she could run straight out the door and yell, find something to break or punch or kick.

"Come *on*." Ellen tugs at her husband.

"Skint." Dinah looks at Skint standing there, tall, his face looking like nothing. Skint says nothing, just looks at Ellen.

"Skint?" cries Mr. Gilbert. His head snaps toward Dinah. He's beaming with delight. "Did you say, 'Skint'? I have a son with that name!"

Dinah's heart breaks in two.

Oh, Mr. Gilbert. Oh, Skint. Her Skinty, her Skint, her favoritest Skinty Skint. Puzzled staring eyes of his dad. He does not remember her Skint.

Dinah can't bear it, Skint having to be here for this. Grab him, escape; get away from them. Go!

"Let's freeze the dough, Skint," she cries, "and bake the cookies later. We'll do the parcel in parts, the cans part right now, and then later the cookies. Come on, Skint, let's go." Moving. Fast walking. That helps him—they'll go right now.

"That's your son, mister," says Ellen as Dinah whirls around the kitchen like a mad thing. Cover the bowl—dough in freezer—put the milk away. "The tall one. Come on."

Mr. Gilbert looks incredulously at his wife. "I have *two* sons named Skint?"

"No, no," says Skint. "Just one, Dad. Just me."

"But my little boy is five!" Mr. Gilbert cries.

Out. Run. They can make up rude songs about their classmates or skip stones; she'll do pratfalls. She'll sing. Then they can come back here later, play with Beagie, when the ghost of all this is gone.

"Used to be," says Ellen. "You've missed a few years in between."

Skint flinches.

"Let's go, Skint." Dinah pulls at his sleeve. "We have to get our act together; come on."

Dinah tugs at Skint's sleeve again. He doesn't budge. Mr. Gilbert does, though. He looks outside and steps carefully onto the porch.

Ellen follows him. "Come home whenever," she says over her shoulder to Skint. "Everything is peachy. I'll just head back to the house with the—"

Skint cuts her with a look.

"I'll head home with your father," she says. "You and your friend can do what you need to do."

"The parcel, Skint," Dinah chatters. "Let's arrange your box of cans."

"We'll do it later, Dinah," says Skint. "I'll come back and meet up with you later."

"Don't even," says Ellen sharply. "We're fine. Just stay here with your—with her."

Skint looks at Ellen. He leans out the door. "Dad?" he says softly. "Dad?"

Oh, Skint. How can Mr. Gilbert have gotten so much worse? Please let her magic him better; make him remember her Skinty Skint. *Make him remember, make it different, make it the way it ought to be.*

All this wearing out, giving out, people leaving and being left; people leaving, gone forever so you can never be with them again. Never any more singing or holding their hands. What a way for things to be.

She won't have it. No. Not for Skint. *Outside; let's go.* She'll cheer him up better than ever—who cares about neatness—they'll bring Skint's cans now to the Rural Routes and leave them on the porch—then onto other plans—monk letter-writing, maybe. Running around outside and looking for things in the woods. At the end of the day the rest of the parcels, done up nice and also the cookies.

"Skint!" she cries, and tugs again at his wrist and arm.

"We're out of here, anyway," says Ellen. "See you later."

The Gilberts are gone.

"Give me the sponge!" Dinah cries. She gives the counter a frantic swipe and tosses the measuring cups in the sink. "Come on!" She pulls on her coat and grabs up her own keys and flings open the door. "Let's go!" She pushes Skint out onto the porch and grabs up his box of cans. She tugs him harder, and they're away at last; they're gone.

"Skint." Dinah's voice is chittery: all these cans and also running.

"What." Skint's voice is chittery, too.

They reach the bridge. "Stop," Dinah pants. "Stop." Overhead, icicles creak from the evergreen branches; gray clouds up above and wind. The air slaps at their cheeks. "Skint."

Skint stops. He kicks at a stone.

"Skint," says Dinah. "Skint."

Eyes streaming. Buzzy singing and eyes closed under blankets on the chair. Mr. Gilbert's brain undoing; Mr. Gilbert's coat.

Skint is still. When he speaks, his voice is so quiet she has to strain to hear it over the wind. "You can understand her, though, can't you?" he says. "She loves him. She had to take care of her brothers all those years when her mom was sick. She thought my dad would be taking care of her."

"What?"

"My mom," says Skint.

His mom? Muffled big sound and a tree branch is crazy shaking, like someone grabbed hold of it and is swinging. Snow shed, naked king bones gray.

Mr. Gilbert. Backwards Aging, but perverted; mind falling backward but erasing as it goes, his body falling forward, stumbling into decline.

"Backwards Aging," she stutters. "Oh, Skint. Your dad. Your dad."

Backwards fucking Aging? She wants to invite his dad to do Backwards fucking Aging?

Panic threatens to explode Skint's brain, his skull, but his chest sears in and holds it. What's he going to do, though? Even Dinah doesn't see. He can't keep leaving his father alone with Ellen. He can't keep her contained.

Skint's face is blank and dark.

"The Center," says Dinah. "Skint. My mom would know how to make things nice for your dad."

"NO!"

Dinah stumbles back as if he's pushed her.

"Don't you say a word about this to your mom!"

Of course not—what was she thinking? Skint doesn't want to talk about this any more than he ever did. Why would she make that worse by spreading it around? Stupid, insensitive Dinah!

"Let's write to Walter!" she cries frantically. "Let's make him a fan club! Of two! Us!"

Skint's face goes blank again. Two red spots rise in his cheeks and spread. He brings his hands to the sides of his face, one of them scraped red and raw.

"What?" Dinah is bewildered. "What?"

The Rural Routes' house is still dark, no lights on, no smoke. The box of cans is heavy, and Dinah uses her knee to shift it higher.

"Nothing," says Skint. He mashes his cheeks in with his fists. "Nothing. Come on. Let's just go."

In the box, cans slide over each other and resettle from the shifting. On top is a small one, squarish with rounded edges.

LE SARDINE D'ITALIA, it says on its label, and underneath, in parentheses, SARDINES.

TWENTY-TWO

Skint?

Skint?

Skint is the food pantry break-in person?

He broke in to steal *sardines*? The ones she donated at Christmas?

Dinah's head squashes in on itself, a tangled nerve jangle of kitchens and coats. Skint and forgetting and his dad fading away; and now Skint has become a thief?

No! No! That can't be right. The reverend said nothing was missing. Skint must have bought the sardines himself because he knew it would make her laugh. But as soon as she thinks that, Dinah knows it's not true. Of course Reverend Michaels said nothing was gone; why would he notice if something were missing from the Pantry? She glances into the box. Beets, potato sticks; she's seen them all before. Alphabetized and color-coded. Skint stole every one.

He's watching her face. He knows she knows.

"Skint?"

Skint puts his hands in his pockets and rocks on his toes.

"After the Friendly?" She searches his face. "Was it because you were mad at Bernadine?"

"No," says Skint. "Don't be stupid."

"Why, then? Why would you bust into the church and steal?"

"Oh, come on, Dinah. It wasn't like *stealing* stealing."

"What kind of stealing was it, then?"

"For fuck's sake, Dinah! It's cans, not the Hope Diamond! It wasn't stealing for personal gain! I took the stuff for the Rural Routes, Dinah. They deserve that food as well as anybody."

"Skint, you busted down the door!"

"It can be fixed in five minutes with a nail gun and a strip of plywood, Dinah."

"You scared the pastor!"

"Jesus Christ, it's not like I burned the place down!

It's only giving what's needed to the needy! You're acting like I set off a bomb."

"We have cans at home we could have given," says Dinah. "I would have given the Rural Routes all our cans." Skint is a smasher of churches, a break-in robbing thief. Dinah's head is about to explode.

"But not sardines. You don't have sardines at your house," Skint says, and baps her with his elbow. She pulls away but then remembers about his dad and does not know what she should do.

"Don't you want the Rural Routes to have your most favoritest food in the world?" he asks wheedlingly.

"Backward reason-making," Dinah starts to say, but this is more than backward reason-making. This is wrong; this is more; this is too much; this isn't Skint. This is not normal angry Skint, mad about monks or Bernadine. Skint has busted up a church.

Is he right, though? Maybe it does not matter if it was only cans. Skint was going to give them away again—isn't he more Robin Hood than robber?

Dinah shakes her head hard. She is used to angry sad Skint, angry and sad about people, but he has never been destructive or a robber. Unless you count him swiping the Pop-Tarts yesterday and Dinah does not count him taking those Pop-Tarts.

Skint rears his own head back and looks at her, defiant. "Are you going to tell your dad?"

"My dad?"

"Because I don't care if you do," Skint says. "I stand by my actions."

Dinah's eyes prick. She is not much of a crier but here are all these tears anyway, grown large and threatening to betray her by spilling.

Skint wilts.

"Don't, Dinah B. Stop. Stop, Dinah! I'll fix the door!"

"My stomach hurts," she says, bending over. The box drops to the ground.

"Dinah, stop. Don't be sick. We can take the stuff back. Immediately. Right now."

"No! What if someone sees?" Not the Vole but Skint led out in cuffs and booked on charges, maybe even jailed. How do you break someone out of jail? Obviously not the same way you spring them from the Pit—

"You heard your dad—nobody thinks things were taken," says Skint. "If someone sees us, they'll just think we are helping with donations, that kind of thing."

That is probably true.

"And after that we can raid our own houses for cans for the Rural Routes," Skint continues, searching her face. "Though I can tell you right now all I have to offer is a near-Paleolithic can of tuna."

He baps her again and makes a smile. Dinah manages to make one at him in return.

"Come on," says Skint. "Let's take them back now."

"Okay," says Dinah. "Then after let's just do my house. We have cling peaches, I think, that we could give them. Plus a lot of soups."

"Swell elegant fare," Skint says. "You'll make the Rural Routes very happy."

He looks so beseeching. Dinah can't bear that, either. She takes his arm and squeezes. Her chest is hollow and cold. She doesn't know what she's supposed to do.

Walter and evening and letter-writing and snow. Dinah wishes it were before yesterday ever started and they were at the donkey dance again, or even yesterday morning before church cleaning, with none of this having happened. Only she and Skint, alone, outside, maybe. Walking. Listening to the ice shift in the river and being glad about no school.

TWENTY-THREE

Soul-deep pleasure of wood bursting beneath his palm; crack of the lock and his boots in the dark. Fuck, yes, it was him. *Fuck, yes.*

TWENTY-FOUR

Dinah looks up the hill to the church and freezes.

"What?" says Skint.

Dinah points. The parking lot is full and more cars line the road. They forgot about it being church hour. St. Francis will be full of people, the nave full of grown-ups and the nursery full of babies, even the basement stuffed up with kids in Sunday school.

"So what," says Skint. "We'll use the side door."

"No!" She doesn't want him anywhere near that side door. "Too risky! What if the police are in there, investigating?" Hiding in the cupboards and dangling from the eaves, ready to pounce and lead Skint away—

Skint rolls his eyes. "I think you're seriously overestimating the fuzz's response to this, Dinah." But he swallows.

"I don't want you to have to live on the lam!"

"I'd be great on the lam," says Skint. "I'm a fast runner. Faster than the fuzz, anyway."

Anybody would be faster than the Aile Quarry fuzz. There are only the two policemen in town and both of them are rather thick of middle. Dinah is comforted by the thought.

"I'd have to keep bringing you parcels of food, though," she says.

"Nah," says Skint. "I'm very resourceful. With my mad church-cleaning skills, I'd get a janitor's job with no problem."

Not in a stripy suit with a leaden ball chained to his ankle, he wouldn't. But Dinah says only, "No one would hire a fifteen-year-old janitor."

Skint shrugs. "Everyone thinks I am older the whole time. Who'd question me?"

"Stop." Dinah jigs from one foot to the other. "Let's just take the cans and go back to my house right now."

"No," says Skint sharply. "I don't want that box to be anywhere near you or on your person. I was stupid to bring it over there to begin with. I'll take it back home with me."

"No," says Dinah. "I don't want it near or on you, either."

They fall silent, staring up at the church.

If he's caught, it won't go on his record, will it? Don't they overlook that if you're under eighteen? Oh, please don't let Skint get caught. His life will be wrecked even more than it already is. What got into him to make him so dumb?

But Dinah knows it's more than stupidity. It's anger. Look how upset he was about the monks. The business with turkeys on top of that, and then the Friendly meeting—curse that Bernadine! And all of it mixed with the new worry about the too-thin Rural Routes and the way that nobody helps. It put him over the edge.

"We'll hide the box someplace and take the cans inside another time, when it's all clear," says Dinah. Meaning she will take them inside. Dinah alone when Skint is home and not anywhere nearby.

"Like where?"

Dinah looks around. "What about behind the bulkhead? It won't be for very long, and if anyone sees the box they'll just think it's a donation someone brought by when the pantry was closed."

"Until it is brought in to Bernadine. Who will recognize the contents as those missing from her Inventory." Skint kicks at a piece of ice. "Not that I care," he adds.

"We'll wait, then," says Dinah. She picks up the box again. "We'll wait with it over there by the bulkhead right now until the service is over and everybody clears out. It's almost time for it to be over, anyway. Then we'll quick go in and put the cans away."

"Whatever. Fine." Skint reaches for the box. "Let me take it."

Dinah swings away from him. "No."

Skint shrugs and puts his purple hands in his pockets.

The wind is strong on the bulkhead side of the building, and even though the sun is shining now, it is freezing, so cold Dinah's nostrils feel as though they are lined with straw. It's too cold for Skint to wait out here with no coat. What can she do?

Dinah points down at the squat little corner formed by the bulkhead and the church. "There is even a tarp we can cover the box with." They'll cover it, and then she can send Skint someplace warm to wait.

"This is one crusty, manky tarp." Skint peels back its edge. "Ugh. Put the box down."

Dinah releases it and shakes out her aching fingers.

Skint tugs the edge of the tarpaulin over the cans and wipes his hands on his thighs.

The wind whips their hair back and forth into points.

"You have sharp hair," says Skint, batting it away with his hand. Dinah catches it in one fist.

"Go to my house to wait," she says. "I can do this part."

"No," says Skint. "You go. I should be the one to do it, anyway."

"No," says Dinah. "It's freezing out here. You can meet me here after the service."

Skint looks dark-eyed again and tired. "I'm not leaving," he says. "No."

Dinah hesitates, then gives in. "Fine," she says, "but I'm staying here with you."

"There's no need for you to." Skint pushes his hair out of his eyes. "Besides, I don't feel like very good company right now."

"I don't need good company."

Skint opens his mouth, then closes it again and shrugs. "Suit yourself." He crouches down by the bulkhead, rests his head against the church and closes his eyes.

Dinah crouches down beside him, her back against the bulkhead. The relief from the wind is immediate. Thank God. At least he won't be quite as cold.

Opposite them is the play yard, with its wooden climbing structure, swings, and trees.

She thwaps at Skint's arm.

"Let's climb to the top like we used to when we were little," she says. "Let's hang down from our knees."

"Hanging like that makes your shirt bunch up around your armpits and leaves your stomach exposed." Skint's eyes are still closed. "I don't really want to add flashing to the list of my crimes."

"We can tuck our shirts in," Dinah says. "Be fun."

"You do it," says Skint. "I don't feel like it right now." He shifts his weight and settles more stolidly against the church.

Dinah would like to poke him but thinks maybe she should leave him alone. She gets up and makes for the structure.

Skint tucks his hands into his sleeves. Thank God. He can finally breathe a minute, be alone. Not think about cans or churches or Ellen or the bank; not about the money or not getting it and losing his—

No. Stop. Breathe.

The weather-beaten shingles are rough against his head. He's nearly asleep, near dreaming of Dinah hanging by her knees, hair floating down. The gray man is in front of her, hand on Walter's neck. A second Walter stands solemn next to Skint, facing away from him toward the woods. Skint's cheek is against the donkey's and Skint breathes into the petal of his ear.

"—go—"

Sunlight breeze and stones in Dinah's hand.

TWENTY-FIVE

Dinah holds her coat flat against her stomach. Trees upside down, snow drifting in the wind. Drifting down, sifting down, ground overhead like a sky. Her eyes and nose stream in the cold, tears heading templewards into her floating-down hair.

Blood rushes to the top of her head and fills the whole of her mind, stilling her chatter and frantic planning.

Nothing. No more thinking right now. Just hang and sway. When they were five, she and Skint used to hang upside down like this until their noses felt like fire and their cheeks sagged up into their eyes, marveling across the yard at the tops of the apple trees swaying weirdly below their knees.

Great-Granny always sang when she ran the vacuum in the nave. When Dinah was big enough, in kindergarten, she came along and helped with the singing. She also held the dustpan for Granny when she needed it. Each Saturday, when they were done with the cleaning, Granny took Dinah outside to play.

Almost every time, Dinah climbed the apple trees.

"Would you look at that sky," said Granny. "I have a mind to get up that tree with you and get a closer look, Dinah."

"You can't, Granny!" said Dinah. "Your shoes are too slippy. You need to wear sneakers to climb up this tree. Plus you need to be a good climber, like me."

Dinah leaned back against the trunk and pretended about flying while Granny closed her eyes and rested on one of the swings.

Dinah was supposed to be at kindergarten, but here she was in the churchyard instead, breeze on her face and apple branches overhead. A petal drifted by her nose and wafted away across the play yard. Three stones rested in Dinah's hand.

This one was for Skint. This one was for Granny. One more in her pocket for if she saw her granny's shoes.

Pear-smelling cotton buzzy singing overhead.

Dinah's eyes filled with tears.

Two feet in sneakers stood in front of where she lay. Skint crouched down beside her.

"Why are you on the ground?"

Dinah didn't answer. Petals fell from the trees like soft and scented snow.

"Are you angry?"

Dinah was quiet.

"Are you sad?"

Tears spilled across Dinah's nose onto the ground.

"Do you want me to get your mom?"

Dinah shook her head no against the dirt. She reached over and put the stones on top of Skint's shoes.

Shuddering. Dinah couldn't catch her breath. All this stuff coming out of her nose. Her dad wiped it away.

"Me, too," he said, holding her close. "I want her back, too."

Skint was gone. "He won't be back for first grade," Dinah's mother said. He moved away, far away, with his dad and his candy and his mom who hugged him hard and was always saying it was time to go home and slop him.

Dinah sat in her closet and palmed her stones to wait.

TWENTY-SIX

Now the wind is tangling in Dinah's floating-down hair. It's hard to breathe, dangling upside down like this, so Dinah pulls herself back up to the bar and then drops to the ground. She starts back across the play yard toward Skint, who is still sitting hunched and unmoving by the bulkhead.

Someone else is moving across the play yard, too, someone small in a too-big coat with a skull stitched onto the back.

"K. T.!" Dinah calls.

K. T. stops and turns around.

"Hello," says Dinah as she catches up to him. "How are you? Aren't you supposed to be down in the Sunday school?"

"I'm being out here right now instead."

"How come?"

K. T. doesn't answer.

"Skint's over there," says Dinah. "Want to come with me and say hello?"

"All right."

Skint's eyes open at their approach.

"Hey, there, my friend," he says, and holds out his hand to K. T.

K. T. doesn't take it.

"I waved to you yesterday," says K. T. "On your bike."

"I know," says Skint. "You were standing by your mailbox."

"You didn't wave back."

"Yes, I did," says Skint. "I turned around and waved, but you were looking at the ground."

"You did not," says K. T.

"I did," says Skint. "You just didn't see me."

K. T. thumps his mittened hand against the wall of the church by Skint's head.

"Is something wrong, K. T.?" Dinah asks.

"I don't like it in there," says K. T. "The Sunday school lady doesn't like me."

"Who couldn't like you?" says Skint. "You're great."

"I am not."

"Yes, you are. Me and Dinah think so."

"Does the Sunday school lady know you're out here?" asks Dinah.

K. T. shrugs and thumps his hand.

"Hey!" says Skint. "I almost forgot!" He works something out of his pocket and tosses it up to K. T. "Catch."

K. T. catches the object, but it falls out of his hand and bounces away. "My Super Ball!" he cries, scrambling after it. "I thought I lost it!"

Skint grins at him.

K. T. stands back up but he is not grinning. "Why did you steal my Super Ball!" he shouts.

"Easy, kid," says Skint, his own smile fading. "I didn't steal it. It rolled under the cabinet in the food pantry yesterday. I fished it out to save for you."

"It's mine!"

"I know," says Skint. "That's why I kept it in my pocket for you."

"I hate you!" K. T. cries.

"For finding your ball?"

"You were going to keep it!"

"Never," says Skint. "What's the matter, K. T.?"

K. T.'s nose starts to run and his eyes fill with tears.

Dinah and Skint exchange glances. Dinah touches K. T.'s shoulder, but he jerks away from her. Clutching his Super Ball in his puffy blue mitten, he hurls it awkwardly against the bulkhead. It bounces off with a clang and hits the side of the church, high up near the window, and thonks back down to the ground. Skint pops up and catches it in one hand.

"They'll hear you in there," he says and takes K. T.'s hand. "K. T., what's bugging you?"

"Give me my ball!" K. T. grabs his hand out of Skint's, his brow anguished and creased. There is an eyeball drawn in marker on the palm of his mitten.

"K. T., what's *wrong*?"

K. T. snatches the ball from Skint's hand. Then he smashes it against the ground so hard it flies up and hits him squarely in the head.

K. T. sobs.

Dinah squats down beside him. He pushes her away, and the force of the push tips them both backward onto the ground.

Skint scoots over and puts his hand on K. T.'s arm. "Tell us what's wrong, K. T."

"You don't even know how you're supposed to bounce that kind of ball!" K. T. gulps raggedly through his tears.

"I'm sorry," says Skint. "Do you want to show me how?"

K. T. shakes his head and weeps.

Dinah pats his head, and this time he lets her hug him to her. "What's the matter?"

K. T. hiccups indiscernible words into her armpit.

"What was that?" asks Skint.

K. T. lifts his head.

"I'm not allowed to see my mom anymore," he sobs.

"What? Why not?"

"He came to pick me up this morning—"

"Your dad?"

K. T. digs his skull into Dinah's chest and nods.

"And I couldn't find my little guys." His face creases again with weeping. "My mom was helping me find them, but my dad was yelling at me because of being late for church. And my mom—" He gulps. "My mom was upset because of my dad yelling and then my dad hollered, 'That's it! I'm sick of this!' And he said she can't have me visit there anymore." K. T. sobs again. "I hate my dad!"

Skint lays his hand gently on K. T.'s head.

"He said he was going to make it so she can't see you?" he asks.

K. T. nods, weeping.

"K. T., I don't think he can do that. He was mad, and that's probably why he said that, but I don't think he'd be allowed to stop you from seeing your mom. I don't think that's legal."

K. T. lifts his head. "What's 'legal'?"

"It means it would be against the law for your dad to do that. It means your mom has the right to see you, and if he doesn't let her, your dad would be in trouble."

K. T.'s face crumples again.

"My dad said my *mom* would be in trouble. He said the police would take her to jail if she tried to come get me!"

Dinah hates Mr. Vaar. Swelling around in his stupid zippered shirt—

She and Skint meet each other's gaze.

"This," says Skint, "is not acceptable."

"We'll talk to him!" Dinah cries.

"Sure," says Skint. "That'll work. Because he's so kind and so rational."

K. T.'s eyes stream. "I want my mom," he weeps.

"K. T.!"

It's the Vole. He's come around the side of the building and stands stock-still when he sees Dinah and Skint.

Dinah adjusts herself and K. T. so they are sitting more solidly in front of the tarped box. She fans out her elbows to hide it better. K. T. burrows his head into Dinah's chest and refuses to look up.

"K. T.!" barks the Vole again.

Dinah glowers at the Vole, who snorts and looks past her to Skint, who looks evenly back at him. Skint looks like he is about a hundred years old.

"K. T." The Vole turns away from Skint. "What the hell are you doing out here?"

K. T. doesn't answer.

"What is wrong with you? You can't just run away like that. You have to get back in there."

"No."

"Leave him alone," says Skint.

"Shut up, Rotmouth."

"He's upset, fungus."

"My brother is not your fucking business."

"What's 'fungus'?" K. T.'s muffled voice.

"I guess you're right, Avery," says Skint. "His lachrymal effusions already speak so movingly to your family's compassion. I'll just step back and let him be cradled in its palm."

"Shut up, ass-wipe. Come on, K. T. Cut the crap. Get back in there and act like a normal kid."

"What name did you call Skint? What did you call him with 'mouth'?" K. T. lifts his head at last. His eyes are swollen and damp.

The Vole hesitates. "What's going on?" he asks.

K. T. looks down again and shakes his head. He pulls his mittens halfway off so the drawn-on eyes cover the tips of his fingers.

The Vole doesn't say anything. Then: "Come on," he says, not unkindly. "I'll walk you back in."

"No."

The Vole looks at K. T. "Did something happen? This morning?"

K. T. shrugs.

The Vole glances at Dinah.

She glances back at him and then turns to K. T. "You

want to stay out with us here a minute, K. T.?" she asks. "You can tell his teacher he's with me," she says to the Vole.

"No!" K. T.'s head snaps up. "Don't tell my teacher!" His voice breaks. "That dumb lady doesn't even call me by my kindergarten name."

"Your kindergarten name?" Skint asks. "What's your kindergarten name?"

K. T. doesn't answer.

The Vole puts his hands in his pockets. He glances at K. T. again, then at the ground. "Come on, K. T.," he says at last. "I mean, Kevin Todd. Come on. I guess we can stay out here a minute. Let's go swing or some shit."

"Will you tell, Avie?" K. T. asks anxiously. "Avie, will you tell?"

Skint raises his brows at the "Avie."

"No," says the Vole. "Whatever. Come on."

K. T. gets up off Dinah's lap. "Okay," he says. "I'll swing."

"See you later, K. T.," says Skint. "We won't forget your problem. We'll think about what we can do."

"My brother's all set, Gilbert."

"Right," says Skint.

K. T. and the Vole make their way to the swings.

"I hate mankind," says Dinah. Her rear is freezing from sitting on this concrete.

"So do I," says Skint. "Let's get rid of them all."

He pushes himself up off the ground.

"I'm going," he says. "If you really don't mind doing the cans by yourself."

"I don't mind," says Dinah. "But what about the pantry-raiding at my house?"

"Later, maybe. I want to be by myself awhile."

Dinah bites her lip.

"Do you think the Vole noticed the box of cans?" she asks.

"I doubt it, what with your great heaving self in front of it the whole time. I don't think he'd give a shit about it if he did, Dinah." Skint brushes off his pants. "I'm off."

"I'll call you?"

"Later, I guess. If you want to."

He's already gone. Dinah watches as he hunches away down the road without looking back at her at all.

TWENTY-SEVEN

Everybody's gone at last except the choir in the nave; another rehearsal, a long singing day. Dinah sets the box of cans down on the floor in front of the bulletin board inside the incense-smelling church.

Nobody ever deals with the outdated notices on this bulletin board, she thinks. *They just staple new ones over the old.* Though maybe she is the one who is supposed to weed out the old ones. Maybe it is technically in the domain of the sexton.

Rip. Off go the old Auxiliary Aid minutes and the call to donate cans for the Christmas food drive. *(Shut up about that right now; stop stop stop.)* Off, too, goes the notice about last week's choir rehearsals, written in Dinah's dad's beautiful, even hand.

"Donkey Minuet" reads another notice, and Dinah carefully loosens that one, too. She folds it up and puts it in her pocket and heads toward the food pantry.

". . . he went up to his chamber . . ." the choir sings as she steps into the Pantry. Dinah doesn't know what she was expecting in here. Things tossed about, perhaps, cans lying where they have rolled to a stop. But if you didn't know better, you'd think no one had touched a thing. The Pantry looks just the same.

Except there. The side door. The doorjamb busted and a strip of jagged torn wood; new wood exposed and sharp under splintered brown paint.

Skint, in the dark, walking up here, fast and angry. Not monk kind of angry but angry with a goal, angry he can't keep in or call her up and tell her about, a bigger kind of angry than she's ever seen. Skint, in the dark, hitting the door as hard as he can; ragged splinters cutting up his hand.

What can she do? What is helping?

Make Skint not be so angry. But she doesn't know how. All she can think to do is take Skint's hand in hers and hug the part that is scraped.

The choir moves into that difficult fugue with the notes that sound like crying.

". . . Absalom, my Absalom . . ."

One by one, Dinah puts the cans back in their proper spots on the shelves. One of the tenor voices breaks over the rest like a waterfall, his voice lambent and clear. Who is that? Mrs. Wattle is singing a bit more quietly than usual, and even though other people are missing notes here and there, it all does sound sort of nice. Her father's work is paying off.

The cans away, Dinah moves back into the foyer and peeks through the door into the nave. All of the choir is looking intently at her dad as they sing. Mr. Beach's hair sticks straight up as he works his shoulders and hands to direct them. The lovely tenor voice is breaking, falling; which man is it?

That one, there, eyes locked with her dad, his music clutched tight in his hand, singing as if his life depended on it, as if this song must be sung now, and by him.

Mr. Vaar? How can he be that voice?

". . . would God I had died for thee . . ."

Suddenly exhausted, Dinah leans away from the nave. The basement. No one will be down there, and if she puts three chairs in a row, she can lie down on them, sort of; she can fall asleep for just a minute. Then she'll wake up and be ready for thinking. She'll be able to figure out what to do.

She heads slowly down the stairs, palming the tin in her pocket, square with rounded edges.

TWENTY-EIGHT

Skint would rather be on his bike, but walking will have to be good enough; hard fast walking. It's freezing out here, ground too hard, sky too bright. Skint puffs down the road, walking faster and faster until he's jogging, running jogging running. The Rural Routes appear in his mind, then fade; empty porch gray and dark.

Fucking humans. Fucking humans letting each other freeze. What is wrong with us?

We suck, as Ellen says. Or used to say, whenever his dad would get upset and unhappy and need to write another article. "Have you looked much at humanity lately?" she said once. "Because pretty much we're shits. We only care about ourselves or our own little families and we don't do anything for anyone else. Won't make do with less for the sake of someone else. Me included."

Her included, me included, all of us included. Monks made to stand in tubs of shit, shot, tortured, in *hell*, and Skint does nothing, *nothing;* all he does is rage with Dinah. Monks in shit and kids made to be sad; K.T., so happy to be baking with his mom and his ass of a dad comes in and takes that away—Skint can't bear it. He can't, the happiness fading from K. T.'s eyes and his chest gone hollow, his face gone hot, tears in his eyes and that asshole of a man loving to crush his own little boy.

Hurt of K.T., hurt of those monks, unbearable hurt when he thinks of his mom in the store picking out those plush frogs, the longing and grief and pain and grief. And his dad, his dad.

"I look just the same," his dad told a friend on the phone a few months before they moved back here. "If you saw me, you'd think I was fine."

"Listen to him," said Skint's mother. "The conditional in place, even as memory fails."

His dad smiled a little. Then his eye fell on Skint and his mouth corners dropped, fell down; uncurled themselves down. His eyes unbearable, worse than sad. Devastated, despairing, gone.

"My God," said his dad. "My God." Eyes creased and watered and his hand at his mouth. "My God," he said, still looking at Skint. "My God."

He got up and left the room.

Footsteps thumped up the stairs and overhead, then stopped. From above came ragged sounds of weeping. "My son. My son."

Too much. Too much hurt and not eyes enough to see; too much pain and not hands enough to help. Skint can't take it anymore, he can't. Full of enough crying for eleven crying heads, all of them raging—but he won't do it, he won't. He won't start, because if he does he'll explode; he'll never fucking stop.

TWENTY-NINE

A horrid smell of hot vinegar and cheese hits Dinah as soon as she opens the door to her house. Artichoke dip. Dinah's parents make it for every occasion. Panicked and sore-backed from her too-long nap—two hours, it turned into!—which she took crumpled up on the wooden chairs, Dinah finds the smell too much to bear. And the nap didn't even help. She has no more ideas now than she did before.

At least her parents will be out at their book club potluck for the evening, so as soon as Beagie is asleep, Dinah can be alone, alone, alone. She doesn't want to have to talk to a soul. Except for Skint. She has to talk to him. She'll call him once the house is clear.

"Dinah, darling!" Mr. Beach calls from the kitchen. "Come and have speech with us!"

Ugh. But if she doesn't go in there, they will only hunt her down to say hello. Feeling undarling and hollow, Dinah steps into the kitchen.

"Hello," she says.

"Hello, Dinah!" her mother calls from the pantry. Her father is sitting at the table, tea mug in hand, an old book of songs open before him.

"I need to hang up my coat," Dinah tells him, twisting her feet. "Is it okay, please, if I at least hang up my coat?"

"I forbid it," says Mr. Beach. "I forbid it most specially. You must first regale me with tales of your day."

"I don't have any," says Dinah.

"Then I will regale you with mine. Church was lovely. And the choir is shaping up rather nicely, I think. I have contained the Wattle and Mr. Vaar is leading the tenors quite beautifully—"

"I hate the choir."

"So do I, of course. But I hate them less today. And you only hate them because of your dreadful, dolorous singing voice. You are afraid you would fit right in. You—"

"Bill," Dinah's mother's voice admonishes from the pantry. She thinks it is awful for Mr. Beach to twit Dinah for her lack of tunefulness. Normally Dinah would seize the opportunity to sing with great purpose and volume, but not right now.

Mr. Beach takes his hands down from his ears. "What?" he says. "Not even one note? So to speak?"

Dinah crosses and uncrosses her feet. "I do not feel much like singing."

Two other feet, stampy and small, emerge from the pantry and race toward her. A small head burrows into her leg.

"What were you doing in there, Beagie?" Dinah picks him up and kisses him. They regard one another soberly.

"I was letting him sort Tupperware," says Mrs. Beach, emerging with a casserole dish in her hand. "It bought me fifteen minutes to get on with things. Because some people would rather thumb through the shape-note songbook than do their bit to stir things on the stove."

Mr. Beach looks guilty and closes the book over his thumb; long and faded blue, it's Granny's old book, a harp gilded on its cover.

Dinah's eyes prick and grow warm. *Do not, do not cry, you.*

Beagie rests his head on Dinah's shoulder. She takes his small foot in her hand. Small as a dinner roll and soft as one, too. One day it won't be so; it'll grow big and smelly, tendoned and knotted with veins. What if they hurt him when it's cold out, or damp? What if walking grows hard?

"Is something wrong, Dinah?"

The whole thing is wrong; all of it's wrong. The whole stupid way we are.

"When do you leave?" she asks. She needs to call Skint, talk to him, now.

"Never," says Mrs. Beach levelly, setting down the dish. "We've decided to stay home and spend the evening with you instead. We'll start by braiding your hair—"

"I'm to tie on the bows," agrees Mr. Beach.

"Then we'll work out an interpretive dance for us to perform as a family."

"Please, just when are you leaving?"

"Dinah Christine, why are you no fun?"

Because she is, right now, an egg with a too-thin shell, a glass of water barely gripped.

Beagie rears up his head and applies his plush horse forcefully to her chin. "Iss!" he says. "Iss!"

The horse smells awful, of old food and drool. Dinah kisses it. "Someone should wash your horse, Beagie."

"I shall scrub it in my old tin tub," Mr. Beach agrees, "directly after I have told you some more about the day's triumphs with the choir."

The choir; the choir; can he talk about anything besides that choir?

(trickling, breath-caught notes from the nave—". . . and thus he said, 'O, my son . . .'")

Oh, Dinah doesn't want to talk about the choir.

"Although I sense the topic is not fascinating to you," says her father.

"Could you chop the rest of the artichokes, do you imagine, Dinah?" Mrs. Beach indicates a stinking pile on the cutting board.

"I will!" says Mr. Beach, eager to make up for his lack of stirring. Mrs. Beach hesitates and catches Dinah's eye. Her father wielding a knife is a clumsy, terrifying thing.

"I'll do it," says Dinah. Better to do it quickly and be done and out than have a production about not and have to tend to her father's inevitable wound. "Hold my brother, please." Coat still on, she passes Beagie to Mr. Beach and moves to take up the knife.

"Wugh!" Beagie protests, so Mr. Beach sets him down on the floor instead. Beagie lies down straightaway and drums his heels on the floor, sucking absentmindedly on his horse.

Chop chop chop chop chop.

"So we met about the break-in," says Mr. Beach.

Dinah's stomach jolts, but she covers it with chopping. Did Skint leave evidence? Fingerprints? What if his boots left distinctive prints in the snow?

Be calm, Dinah Beach. Even if they found fingerprints, Skint does not have a record they could match them to, and there are so many footprints stamped around that door all the time it wouldn't matter if he left some of those, too. And if he tracked any snow inside, it would long since have melted. Skint ought to be safe.

Unless he left some other enormous clue because he was too mad to take good precautions. Or just didn't care.

Those defiant eyes, that head tossing, almost glad. Dinah is terrified she is the only one to whom it would matter if Skint gets caught.

"Are there any other clues?" Dinah asks carefully, trying to sound offhand. "As to the perps?"

That was clever, her use of the plural.

"No, none," says Mr. Beach.

Dinah sags inwardly with relief.

"But I don't know that anyone thinks it is much of a mystery," Mr. Beach continues. "You know this town. I'm sure it was high-school kids who probably got scared off. Area teens."

Good. Let them keep thinking that.

"It was area teens last year," she says.

"Thank God you are sensible, Dinah," says Mr. Beach. "We never worry that you will become part of a pack of ravening kids."

Dinah flushes red. She knows she is more dork than sensible. And she makes mistakes the whole time. They are just not mistakes about drinking. She is not interested in a lot of those things, which is hard in a different way, at least at school. She is lucky that Skint doesn't care about any of that either, because otherwise she would be pretty much the only one.

"Dump those artichokes in the pan, Dinah." Mrs. Beach nods at the casserole dish on the counter.

"Did the police come out in force?" Dinah asks, scooping up handfuls.

"Oh, in force. Both of them." Mr. Beach smiles briefly. "Any thoughts, Dinah, about who it might be?"

"No! Why would I have thoughts?"

Mr. Beach raises his eyebrows. "Because you and Skint are generally popping with commentary on the daftness of your peers."

"Well, I am not popping right now. You shouldn't grill me."

"I'm not grilling you, cranky," says Mr. Beach. "Aren't you going to give me a cookie?"

Dinah's stomach falls. "No," she says.

"Not one?!" Mr. Beach hauls himself to his feet. "Not even one for your aged papa?"

"My aged papa is always saying he has got to watch his middle," Dinah says. "Plus we . . . we didn't finish them yet." She puts her hands in her pockets. Her left hand hits the tin of sardines. "Could I *go*, please? Your dip smells awful."

Beagie scooches backward toward her across the floor and places his horse on her foot.

"Dinah Beach, you are rude." Mr. Beach glowers with the aid of his eyebrows. "And strange."

"You are the one who lies down on the floor the whole time."

Her mother furrows her brow.

"Is something wrong, Dinah?" she asks. "Did something happen with Skint?"

"Why would you think something happened with Skint!"

"Easy, there, old thing!" says Mr. Beach.

"You two always think something is wrong with Skint!"

"We never think anything is wrong with Skint!" Mr. Beach is indignant. "I adore him. I think he's a capital kid. You, on the other hand. Cranky and morose and all the time difficult."

"Well, why don't you let me just leave, then?" Dinah's eyes threaten to fill, but she will not let them, she won't. "You never let me just leave."

"Dah!" Beagie pulls himself up on her legs and tugs at her hands, marching pleadingly in place. Dinah picks him up, gulping, but she can't stay in this kitchen for another minute. She hands the baby to Mr. Beach and leaves.

Beagie wails.

"She's a peevish, grumpy old thing," says her father in the kitchen.

"I hate you," Dinah whispers as she goes up the stairs.

Nose running and stupid weeping eyes. All this crying all the time, all these tears and no more laughing.

Go back, go back. Undo these days and let us go back to before.

An hour later her parents are prowling around, getting ready to go to the potluck. Dinah sits in the living room window seat, sardine tin in her hand. Her bones are as heavy as lead. She wants to call Skint, but she can't while her parents are still here. She needs to be able to concentrate, to listen for if he is angry or sad.

"Dinah Beach!" Her father is in the doorway. "Are those *sardines* in your hand? The fancy ones from Christmas?"

Dinah stares at the can. Visions of Bernadine and her Inventory flash through Dinah's head. What can she say? Does her having the sardines in any way implicate Skint?

"But you donated them!" her father squawks. "You gave them away!"

Help! Dinah considers saying that there is more than one can of sardines in the world, but there isn't, not in the world of Aile Quarry, anyway, especially not one labeled in Italian. She can't pretend she bought these herself in town, and if she were to pretend she bought them anywhere else, she'd also have to pretend she stole the car, and also that she'd learned, illegally, to drive. And forget saying she got them online—that would mean packages and deliveries and her mother or somebody would have had to have signed, oh, help, help, help.

"I never did donate them," she says finally. "I hid them." She swallows. "I wanted to hog them for myself."

Her father looks at her, one eyebrow raised.

"On account of how I love them. I filched them out of our donation box before I even brought it to the Pantry."

She is lying all over the place and feels oddly awful that her father will think she is grasping and greedy but she can't care about that right now. Better that than he starts dusting for prints in the Pantry, or remembering about the cuts on Skint's hand.

Skint.

Dinah gives the can a surreptitious rub on her thigh to erase all fingerprints and holds the can out to Mr. Beach. "Here," she says. "Take them. I'm sorry."

He waves the can away with his hand.

"Please," she says earnestly. "I don't want them. I'm sorry."

"This is not like you at all, Dinah. What's got into you?"

"Nothing has got into me."

Her father's brows draw in. "Dinah Beach, you have been known to be shouty and hyperbolic, but never a liar. I have seen and coveted those sardines in that Pantry, many times. You did donate them. I don't know why you are saying otherwise."

Dinah is silent.

"Twice taking food from the Pantry, Dinah? In as many days?

"Twice?"

"Yesterday," Mr. Beach says. "With your odd snack-giving for that little boy—"

Oh. She forgot she took the blame for that, too.

"—and again, today, to satisfy your insatiable need for sardines?"

"I don't have an insatiable need for sardines!"

"When did you take them?" Her father is stern. "It wasn't last night, was it?"

"No!"

"Is that why you are all upset? Were you part of the area teens?"

"Dad!"

"Did you *sneak out* to join them?"

"Dad!"

Mr. Beach stops. He wilts.

"Oh, Dinah. I'm so sorry. What's the matter with me? I know you would never do such a thing. Forgive me, darling." He crosses the room toward her.

"Don't you have to go now?" she says, near tears, drawing herself away. "Don't you have to go?"

"I truly didn't mean it, Dinah. I am just so worried about you. You are low-moody and difficult and you seem so upset."

"I am not upset. Bring me my brother."

"You are upset. *Did* something happen with Skint? Did you two fight?"

"No."

Mr. Beach is quiet.

"How is his father?" he asks.

Thin Mr. Gilbert. Frightened, puzzled eyes. Spoon in Skint's hand and petals coming down.

Dinah picks at the window muntins and doesn't answer.

"He's fine," she says finally, mindful of her promise. Her eyes fill with tears.

Mr. Beach crosses the room and sits down beside her on the window seat. He rests his hand gently on her foot.

"It's awful, isn't it," he says. "Thomas Gilbert is a very fine man. Skint must be very sad to see him changing."

Dinah takes her foot from under his hand and wipes her eyes with an angry palm.

"It's ridiculous," she says. "It's beyond the stupidest thing."

"No, Dinah," says Mr. Beach. "It's human to be sad. You need to let your friend be sad."

"I don't mean Skint," says Dinah. Though what kind

of friend lets a friend be sad? "I mean the whole thing. People getting old and giving out and getting sick and hurt. It's the stupidest thing in the world."

Mr. Beach is quiet. "I think it's more complex than stupid," he says.

"It's not complex! It's just dumb. What good is it to have everybody die the whole time?" Dinah's breath catches. She holds it and studies the neighbor horse's blanket-coat, slung over the fence at the edge of the yard.

Her father is silent. Then he sighs. "You don't really like my ideas about that, I don't think."

Dinah swallows. The horse blanket blurs, then clears, then blurs again.

Her father moves as if to hug her, but she jumps up and away from him and heads toward the door. "I'm going to go get Beagie for his dinner."

And she's out of there, she's gone, flying away upstairs.

THIRTY

Beagie stares heavy-eyed out the window toward the neighbor's yard. His cheeks are smeared with peas.

"Oss!" he shouts, waving his hands and feet. Dinah switches on the light and he turns toward it wonderingly.

"Not your feet," Dinah tells him. "That was me, pulling the switch."

Beagie grunts briefly and turns back to the window. His face crumples. "Oss!" he wails.

"He must be asleep in his shed, Beagie. It must be

the horse's bedtime. You can see him again tomorrow."

Beagie turns back to her and opens his mouth for more peas.

"That was good talking, though, Beagie Bee. Horse, horse, horse."

"Oss."

All Skint took was cans. To give is why he took them; to give, to help. He couldn't have wanted to break anything.

But he did want to. He must have. Otherwise he could have gone in the Pantry the normal way if he wanted to pilfer from it: in the daytime while they did cleaning, or right before the Friendly.

The distant look Skint had on his face, hard and far away. Dinah doesn't know what to do.

Beagie slaps at his high-chair tray. "Duh, duh, duh!" he sings.

"Duh, duh, duh!" Dinah joins in for a bit, but her heart isn't in it and she trails off. She wipes the peas from Beagie's cheeks and fingers. He extends an imperious foot when she's finished; he always demands his toes be wiped, too.

Her father and his believing and heaven and God and design. She understands, though. She understands why her father believes. He believes because it is too terrible not to.

It's too awful to believe that dead is just dead, that

the people you love are just gone. That their bodies just gave out or gave up and you'll never have them to love or hug or be near again. That there is no reason for it or anything else, none but the reasons people make up for themselves. The only real things are the things people decide to do and what other people decide to do to them. And nothing is enough to keep anybody safe, to keep anybody well or alive. Believing there are reasons for things keeps the hell of all this away. Believing keeps people alive.

"Buhh!" Beagie demands to be freed from his chair. Dinah lifts him out and stands him on her thighs. He grabs at her head to steady himself and pushes his forehead against hers, crowing to see her go one-eyed.

"Praying brings Granny near," Dinah's father used to tell her. He believes that, too, that his words are magic, that they can change things, make something less dead than it is.

He's so lucky he thinks that.

It doesn't happen often, but every once in a while, just for an instant, Dinah wishes she still believed, too.

Dinah catches her breath. No tears, no. But she can't help it. *All of us are like Beagie, wishing his feet were magic, believing he is the boss of light.*

THIRTY-ONE

It's dark. Skint's still walking, away from Main Street and town. There's the Rural Routes' house, shut-up-looking and cold.

Why doesn't he go up there? Right up to the door? He'd like to meet them. Hear if they have actual voices.

Clomp stomp jump—he's up on the porch. Skint cocks an ear toward the house and lifts his hand to knock on the door. Stillness inside; no voices or rustling. Skinny little house narrow one-room deep; where are the Rural Routes if not inside?

Skint glances in the windows, leaning in, looking. The road over his shoulder is oddly far away. He and Dinah must look like action figures to them, like pretend kids walking by. Spindly legs scissoring along the road; Dinah's cloud of dark hair shining.

Anybody in there? Anybody home? Skint touches the door. It opens beneath his hand.

"Hello?" he says. Ticking, from inside. Musty, dark. Furniture, doilies, an andiron like an owl.

Why not just go in?

No.

Skint closes the door, tight and fast. He jumps off the porch and bolts up the road, striding, running, running.

THIRTY-TWO

Beagie is asleep at last. Dinah goes into her room and calls Skint.

"Hello," he says.

She sags with relief.

"I have a possible FoE for us," she tells him. "A magic show. On Saturday, at the library. I just saw it in the paper. Mr. Presto the magician with a troupe of beginner Portuguese dancers. It will be perfect! Skinny little girls with knee socks, dancing in circles. We will love it."

"I want to go somewhere," says Skint.

His cellular telephone is not a very good one. Dinah can barely make out his words.

"Come here, then," she says, sitting up straight. "Why don't you just come over here?"

"I mean I want to go someplace *big*. I want to go someplace and *do* something. Flarping do something about all this crap."

"What crap?"

"All of it. Refugees, people. All the stuff I talk about the whole time." He pauses. "I want to go overseas."

Dinah's stomach drops. "Overseas? What would you do overseas?"

"Help those monks. Help. Do something to stop all this insane crap."

"How do you do that? Who would take you?"

"What do you mean, who would take me? I would take me."

Dinah sits up straight. Does he have a secret money stash she doesn't know about? Does he have friends to help him overseas? "How can you, though, alone?" she asks. "People will notice you are only fifteen."

"You know no one notices that, unless they already know me. I'll work, talk my way over."

Dinah doesn't know what to say. Her only idea to distract him and cheer him up was the Portuguese dancers. She twines the edge of her blanket around her hand.

"Why can't I?" cries Skint. "Why can't I just go? It's what I want to do. What is there here to keep me?"

Dinah swallows.

"I would miss you," she says.

Skint's voice is defeated, edged with cold. "Well, it's not like I can do it anyway."

Dinah shifts onto her knees. "Where are you?"

"Outside, by the river. It's beautiful."

"I wish I could come see." She pauses, but he doesn't say he wishes it, too. "Skint, it's too cold for you to be out so late."

"I'm fine."

"Come over," she says. "Please."

"No."

Dinah twists and twists her blanket. "Are you mad at me?" She hears his boots crunch in the snow.

"No."

"We could play a game or something," she says.

"I'd rather swill bourbon."

What the heck kind of comment is that? Does that mean he'd rather swill bourbon than come, or swill bourbon than do a game?

"Besides," he continues, "if I come over there in the dark of night, your parents will think we are secret lovers."

That's more your mom's purview, thinks Dinah, but she says only, "Of course they won't think that."

Skint sighs. "God knows that's true."

What does that mean? That she is a sex moron? Dinah's cheeks flame. "Just come. We can plan about the parcel."

"No." Crunching. "I went by the Rural Routes'," he says suddenly.

"You did? Were they in their regular spots?"

"No. They weren't home."

"How did you know?"

"I went up on the porch."

Dinah sits up straight, her neck searing with alarm. "You did?"

"Yeah. Not for long, though. They weren't there so I just left."

Dinah sinks back down, relieved. "I don't think of the Rural Routes as having evening outings," she says.

"Me either," says Skint. "The house was freezing, Dinah."

Dinah sits up again. "I thought you only knocked."

"I did, detective. I could just tell. No smoke in the chimney. The way the door sounded when I knocked." He's quiet for a minute. "The hell with it," he says abruptly. "If we can't help the monks, we could at least follow through on helping the Rural Routes."

"Yes!" says Dinah, made jubilant by his "we." She grips the phone tightly to her ear. "We can do that. Don't you want to come over? To plan?"

"We should give them blankets," says Skint. "Your crazy crochet hats. Gloves, stuff like that."

"I don't know if we have any extras of gloves." There was that weird box Bernadine gave them a couple of Christmases ago containing seven black gloves—singles, not pairs—all of them sized for a giant. But Dinah thinks her mother already got rid of those. "But I can make some, I bet."

"We'll figure it out," says Skint. "They can have mine. We have a ton of extra blankets as well. We'll give them a couple of those."

"Will that be okay with—" Dinah stops herself. "Swell," she says. "Come over in the morning and we'll plan more."

"Okay," says Skint. Then: "No. Wait. You come to my house. I don't feel like schlepping blankets back and forth."

Dinah opens her mouth, then closes it. *What?* "Your house?" she says. Why does he suddenly want them to hang out there? Dinah can't remember the last time she was inside. Is he forgetting that Ellen will be there, Ellening around the place, jabbing people with looks about their clothes?

"Why the hell not," says Skint. His breath is heavy over the line. He must be walking very fast. "Why not. They'll be out. An appointment at the bank. She's waited forever to get it. She won't miss it. They'll be gone all morning. We can gather all the stuff for the parcel and then we can finish the cookies at your house after."

"Are you sure about this?" asks Dinah.

"Yes," says Skint. "Shut up. I'm sure."

"Okay," says Dinah. If his parents aren't home, then it's a different story, although it'll be odd to be in that house again. She wonders if it will look just the same.

"I'll come by for you," says Skint. "I want to ride first thing in the morning. I'll come to your house on my way back and pick you up."

"Don't you want to meet and go for a walk early, instead of riding? We could go under the bridge and skip stones." Dinah loves to do that, skip stones on ice. They twang as they bounce, with an otherworldly hum.

"No," says Skint. "I'm riding. If you weren't such a candy-ass, you could come with me."

"I'll get my brave ass back in the spring," says Dinah. She relaxes a little, and leans back against her headboard.

"I'm sure."

Dinah swallows. "Maybe after we do the Rural Routes we can think about ways to expand our helping idea. Like we wanted to with the Friendly."

"Why not," says Skint. "I'll be old enough to get my permit soon and we could have a wider scope."

"Old enough, schmold enough!" says Dinah. "That is not the talk of someone who has promised to Backwards Age!"

Skint is silent.

"I'm sorry," she says rapidly and swallows again. Skint in his black sweatshirt and jeans, outside in the cold, biking too fast over ice. "Come over, Skint. Please."

"No," says Skint, "I have to go. Bye." He hangs up without even saying he'll see her tomorrow.

Dinah hangs up too. She feels unhappy again, unformed and sad, like a child whose balloon has come undone from her wrist. She is not entirely sure why she feels this way, though, or what she meant when she said she was sorry.

She goes downstairs to pilfer the kitchen. All of the best things will be given to the Rural Routes.

THIRTY-THREE

Bourbon. Bourbon. Skint remembers sixth-grade Dinah and her bourbon, stuffing liquor-soaked towels in his mouth for his tooth. And that god-awful poultice; what was that stuff? Some kind of spice, he doesn't remember.

She was supposed to tell her mom. He waited for the phone to ring but it never did. Not until he got caught.

"What were you *thinking*, Skint?" the teacher cried. "What got into your head?"

He wanted to say, *I am a demon for liquor.* He wanted to say it was adolescent experimenting. But before he could stop himself, he heard himself say, "I read it was good for teeth."

"What do you mean?" the teacher asked.

But the principal knew. Skint was made to open his mouth.

"Fabulous, Skint! Thanks ever so! Now they think I don't watch out for my own kid." Ellen burst into tears. She has never forgiven him about that social worker being sent to their house.

Infection in the bone. The dentist pulled out the tooth and did surgery on Skint's jaw. Three weeks later he was fine; he was dandy, he couldn't believe how much better he felt. He felt light as a feather, floating in air.

Dinah brought him treasures and ice cream and parcels of treats while he recuperated. She sobbed and sobbed.

"It's okay!" he told her. "Look what great shape I am in now!" He thumped out a rhythm on his cheeks until she laughed through the crying.

Dinah; Dinah; this girl was Dinah. Dark-haired girl with ponytails to steer her turned into this girl with the hanging-down hair. All those games with stones and snow, pretending about trees being kings. He wondered about her when he was in Kentucky. He hoped she would still be here, if you really want to know. He thought about her all the time.

Dinah sounded so forlorn on the phone just now that Skint can't bear it. He also hates her and he can't bear that, either, nor the thought of her playing or her whimsy or anything else about Dinah right now. All he wants is to get on his bike, not wait until morning, just get on his bike and ride hard in the dark, down frozen dirt roads, tearing from ice chunk to rut, jumping over rocks and nearfalling downhill.

What is the point? What is there to keep him here at all? What makes him not just off himself and be done? His eyes burn and he covers his face in his hands.

He loves them all so goddamned much.

Oh, go to Dinah's, be over there with her right now. Be with her and stop there, suspended; never get older or go home. He can't, though. He has to go home.

THIRTY-FOUR

Skint enters his house through the kitchen, his goal to steal soundlessly up to his room.

The kitchen light flicks on. Ellen gazes at him steadily. There are circles under her eyes.

Skint is silent.

"How stupid are you?" she says. "What the hell were you thinking? Delaying us in that kitchen! Of all the people to get a load of your father it would have to be the one with the mother—"

"I'll try to hang out only with orphans in the future."

"Don't be smart. Don't you be smart!" Ellen raises her voice to a whisper-shout. "Don't you know what tomorrow is for us? Do you *want* him taken away from us? Do you want some social worker coming around again?"

Skint's chest constricts so tight and fast it's as though it's been squeezed by a fist.

"Do you?" Ellen asks, neck craned forward. "Because your actions sure as hell suggest—"

"*My* actions?"

"What's that supposed to mean?"

"It means you. It means if you want to talk about actions, let's talk about yours. How hard would it have been for you to just take the key and walk Dad back out to the car and go? Why did you have to make such a big deal over his coat? You could have left right away. But no. You had to—"

"Don't you dare. Don't you dare. You're the one who took off at the crack of dawn to get away from us. You're the one who left before the whole process of trying to get your father dressed and—" She breaks off. Then: "What did your dotty girlfriend have to say?"

Skint's stomach clenches. "Nothing," he says.

"Oh, come on."

"I'm serious." Eye sockets hot and clenched, his head aching. "She was oblivious."

"You don't know that," says Ellen. Her eyes grow dark and she covers her mouth with her palm. "You don't know what she thinks, or who she'll say something to."

"I do know. She won't say anything." Dinah promised not to

say a word about his dad, and he knows she won't. And in any case—"Believe me," he says bleakly, "Dinah didn't notice a thing."

Ellen stares straight ahead, taut-boned and thin.

"I can't lose him. I can't bear the thought of—" Her voice breaks. "I've been waiting for her mother or someone to call all day. I'm exhausted."

Skint rubs the side of his hand. He has no energy left to confront her about whatever it was that happened last night. "So go to bed, then," he says. "Go."

THIRTY-FIVE

My heart breaks for that poor man." Mrs. Beach's voice floats out from the kitchen as Dinah comes down the stairs early the next morning. "Seventy-three years married. Seventy-three! I can't imagine how he'll live without her. Here, grate this cheese, please. No, wait. I'll do that; you do the eggs."

"I can work the grater safely," Mr. Beach says indignantly as Dinah enters the kitchen. "Good morning, dear Dinah!"

Why is he always so appallingly cheerful?

"Who is dead?" Dinah asks.

"Ruth Ennethwaite," says Mrs. Beach. It's Monday, so she is in her professional aspect, ready for work in pants of a businesslike material and an unstained shirt. "Ninety-seven. Set the table, please, Dinah."

"No," says her father. "I need her to run to the mini-mart and get me the paper. I want to make sure they ran the announcement for the Evensong. I don't want to have done all this work with that choir only to play to an audience composed of the two of you."

"What am I, some kind of lackey?" Dinah cries.

"No, you are some kind of dependent child that I feed daily at enormous cost to myself and feel strongly can do her part every once in a while."

"I do my part the whole time."

"Go get the paper, Dinah."

"I'll get Beagie up and change him instead."

Mr. Beach frowns. "You will go get that paper or be fed nothing but sink scraps until further notice."

"Who cares." Dinah grabs her coat from the hook by the door. "Food is stupid. Give me money."

Her father glowers at her. She pulls her coat over her pajamas.

"Dinah Beach, you go get dressed!" says Mrs. Beach.

"No," says Dinah. "Flannel is warmer, anyway." She's got her boots pulled on and the door open, and is holding her hand out for her father's folded five-dollar bill.

"What an enormous pain in the neck she is," says

her mother as Dinah goes through the door.

"So are you, Mrs. Beach," Dinah mutters darkly to herself on the porch.

"She is indeed a pain, our Dinah," says her father, wrongly imagining her out of earshot as he moves to close the door behind her. "We are lucky, though, that she's such an odd little duck. Imagine if she were out there stirring up trouble."

Dinah stops in her tracks.

Odd little duck?

Punching!

THIRTY-SIX

Skint can't concentrate on the news this morning. Did he even sleep last night? Some twilight minutes, maybe, licking at the edge of a dream, but always coming back to awake. Doesn't matter, though. It's getting light out again, finally. He can go out and ride.

Skint cocks an ear toward the hall. Voices; they're awake, too. Ellen must be giving herself plenty of time to get his dad ready for the appointment at the bank. He can't catch her tone from here, though, so he folds the paper and gets up and eases down the hall.

The bathroom door is open. Mr. Gilbert stands in the bathtub, leaning against the wall by the window, his fingers spread over one of its panes. Ellen, her back to the hall, mops a puddle from the floor with a wad of paper towels under her foot.

"This is a new one," she mutters. "Peeing is one we haven't had before. You can't do this, Thomas, not unless you want to send me right over the edge."

Skint's chest seizes.

Mr. Gilbert is silent, eyes on the trees. Then: "What for a world," he says softly. "What for a. For."

Dad.

"Jesus Christ," Ellen says, wiping. "Come on, Thomas. We have to get you dressed. I have to be there on time. We need that money."

Mr. Gilbert stares out the window.

"Especially if I'm going to have to add Depends to the budget."

Skint's heart pounds. Mr. Gilbert is still.

"Thomas."

Skint's father turns and looks around the bathroom, his brows knit. His gaze falls on the bottle of bleach sitting at the edge of the sink, and he starts.

"Don't throw that!" he cries. Skint jumps.

But Ellen only picks up the wet wad of paper towels off the floor and flushes it. She begins again with a dry one. "Come *on.* You have to get out of those pajamas."

Mr. Gilbert's eyes are puzzled. "Why is it all wet down there?" he asks.

"Because I was trying to make the tiles slippery enough that I'd fall and crack my head open," says Ellen. "I long for the sweet release of death." She throws the second wad in the toilet. "Jesus Christ," she says, looking into the bowl. "The last thing we need is a clog."

But Mr. Gilbert has already turned away and is staring out the window again.

Ellen leans over and grabs at the hem of his pajama top. "Come."

Mr. Gilbert doesn't move.

"Come!"

He bows his head.

"Thomas. We have to *go.*"

"I can't." Mr. Gilbert's voice breaks. "How can I go, when so many others have no recourse but to stay?"

Skint's heart drops like a stone.

Ellen jiggles the toilet handle. "I'm sure everyone would want you to go."

"How can you say that, Gus? How can you say that when you've never even come over here to see?" Mr. Gilbert's eyes fill with tears, and Skint lays his palm on the wall. *Dad.*

Mr. Gilbert's tears recede, and his gaze grows hooded and dark.

"Come *on,*" says Ellen. "Let's *go.*"

Skint's father leans his head on the glass.

"Tom! Get out of that tub!"

He is still.

"I said, get *out*! Come *on*! We've got to get out of here; let's go!"

Skint steals away down the hall. Grabs his bike. Goes.

THIRTY-SEVEN

It's only seven thirty. Nobody else is up or out yet. Dinah, newspaper in hand, picks her way down to the river's edge in her pajamas and boots. She wants to skip a few stones. The bridge is above her, to the left, and the river in front of her is frozen. You'd never know, to look at that expanse of solid white, that underneath it there's water rushing, waving riverweed and silt. Up here everything is quiet: wind small, the just-risen sun. None of the winter birds are singing.

The stillness doesn't last for long, though. As Dinah stands silent by the bank, there's a tremendous sound, like iron; deep; a sound as large as an avalanche.

Wharnk.

The river. The rushing water underneath makes the ice buckle and crack. The tectonic breaks sound like the singing of an otherworldly creature; spare, eerie, sad.

Wharnk.

Wait. Someone is out on the gray-blue surface of the ice. It's not uncommon to see, especially in a winter like this, a winter so cold even the oldest people in Aile Quarry aren't talking about how different things are now because of climate change. They should be: climate change is the reason behind this extra-cold winter, too. But it's beautiful. It's beautiful, the cold: pervading, like an understanding in the bones.

The walking person is no ice fisherman, though. He has no equipment, just a body, tall and gray against the snow. You have to be careful, walking on the river ice, not because of thin spots but because the ice is not smooth. It's full of ridges and swirls, ready to trip a person down. But the person doing the walking is stepping without care, walking like he's slouching along any dirt road.

Skint? Dinah cups her mouth to call, imagining his breath coming out in ice clouds, his inward-turned eyes; pockets stuffed with rock candy and pens. She should walk out over the ice to meet him. But he wouldn't want her. He wouldn't tell her so, but she'd feel him freezing inside, cold to the core and being too polite.

The figure bends at the waist. Dinah's vision snaps

and she sees, clearly, that the figure is much too old to be Skint: dressed all in gray, an adult, a man, wearing a coat, even; some ice fisher, probably, just checking the ice. How could she have thought it was Skint?

She drops her stones. She doesn't feel like skipping them anymore, not all alone, not by herself.

Dinah climbs back up the embankment to the road and then walks along past the Rural Routes' house (zero Rural Routes out; when was the last time she waved?). She passes their mailbox with its faded letter *E* and heads up the hill toward town, past the little gray house where Bernadine lives with her mother.

Framed in their window, kitchen light on, Bernadine and her mother sit at their table. In front of each is a cup of tea; a clock is frozen above them on the wall. Neither woman sips or talks or moves. Still as snow, they perch as solitary as owls. Each might as well be alone.

Bernadine moves her head suddenly and stares out the window. Dinah freezes. Does Bernadine see her? But Bernadine's face looks like nothing.

Unhappy. Unhappy. All Dinah's fault. She's made everyone be extra all alone.

Dinah reenters her house by the front door to avoid the kitchen and its denizens and goes up to her room. She takes up a skirt flung over the back of her chair but is distracted from dressing by the sight, out her window, of a lanky, coatless Skint pushing his bike up the driveway.

Dinah sticks the skirt on over her pajamas and runs down into the kitchen, shoving her arms into her coat sleeves again on the way.

"Where's my paper?" wails her dad.

The river's edge, cold; paper blowing in the snow.

"I left it outside," Dinah says, grabbing up the tote full of food she gathered last night for the Rural Routes. She flies out the door toward Skint.

THIRTY-EIGHT

Skint's head is sweaty, his hair sticking up from his forehead in spikes.

"You must have been riding fast," says Dinah, thumping toward him down the driveway. She stops short when she reaches him, staring at his knee. Skint's jeans are ripped, the edges of the tear crusted in red.

"You're hurt!" she exclaims.

Skint glances down. "I'm fine," he says.

"But you're bleeding!"

"No big deal. Perils of biking. Come on."

He starts down the road, pushing his bike. Dinah hurries beside him.

"Well, I am going to dress that for you as soon as we get to your house." Skint tumbling, sliding, bike end over end, gears slashing, Skint falling, crashing down. Dinah's own knee knifes beneath her skin.

Skint glances at her. "Probably would have been better if you had dressed yourself."

"It doesn't matter," says Dinah. Peroxide. Gauze. Tape to hold it in place. She hopes they have all that at Skint's house. "You're the only one who's going to see me. Right?"

Skint nods. "Their appointment is right now."

The road ahead of them is rutted and full of ice.

Skint steers his bike with purple-knuckled hands. Dinah touches the scrape on the side of his hand with one forefinger.

"How are you?" she asks awkwardly. "I mean, are you . . . good?"

"I'm fine," Skint says shortly. He glances at Dinah's tote. "What did you bring?"

"Soup," says Dinah. She tugs her tote open so he can look. "Tea. See? And those crackers you like with pepper in them. Lots of other things."

Skint stares incredulously at the sight of a plastic bag on top of the rest. "Craisins? You brought them *Craisins*?"

"Yes," says Dinah firmly. "For an additional treat

besides the cookies. People need more than one treat."

"Something that looks and tastes like little sacks of nearly coagulated blood is no treat, Dinah."

"Grargh." Dinah makes as if to Handcreature his nose, but he shies his head away.

Skint's house sits gray and dark, garage door down, heavy under snow. He unlocks the front door and they go in.

The living room smells stale. But underneath that is the Skint-house smell Dinah remembers from when they were small: breakfast cereal and heat coming through the vents. The couch is crumpled under a blanket, a nightgown tossed over its arm.

"The extra blankets are in the hall closet," says Skint over the clatter of Dinah's bag of cans and the wiping of their feet.

"To the bathroom first," says Dinah. "We have to do your knee."

"Shut up, dork. I'm fine. Come on."

He starts down the hall and Dinah follows, cans clanking and banging. She remember this hall, its walls lined with books: fat ones about countries and politics, some plays.

Skint stops short. He puts his hand out behind him to stop Dinah. Her bag of cans hits her in the knee.

"What's the matter?" she asks. Then she notices it is

wet underfoot; water is trickling toward them from the bathroom, stenching.

"I'll get paper towels from the kitchen," Dinah says, turning.

"Shh!"

Voice ahead of them, from the left, from Skint's parents' room.

"—every goddamn day? Every goddamn *day*?"

Skint is motionless in front of Dinah, one foot raised.

"*Two* fucking *hours* now, for pants?" cries the voice.

Skint wheels around. "Go, Dinah!" he whispers fiercely. "Go!"

From the bedroom, louder:

"Can't even get out the door without you peeing and fucking yourself up—"

Ellen?

"—and now it's two fucking *hours* to convince you to dress?"

Who is she talking to? Mr. Gilbert?

"Dinah!" Skint's whisper is a piston. "Go!"

"Are you going to wet yourself and the floor every fucking day now? Are you?"

Wet yourself? For an irrational instant, Dinah thinks Ellen must be shouting at Beagie. *What is going on?*

"Toilet overflows and I can't even deal with it because of you? Get over here!" Ellen's voice rises and rises.

Skint: "Dinah! Go!"

"No more of this fucking shit! No fucking more! You overgrown, useless fucking infant of a man!" Ellen is screaming.

Dinah's heart pounds. *Mr. Gilbert. Mr. Gilbert.*

"Get the fuck over here! Get the fuck over here, now!"

Skint grown enormous—"Go, Dinah! Go!" His face is fury, frozen, pushing at her—"GO!"

But Ellen's screams are louder, tearing out into the hall.

"I said FUCKING GET OVER HERE! GET OVER HERE, NOW!"

Ellen. Mr. Gilbert. Screaming. *Skint's dad.*

Skint pushes toward Dinah, blazing, pushing—"Go!" he yells at her. "Go!"

Behind Skint—Dinah lifts her hand.

Mr. Gilbert, bent. Backing up, inching backward out of the bedroom into the hall.

bent back; thin legs; bowed body; bent

Naked

shoulders bent, gray chest; inching backward into

the hall

Naked.

Dinah lifts her hand; mouth open, no sound. *No. Skint; don't turn around. No.* She grabs Skint's wrist to pull him toward her with all her might.

But Skint's already turning around.

* * *

Ellen flashes in the doorway and cranes her neck until she's screaming into Mr. Gilbert's face. "GET OVER HERE NOW YOU FUCKING USELESS—"

Mr. Gilbert flinches. Dinah's legs buckle, and she falls to her knees. Ellen's head whips around. She howls, an otherworldly sound.

"GO!" screams Skint at Dinah. "GO!"

But Ellen is coming at Skint, coming at him, pushing. She pushes him, pushes, pushes.

"Get that"—push—"bitch"—push—"OUT OF HERE"—push—"NOW!"

Skint stumbles back, and Ellen pushes at him more, two hands on his chest, pushes harder, her face twisted red and hot.

Skint falls over Dinah where she dropped, where she's kneeling on the ground.

Tears run down Mr. Gilbert's cheeks.

"Get out!" Skint screams at Dinah over their jumbled, tangled legs. "Get out!"

"Your dad—your dad—"

"Get out!" Skint kicks at her. "Get the fuck out!"

Behind them there is an awful sound. Mr. Gilbert's on the floor.

Dinah crawls until she's standing, stumbling, running, out the door and gone.

THIRTY-NINE

Dinah crashes through the door at the Center.

"Mom!"

"Dinah!"

Dinah's gasping, can't breathe.

"Dinah, darling, what's wrong, where's your coat?" Her mother hurries to her. "What's wrong, darling, what happened?"

Her mother's eyes, brown in their sockets. Her face. Those bones.

"Tell me, Dinah, what happened; honey, tell me, what's wrong!"

Dinah's breath is a side-crushed keen.

"Is it Skint, Dinah? Is something wrong with Skint?"

Dinah shakes her head, then nods it, *yes yes yes*.

"What happened? Is he hurt? Tell me, Dinah! What?"

"Ellen—" Dinah squeezes out.

"Ellen?"

"Mr. Gilbert." Eyes filling, voice breaking. "Help me, Mom! Help! I don't know what to do!"

"How can I help, darling, tell me! What do you need?"

screaming naked pushing wet—"Go there—help him! Help Mr. Gilbert, go!" Snot streams and tears sheet down Dinah's face.

Mrs. Beach is already moving. "Call Gail," she says to the girl behind the desk. "Tell her to meet me. The Gilberts on Pine. Dinah, call your father! Wait for me at home!" No coat on but her cell phone in her hand, Mrs. Beach races out the door.

The door swings shut. Dinah sinks down, face in her hands, hair hanging down.

FORTY

Skint grips his dad's arms in his hands.

"Dad," he says. "Dad."

Mr. Gilbert weeps. No words. Only tears. Ellen on the floor, face buried in her knees.

One arm beneath his father's shoulders and one beneath his knees. Skint lifts him. Takes him in the bedroom. Lays him down. Finds pants for him, puts them on.

He kneels, forehead on his father's knee bent at the edge of the bed. The bone is close beneath the skin, dry and brittle thin.

"Dad," Skint whispers. "Dad."

Skint never should have left this morning. He never should have left.

"You fucking useless kid," Ellen weeps in the hall. "You fucking stupid kid."

"Dad," Skint whispers. "Dad. Please."

Thin fingers in his hair, resting light as feathers. "I can't let you climb that, sweetheart," his father says. "That branch isn't strong enough to hold."

God. God. Please just let Skint take him. Let him lift his father up, bones thin and spare in his arms; lift him out and walk away with him, swift running down the road; let him run until they lift, until they fly, until they're gone.

Long time quiet. Ellen sobs. Skint's father, unmoving.

Someone's at the door.

Skint lifts his head.

"Don't get that!" he shouts to Ellen.

His mother doesn't answer.

"Mom, don't!"

Skint jumps up and races into the hall, past Ellen, crouching silent in her spot against the wall.

"Skint?" Muffled voice through the door.

Mrs. Beach.

Before he can get to it, the door opens slowly. Mrs. Beach's hair is all over the place, her cheeks red. Cold streams through her into the room.

"Hello, Skint," she says.

"What are you doing here, Mrs. Beach?"

Mrs. Beach's eyes are worried. "I just thought I'd—are you—is everything all right?"

"Everything's fine," says Skint. "What are you doing here?"

Mrs. Beach's eyes travel around the room.

"May I come in?"

"I'm afraid we're busy just now, Mrs. Beach. I'll let my mother know you stopped by."

Mrs. Beach nods but breaks off with a start, her gaze locked on something over Skint's shoulder.

"Thomas?" she cries. She's in the room and moving swiftly, past Skint into the hall. "Thomas! Are you all right?"

Bruise blossoming on his temple, Skint's dad stands in the hall.

FORTY-ONE

The hospital gown, untied, dangles around Skint's father's neck, gray chest hairs exposed over his too-thin bones. *Oh, Dad. Dad.*

"They have to check him, Skint." Mrs. Beach is sitting beside him. Ellen is in the chair across the room, by the window. She hasn't said a word. "They have to be sure he doesn't have a concussion."

"He's fine," says Skint. "He's fine."

Mr. Gilbert's eyes are troubled. He puts his hand on Skint's head. "Don't worry, Dad," he says. "My own fault. Branch too weak to hold me."

Skint's head is too heavy to hold. He rests his forehead on the bed.

A cluster of voices rises outside the door, a couple of nurses and someone else whose voice Skint doesn't recognize: a man. The door swings open and the voices grow louder. Skint turns to see who it is.

It's the police.

Food pantry; cuts on his palm—

Skint leaps up and away from his father's bed.

"I'm sorry!" he screams. "I'm sorry!"

"It's all right, son." Huge cop with a mouth full of ecru teeth. "No need to be sorry."

"What are you doing here?" Ellen cries. "Who said you could come in this room?" Skint's mother will kill him, he'll be in jail, he'll never see his father again—

"Mrs. Gilbert—" the policeman begins, but Skint can't hear the words.

"Please!" he cries. "I'm sorry!"

Ellen's face shifts from rage to blank to terror.

"Young woman?" Mr. Gilbert cries, sitting up. "Young woman? What's going on?"

Mrs. Beach tries to get an arm around Skint, but he snatches himself away. "Get away from me!" he cries, and wheels round to face the cop. "Please don't tell my dad!"

Ellen slides out of her chair and onto the floor. "Are you going to arrest me, arrest me; jail?" she chatters. "Are you taking me, arresting me; jail?"

Nurses all over the place, one of them going to his dad, the other squatting down beside Ellen.

They're going to clear the room so they can get him alone, question him, make him confess—

"Skint!" cries Mrs. Beach. She takes his shoulders in her hands. "Listen to me! The police are here to help! They're here to help your dad!"

Skint stares at her. His dad? His dad?

"They need to talk to your mom, Skint; they want to help your dad!"

This is not about the food pantry?

Ellen, screaming: "Stay away from my husband! Thomas. Tom!"

FORTY-TWO

The room is quiet again. Skint sits by his father's bed, his dad's fingers in his palm. One of the cops helped his mom out of the room a while ago. Skint can't figure out how long, but now the cop's back, alone.

"Mrs. Beach, here, was pretty worried," he says to Skint. "She gave us a call to come around."

Skint raises his head and looks at Mrs. Beach.

Her face is red, her hair a mess. "I'm a mandated reporter, honey," she says. "That means I'm required to call."

Skint stares at her and says nothing.

"Penny here works with us a lot to help the elderly, people who need help," says the cop.

Skint drops his head. The edge of the rip in his jeans has dried to a dull, dark brown. The knee itself doesn't even look real. Too skinny, too angular; disarticulated from the rest of Skint's leg.

His father has fallen all the way asleep, breath light, chest rising, falling. His hand grows insubstantial in Skint's and his fingers fall from Skint's palm. Over Skint's head the cop is talking, going on and on. It's been tough at home, huh, son? How have things been at home?

Skint toys with the edge of the tear in his jeans. The denim has dried to his knee. It'll hurt like a motherfucker when he tries to peel it off.

"Mom was angry this morning, huh, son?"

"I'm not your son."

Skint rips the fabric off of the cut. Shit. Now he's bleeding again.

"It's fine," he says, pushing Mrs. Beach's hand away.

"Pardon," says the cop. "I don't mean to offend. We just need to get what all happened, what led up to this trip to the hospital for your dad."

Skint straightens and bends his knee.

"Skint." Mrs. Beach. "Officer Craig is talking to you, honey."

Skint glances at the cop.

"Do you know how your dad got that bruise there on his head, Skint?"

"He fell."

"Oh," says the cop. Then: "What made him fall?"

"How the fuck should I know?"

"Skint."

"The floor was wet," says Skint. "He slipped. He fell."

The policeman glances at Mrs. Beach. *What? What? Where's Ellen?*

Where's Ellen!

Skint leaps up. *What is going on?* Do they have Ellen in *jail?* Are they bringing her up on *charges?* "My mom didn't hit him!" His voice doesn't even sound like his own. "My dad just fell and hit his head!"

The cop glances at Mrs. Beach again, then at Skint. "How did that come about, Skint? Can you tell us?"

Ellen's blotchy face, ponytail sliding. Neck craned forward, contorted mouth. His dad, backing up.

"Leave me alone!"

Forty-Three

Dinah's father and Beagie came and got her at the Center hours ago, but no one will let her go be with Skint. She's been lying here on her bedroom floor forever, waiting, bones leaded and heavy and dead. The rug needs a shampoo. It smells awful, like rotting teeth and crying. There are two uneven yellow threads in front of Dinah's nose and she picks at the shorter one.

Feet creak outside her door. "Dinah? Dinah? Are you asleep?"

"I'm awake," Dinah cries, lifting her head from the floor. "I'm awake!"

Dinah's mother opens the door. "I'm sorry it took so long. We've been at the hospital most of this time."

Dinah scrambles up to sitting. "Is everything all right? Where's Skint?"

Skull against the bedspread; all the blood has rushed to Skint's head. Mrs. Beach and the cop going on and on about how his father needs care, as if it is news. As if what he needs were some kind of goddamn puzzle. Food. Showers. Help with his goddamn clothes.

"Your mother—" says Mrs. Beach.

No. Skint can't think about Ellen right now. They've questioned her but they aren't holding her, they said; they can't prove that she did a thing. They're offering her counseling. They think that will help.

"Fuck my mother."

Skint lifts his head. The shift of his blood makes him lightheaded, his eyes staring and feeling like stones. "I can take care of my dad. I already do."

"We'll help," says Dinah, bouncing a little on her knees. "We'll take turns taking care of Mr. Gilbert when he's out of the hospital. We can take turns staying over there, too. I'll do all the cleaning. You and Dad can ask in church for people to help, too. Don't you think that's a good idea? Don't you think people will help?"

Mrs. Beach nods, eyes creased, twisting her fingers

in her hands. Then she stops, and shakes her head no.

What do they mean, his dad needs more help? What, a machine with arms and claws, a putter-on of pants? Or maybe they mean someone to come around to the house, maybe even someone living in. That actually wouldn't be half bad. Skint could give his room to that person and make a new one for himself, down in the basement.

But no. No. That is not what they mean.

Dinah screams.

"No!"

Skint leaps from his chair and it goes flying back, crashing.

This is what she calls helping, sending his dad away! "I watch my father! I make sure he's not unsafe! You don't know shit about any of it!"

He'll punch Mrs. Beach in her swimming fucking eyes. His chest draws in, ribs constricted, jabbing tight.

Dad! Daddy!

Walking. Talking. Hand in his father's hand.

"Where is Skint?" screams Dinah. "Where is he?"

"We tried to get in touch with his uncles," says Mrs. Beach, grabbing for Dinah, who rears back, pushing away. "Bernadine tried and tried!"

"Bernadine?!"

"It was her volunteer shift—she saw Mr. Gilbert's name—"

Please, God, help me, please!

How did they get to this point? How did all this happen? How did they get from cookies and home to people stealing away his dad? How? Who?

"You," Dinah breathes to her mother. "You. This is because of you." Skint in the hospital, her ghastly mother taking his hand, telling him she's called the police and arranged to have his father taken away. Ellen back home and Skint sick with rage, can't stand to be with his mother in that house. "You've wrecked everything! You've wrecked Skint's entire life!"

"Dinah sent me, honey; she sent me" is what Mrs. Beach told Skint before, at the house.

Dinah is how they got here. Dinah ran out the door and told.

Blue flame licking, spitting, rising steady burn.

Dinah told them, she told them, she told them.

"Skint." Mrs. Beach's voice scrapes inside his brain. "If you don't want to go home, you can stay with us, as long as you need, as long as you want, as long as you like."

"Mrs. Beach," says Skint, "I would rather fucking die."

FORTY-FOUR

Skint's staying with Ms. Dugan?

"Bernadine called her from the hospital. She offered and he said yes, Dinah," Mrs. Beach cries. "He won't stay with her forever! Just until we can sort things out! Bernadine will help her!"

"Help her? Sort things out?" Dinah cries into her mother's upturned face. "How can you sort this out?"

If Skint won't live with his mother or with the Beaches, they'll send him away—one of those useless uncles—he'll have to move away from Aile Quarry!

"This is what you call helping?!" Dinah's up and by the door. "Skint won't even come to our house because he can't stand to be near you! I hate you! *I hate you!*"

Dinah bolts from the room.

Feet slapping the road, she tears down to Ms. Dugan's. Her mother is the assiest person who ever lived, the stupidest, least caring—Dinah will get her to undo what she did. She has to; she'll make her apologize to Skint. Dinah will fix it; she will, she will.

Skint's bike is on Ms. Dugan's porch. Good, he's here.

Dinah pounds on the door. She'll make Beagie do that little dance for Skint, she'll—

"He's out." It's Bernadine, not Ms. Dugan, who opens the door. "Come in, Dinah Beach. It's cold."

"Where did he go?" asks Dinah, breathless from running. Behind Bernadine the living room smells like meat and the shelves are full of trophies. Pictures of teams and nephews hang high on the walls, practically touching the ceiling.

"Nowhere. Just out and about," Bernadine tells her. "You leave him alone. Sometimes a body needs to be alone."

Skint is alone all the time, you awful person. What he needs is me.

"Hey, there, Dinah B." Ms. Dugan appears behind Bernadine. "Come on in. Mrs. Chatham's in the kitchen. Come sit with us. Have a soda pop and we'll talk the thing out."

"No, thank you. Please tell Skint I came to see him, please." Dinah's off the porch again and running.

Oh, please, just come stay with us; I'll get my mom to keep away.

The sky is darkening and the clouds are thick with imminent snow. Dinah has looked everywhere. It shouldn't be this hard to find Skint, not if he isn't on his bike, but he hasn't turned up anywhere Dinah can think of for him to be.

Jogging, hustling—past the Rural Routes' house. The man Rural Route is out on his porch. Where is the woman? Dinah has never seen one Rural Route without the other. The man stands, shoulders sloped, head bent down—he's waiting for the woman, Dinah imagines. She's probably inside, putting on that coat—

Stop it, Dinah Beach. You have to get going; hurry. She waves quickly to Mr. Rural Route, but he doesn't wave back; maybe he doesn't recognize her alone, without Skint.

I'll help you but Skint first. I have to find Skint right now.

The road climbs deeper up into the woods until the pavement gives out and becomes the dirt path, littered with fallen twigs and stones. Other than Dinah's footfalls, there's nothing to hear up here but the no-sound of waiting snow. No houses up here and the path isn't cleared, so Dinah has to bash through the icy crust on top of a winter's worth of snow with every step.

Bash, bash.

Wait; ahead of her. Someone walking. Thin, in a hooded sweatshirt.

Dinah freezes.

"Skint!"

The walking person stops. Hollow-looking bones and too-thin skin.

Dinah flails forward, ice cutting at her shins. "Skint!"

The person turns around. It is Skint. But he does not step forward to meet her.

Dinah reaches him, breathing hard.

Crumbs in his eyes, knuckles purple, cheeks smooth and chill as stone. Sneakers soaked through; where are his boots? High above them the peaky heads of the evergreens bend and peer down.

"Skint?"

His eyes look like nothing.

The quiet in the wood is enormous. No more boots sounds, no words, just Dinah's own heavy breathing.

"Skint," she says urgently. "Skint, my mom's an ass. She's an ass but we can fix it; we can think of something—"

Skint's gaze grows distant and he looks over her shoulder, to the left.

Dinah's neck creeps up, freezing. "Skint?"

He says nothing.

Dinah looks over her shoulder, too. Nothing there but a pair of crab-apple trees, standing in the middle of the pines, ice-covered and bent under the snow.

"Those are lovely," she begins, but Skint cuts her off.

"No," he says. His voice is like a gun. "They are in fact not lovely. They are dying; they're dead. They are calcified fucking trees."

"I only—"

"Shut up."

Dinah starts.

"Don't talk to me," says Skint. "Shut up."

"I—"

"I said, shut up. Haven't you said enough?"

Dinah chest sears.

"Skint—I'm sorry—my mom—"

"Your mom? Fuck your mom. What did you think she was going to do? You're the one who screwed everything up."

Dinah's mouth opens. Her head snaps back.

"You run off to her like a crying toddler; what other recourse does she have? Of course they're going to take him, put him in a home! Thanks ever so much, Dinah. You've made everything so effing grand."

"Skint! I'm sorry! I thought—he—I thought—"

"You didn't think. You never do. You don't think. You play, like an overgrown, messed-up baby."

What? What?

"You and those skirts and your parcels and pretending." Skint's voice drips with disgust. "Fuck you, Dinah.

Fuck your willful kid crap."

"Your dad—I was scared for him—he—"

"You poor baby. I don't care if you were scared."

"Your mom—Skint. He needed help—"

"We've been fine without you this long, infant; what made you think we needed you now?"

"Your mom was—"

"Shut up about my mom! Since when do you notice my mom?"

Dinah's brain stumbles, trips. "I don't—what?"

Skint throws his head back, hands in his hair. "Jesus fucking Christ!" He drops his head back down and he looks at her, revulsed. "You fucking *spare* yourself from everything. You avoid anything that tells you that life is not a singsong. Most people don't have it like you, you know—parents who think she's hot shit for breathing and a life with zero crap. Your perfect parents perfect, baby laughing on Daddy's lap. Shit happens, Dinah. People suck."

"I *know* people suck!" Dinah cries. "Don't you know I know that?"

"I don't think you know jack. Grow up, Dinah. Grow the hell up."

"I'm sorry, Skint, I'm sorry! I'll help, I'll—" Steal back his dad, memory him up?

"What'll you do? Punch someone? Distract me with some crazy-ass game?"

"I'll do anything, Skint, I'm sorry! I love your dad, I love him!"

Skint's gaze is ice.

"Then I'd hate to see how you help the people you hate. Go home, Dinah. Get away from me and go home. And never come near me again."

FORTY-FIVE

Dinah stumbles down the path in the falling-fast snow. The truth of herself is fire in her veins. Skint is right. What has she ever done but pretend? All these years of her stupid playing, thinking it made him happy—it was never what he needed. She never even helped him at all.

Dinah's skirt tangles in her legs and she slaps at its stripes. Tears and mucus rise and break. Every word he said was true. She told herself it was him she wanted to spare, keeping Skint away from his own house, away from thinking about his dad, but it wasn't, not really.

She kept them both away from it all because it was too much for Dinah to take, too: She's never liked Ellen, but the truth is she was avoiding Mr. Gilbert just as much; Mr. Gilbert, bent and silver, sad to the bone and gone. She had no idea how bad he'd gotten because she didn't truly want to know.

The trees overhead shake, snow falling down. Snot-smeared and eyes streaming, Dinah staggers down the path, her blood running with the sick of Skint's rage, with her own selfish wrong-help having been worse than none at all. All this time with that going on over there, Skint all by himself in that house with just Ellen—

Now you notice my mom?

Dinah stops moving.

You can understand her, though.

Dinah's sobs slow, and cease.

Ellen. *Ellen.* Skint was upset yesterday because Dinah didn't understand it was *Ellen* that was his problem, not just that his dad was worse. He was telling her. He thought she saw. And she didn't. She didn't. Dinah was too stuck in her own selfish thinking to see what Skint meant. He meant Ellen; he meant her cruelty; he meant how she was to his dad.

She is a hypocrite! A hypocrite! So worried about how Walter was being cared for, but she never once worried about Skint.

No! No! Roots in the path, ice covered and gray. Dinah drops, face in her palms.

What if she hadn't been so wrong? What if she had understood?

Freezing knees; wet to the bone. Ice on her mitten tips, snow falling down.

Forty-Six

Good. Let her go. Stumble out of the woods, Dinah, clatter and stumble away. Skint's chest hammers as hard and fast as if he'd shoved her down the path himself. His throat is full of stones.

Dinah disappears around the curve of the path, and now there's no sound but his pounding chest and his breath, ragged and loud.

Then his heartbeat slows and his bones go suddenly limp. He is spent, exhausted, more tired than he has ever been.

Should he go to Ms. Dugan's and sleep? That house, though. That house. Full of old crackers and gym clothes; Bernadine and her mother always there, too, and the incessant, senseless askings. ("Newspaper, Mr. Gilbert?"—"No, thank you, Bernadine."—"Join me in a run, kid? Get the old lymph system going?"—"No. I'm good, Ms. D. I'm fine.") All of them sipping tea, one sip after another. Sip. Sip. Sip. Sip.

Every day there? Every day counting sips of tea? Never alone, always with them, no more time with—

Crack! A tree branch, snapping in the snow and cold.

Dinah. Dinah.

Stumbling away from him out of the woods, away from him, stumbling away.

Heat threatens the backs of his eyes, flicks at the base of his brain, hollowing his chest to its bones. Can't think about his dad without his body becoming a scream, can't even begin to think about Ellen—

Stop! Hold it in! But he can't. Flames sear up Skint's chest into his throat, bigger than he can quell, and the heat tears through every stick of his bones, draining them of marrow and blood and racing up into his head until his skull can no longer contain it.

Daddy! Dad! Dinah! Oh, God—everybody's gone! There's nothing left to keep him here. Nothing left at all.

Too much. His mind explodes, bursts into eleven pieces, flung away, gone.

Nothing left. Skint in a thousand fragments. Rising, filling the wood.

FORTY-SEVEN

Dinah lies on her bed, her clothes stiff with dried-out snow. It's late; dark. Now is when Skint would usually call her, but her phone is as still as the trees. He is probably out walking, walking. Out in the cold and the snow.

Beagie's bedtime noises sound through her closed bedroom door.

The phone rings and her mother answers it. Mr. Beach is out.

"Dah, Dah, Dah!" Beagie shouts for Dinah over her mother's greetings, but Dinah doesn't get up or answer him, and he stops.

"I wish we had known, too," her mother murmurs into the phone in the lull. "If we had known, I might have—"

Dinah leaps up and flings open her door.

"You should have known," she says clearly. "You should have."

"Dah!" cries Beagie and holds out his arms.

"I'm sorry," Mrs. Beach says into the phone. "The baby—I'll call you back later." Her mother's eyes and her scrubby old bones, her hair a mess, as tangled as Dinah's. "Dinah, it's very complex—"

"What's so complex about it? Didn't you ever think about Mr. Gilbert after he stopped coming to the Center? Didn't you ever think about him at all?"

"Dinah—"

"Isn't it your job to understand about dementia? How it is, how awful it gets?"

"Dinah, don't do—"

"What? Would you prefer me to go look at how pretty it is outside? Would you like me to just not think about anything hard? Why?" Dinah's voice rises to a shout. "So you won't have to either?"

Beagie's face crumples and he starts to cry.

"You're the one who is supposed to care about old people the whole time!" Dinah shouts. "Why didn't you ever go over there? Why didn't you ever see if things were okay?"

Mrs. Beach's mouth falls open.

"Here is what's evil, Mrs. Beach! It's when you know something is wrong and you ignore it and just bash along without doing what someone needs you to do!" Beagie's crying rings in her ears, but Dinah can't stop. Her mother moves toward her.

"No!" Dinah screams. "You stay away from me! Don't come near me again!"

FORTY-EIGHT

It must be almost three in the morning. Dinah hasn't slept a wink. She sits at her desk and stares out the window, feet curled around the legs of her chair. Outside, the snowy driveway is lit dark and blue.

The weird digital bell of their landline ring sounds and Dinah leaps up. It won't be Skint, not on the landline; he'd call her cell. But a call at three in the morning—she flings open her door. Her father's voice echoes in the kitchen, but he's already hung up the phone by the time Dinah reaches him.

"Who called?" she asks.

Mr. Beach starts and swings round, hand still on the phone.

"Denise Dugan." He rubs his eyes. "I was just going to wake you. Skint hasn't been back at her house, darling, not since before you stopped by there this afternoon."

Dinah heart stops. "He hasn't?"

"No. She was hoping he was over here."

Dinah shakes her head. "He isn't. He's not here."

"I know," says Mr. Beach. "We're worried, Dinah. Have you talked to him? Did he tell you where he might be?"

Dinah shakes her head no.

"Do you think he's okay?" she cries. "Do you think something is wrong?"

"Oh, Dinah, I'm sure he's fine!" says her father, crossing to her swiftly. He hugs her. "He's had a terrible, awful day, remember. The poor, poor boy."

"Maybe he went back to the hospital. Maybe he wanted to be with his dad. Call them!"

"Excellent idea," says her dad and he picks up the phone again.

"Or maybe he is out walking! He does that, Dad, when he is upset about something. He walks and walks all over the place."

Her father nods to her as he gives his name to the voice on the other end of the phone.

Dinah listens as he asks them about Skint. She doesn't need to hear the answer from the other end, though. Out in the woods; Skint's implacable face. She knows from the line of her father's mouth that Skint's not there.

FORTY-NINE

It's eerie to have so many people in the kitchen in the middle of the night. Ms. Dugan has come, and Dinah's mother is down now too, in her awful old pajamas. Mr. Beach keeps the kettle on the boil and makes endless cups of tea. But Dinah is too jangled up to drink any.

Where could Skint be? At one of his uncles'? Somewhere even farther away? Could he be trying to go overseas?

Stop. Stop. He's only out walking somewhere people haven't looked yet. (But hours, it has been! Hours and hours alone with no coat!) Walking is what Skint does.

Look at the other night when he called her from out walking.

But this is not the same as what usually is. There is nothing about today or the weekend or any time since Friday when she fished him out of the Pit that is the same.

"I've driven all over kingdom come," says Ms. Dugan. "I didn't see a thing."

"He's not at the church." Mr. Beach hangs up from his latest phone call. "And Bernadine says she drove by the high school and he's not lurking around there, either. Dinah, darling, drink your tea."

The church? The high school? Why are they only looking in stupid places that Skint would never be and not in the place he actually is?

"Can we make a plan to find him, please?" she cries, pushing her teacup away. "Can we please at least make a plan?"

"Honey—" Mrs. Beach begins.

Dinah doubles over, head on her knees.

"Don't talk to me," she says into her thighs. "No."

Hours pass. Outside the kitchen window the sky shifts from coal to smoke to gray; it's dawn, and still no word of Skint. No sign of him at any of his uncles', at Ms. Dugan's house or at his own. There is no sign of him anywhere at all.

Mrs. Beach has gone to wait at the Gilberts' house

with Ellen. Beagie is still asleep. Dinah's brain is raw with exhaustion and too much thinking.

"Rally!" she tells herself fiercely. *Think! Be smart. Make a plan.*

Alert area businesses to be on the lookout for teenage janitors who look older than they are? Smuggle Mr. Gilbert out of the nursing home and place an ad in the paper to let Skint know where to find him?

Childish. Her ideas dissipate like misshapen balloons.

An op ed in the paper, then. Not long. Just "I'm sorry; come home, come home."

"The police will be here in a few minutes," Mr. Beach tells her.

The cup of tea her father made her hours ago is cold now and repellent, oversteeped.

"I thought the police don't help unless someone is gone for twenty-four hours," she says. It is crazy to think that just two days ago Dinah was worried about the police catching Skint and hauling him in on charges. Now she can't wait for them to get hold of him.

"I imagine they get an early start sometimes. When circumstances warrant it." Her father's eyes are tired and red. "It's awfully cold outside," he says. "And Skint had a particularly upsetting day."

"They should hurry," says Dinah. "Did you tell them to hurry?"

"Yes," says her father. "They are just finishing up at Ms. Dugan's with her and Bernadine."

Bernadine.

"I know you dislike her, Dinah," says her father, "but she has been very kind to him today."

Really? What if she tells Ms. Dugan that she believes Skint isn't fit to feed? But thinking about anything connected to Bernadine or the food pantry only reminds Dinah of Skint's and her project to help the Rural Routes. Her eyes threaten to fill with tears.

"The church means the world to Bernadine," says her father. "You can't take someone's whole world away because they make one mistake."

You can if they deserve it. But Dinah is a fine one to talk. She makes mistakes that take away people's whole worlds.

"Come on, darling," says her father. "Let's go wait for them in the living room."

He picks up her cup of tea and carries it carefully into the other room.

The policeman launches a volley of questions at Dinah. Where might Skint have gone? Does she have the names of his other friends? Blarp and blarp and on and on. Dinah's eyes are gritty, and she rubs them with the heel of her hand.

Don't they get it? *Dinah* is Skint's friend. Or was.

And there is nowhere else he would have gone, not if he is not here at her house or out walking or in any of the other places she's named for them a thousand times, made them drive to and call around. Skint is not somewhere usual because nothing is usual anymore. Nothing is usual and it's all her fault. She messed it all up and forced Skint to run away.

"He wants to go overseas," Dinah tells Officer Vane. "He wants to help monks."

"Monks?"

"Burmese monks," Dinah clarifies. "Tortured. Imprisoned, like in Tibet. He wants to help them."

The policeman's sharp shoulders relax, and he smiles at Dinah as though she were Beagie's age. "Well, I think we can rule that one out," he says. "I don't guess he's had the time or the means to get all the way to Burma."

"I didn't say I thought he had got there yet." *Jerk.* Why bother to ask her things if he is only going to make fun of her answers?

More questions, questions that are the same as the questions he's already asked and that she's already answered again and again. Why doesn't he ask new ones, good ones, ones that will get them to Skint? Dinah can't bear it. She can't. Skint freezing outside and full of despair; cut knee, no dad, nowhere he'd want to go—

"It's my fault!" she finally cries. "Skint left because he was mad at me!"

Her father's brows fly up, and Officer Vane looks at her questioningly. "Mad at you?" the policeman asks. "How come?"

"I was stupid. I did the wrong thing!" Mr. Beach moves to sit closer to her on the couch, but Dinah rears away. Her stomach hurts, and she folds her arms over it.

The policeman leans forward, and the chair creaks alarmingly. One of its legs seems to skid. Dinah's father winces.

"What did you do wrong?" the officer asks.

What didn't she do wrong? Dinah blinks helplessly.

"Your friend is in a tough place, Dinah," says Officer Vane kindly. "I don't think anything anybody here did would make him run away."

"I agree," says Mr. Beach urgently and moves close to Dinah again.

"So I wouldn't worry too much about him being mad at you right now," says Officer Vane. "Let's see, could he be visiting someone from his anime club, maybe? Someone he knows from art class at school?"

Dinah buries her head in her hands. Her bones go hollow and thin.

It all goes on and on. No, of course she doesn't think he met someone from the Internet. No, he didn't have his bike when she saw him last. No, she didn't know the bike was no longer at Ms. Dugan's. Yes, he rides his bike a lot. Yes, even in winter.

FIFTY

Noises and voices wake Beagie up. But he doesn't pay attention to them because he is remembering what he was seeing in his eyes while he was sleeping. Pictures of things happening. Dinah singing to him and feeding him peas, Dinah hugging Beagie's stuffed horse, who was much, much bigger in the eye pictures than he really is here beside Beagie in his crib.

Beagie loves Dinah so much. He wants her, right now.

"Dah! Dah, Dah, Dah!"

But Dinah doesn't come.

Beagie kicks his feet, but Dinah only stays a picture in his eyes. He bangs his feet harder and howls.

"Beagie Bee! I'm here!"

But it's his father who has come, not Dinah.

Beagie cries and cries.

FIFTY-ONE

Mr. Beach comes back in the room and sits down beside Dinah again on the couch, Beagie on his lap. "I'm sorry, Officer," he says. Beagie takes a pull from his sippy cup of milk.

"No worries," says the policeman. "A baby needs his breakfast." He smiles at Beagie, then turns again to Dinah.

Go, if you aren't going to help, Dinah wills the policeman. *Leave me alone so I can find Skint.*

"The thing is, Dinah, we're especially concerned because Skint is not the only missing-child report we've had today."

"What?" Mr. Beach sits up upright.

"We received a call just before I arrived here this morning," says the policeman. "Man went to call his child to breakfast, child wasn't in his room. Says the boy often plays in the yard when he gets up, but he wasn't outside, either. Not anywhere. He called the boy's mother—the father has custody—and she doesn't know where he could be either. They're frantic."

Dinah drops her cup of tea. It spreads over the rug and into the cracks between the wide boards of the living room floor.

Mr. Beach clutches Beagie and grabs for Dinah. "Do you think, do they think—an abduction? Two boys in the same day? Officer!" His voice is shaking.

"We don't have a full picture yet," says the policeman. Dinah knows the other boy, he says. Word has it she's interacted with him over to the church.

"Who?" exclaims Mr. Beach.

But Dinah already knows.

"K. T. Vaar," says Officer Vane.

Dinah's heart sinks like a stone.

"My God!" cries Dinah's dad. "Why didn't you tell us right away?"

"One thing at a time, Mr. Beach. We thought we should ask your girl about her friend first."

K. T.'s miserable face. His dad in that windbreaker.

Skint at the church saying "we're stealing all the kids who are stuck with people like that and taking them with."

No. Oh, no. Oh no oh no oh no.

FIFTY-TWO

The policeman leaves, walkie-talkie crackling, boots stamping through the dooryard snow. He's off to look uselessly for lunatics who abduct kindergartners and teens. Dinah has to get out of here. She has to think this through. She jumps up from the couch.

"No!" her dad cries as she flings open the front door. "You are staying in this house until further notice!"

"I'm just going in the yard! A passing maniac won't grab me out of my own yard." Her father's face is creased with worry, but Dinah can't tell him there's no maniac, just Skint. "Please!"

Mr. Beach hesitates. "The side porch," he says. "You may sit briefly outside the kitchen door. But you stay right there! Don't you move an inch!"

It is better than nothing.

Dinah's brain is in a frenzy. The sun is up, wan in the sky and thin, but it is freezing cold outside as Dinah flings herself down onto the top step.

What was Skint thinking? Is he planning to raise K. T. on his own? How will he do that? Skint and K. T. in matching janitor outfits—

No. Don't be ridiculous.

What about school? And food? What about a place to live?

This is insane. If it's found out, it'll be everywhere, all over the news. Talk about felony! Child-swiping leaves church-busting and stealing from the food pantry in the dust. There'll be TV cameras all over, documentary teams, reality shows about the youth of Aile Quarry. Everybody flocking here and Skint routed out, only to spend the rest of his life in jail.

No. No. Not on Dinah's watch. No one will get a word out of her. Never, not this time. Not one single peep.

Behind her the kitchen door creaks open. Her father drops down beside her, Beagie warmly wrapped and asleep again on his lap.

Mr. Beach covers Dinah's shoulders with her coat. "It's too cold out here for no coat, Dinah, darling."

Dinah shrugs the coat off onto the stoop.

"I can't bear to have you shiver," says Mr. Beach.

Dinah shakes her head. "I don't care about a coat." Trembling, she rests her forehead in her hands.

If I had just helped them, stayed there and helped Skint and his family and not blabbed around the place, none of this would have happened. Mr. Gilbert would still be home and Skint would be, too, K. T. in his own yard and all of them okay.

Please let it all work out, let it all be fine; I'll do anything, everything; please let it be okay. But there is nothing Dinah can do, no magic, no one to help her. There is nothing she can do but not betray Skint.

Her eyes fill again and she holds her breath until the tears recede.

"The police will find them," says her father, his arm around her shoulders. "I know that they will." He picks up her coat again. "Darling, please put this on."

"No," Dinah says again, her voice breaking. "I don't deserve a coat."

FIFTY-THREE

The day Skint came back in the sixth grade, Dinah watched him standing across the playground where the other kids were choosing up sides for capture the flag. It was recess. She had been too shy to say hello to him in the middle of class. Besides, he hadn't looked like he recognized her at all.

Dinah crossed the yard.

"Hello," she said. It was so cold that winter day her nostrils felt like she was breathing through a bird's nest. She was warm enough on top because of her enormous coat, but her lower half was freezing. She only had on her skirt with tights that were too thin. "Do you remember me?" she asked.

The game started, and the kids scattered across the field. The Vole grabbed at Sue's hood and she turned, shrieking, and slapped him. Skint looked at Dinah, head tipped back.

"From before," said Dinah. "The play yard at the church. Your dad."

Skint narrowed his eyes.

"Dinah," he said finally. "From when we were five."

His breath was kind of smelly.

"Yes," said Dinah, and smiled. "Welcome back. How are you?"

Above them the evergreen kings looked down, quiet in their robes. Laley snuck up to free the Vole from the other team's prison. But Harlan diverted her, and she ran away, shrieking, leaving the Vole to languish.

"I'm fine." Skint glanced at the top of Dinah's head. "Where are Birdie and Flint?"

Dinah laughed. She forgot about how she used to have ponytails with names. "Gone," she said, tipping her head down so he could see all she had now was just hair.

"That's too bad."

"It is," Dinah agreed. "I miss them."

From the playing field came more shrieking: the Vole washing Laley's face with snow. Laley smacked him, hard, but he put his arm around her, and she allowed herself to be led back into the game.

Dinah reached into her pocket and took out three agate stones and a feather. "These are from the churchyard, actually," she said, presenting them on her palm. "Remember, how we played games with things like this?"

"Yes," said Skint. "We played they were magic."

"Here." Dinah handed him the stones. "For a present, because of you being back."

Skint smiled at her, then laughed. "Wouldn't you rather put them on my shoes?"

Dinah laughed, too, although she didn't really know what he was talking about.

"Let's make the stones be different now," said Dinah.

"Yes," Skint agreed. "Let's make them be talismans. Sacred objects. We'll be priestlings in service of kings."

Dinah's heart rushed as if it were full of petals unfurling. Behind her the wind gathered snow up in a whirl until it rose from the ground like a cloud, like blossoms unfalling from trees.

FIFTY-FOUR

Dinah's mother, back from Ellen's, hastens out of the Beaches' elderly car and hurries up to them on the stoop.

"The police just called Ellen," she says. Her lips are pale, her eyelids puffed and heavy. "A woman near Winthrop told them she saw a boy matching Skint's description out there. A boy riding a bike!"

"Thank God!" cries Mr. Beach.

Dinah's heart threatens to jump from her chest. "I told you!" she shouts, jumping up. "He does that! He does that all the time! He rides when he's upset! Do they have him? Is he home?"

Beagie wakes and cries.

"Shhh, darling." Mr. Beach cuddles him. He takes Dinah's hand.

Her mother shakes her head slowly. "No, honey. I'm sorry. Not yet. They don't."

Dinah's heart falls. But at least he's alive. He's riding. She grabs her hand out of her father's and takes Beagie up and squeezes him.

"There's another piece to it, though." Behind Dinah's mother a chickadee flies toward the Harps' house next door.

"What, darling?" says Mr. Beach.

Mrs. Beach hesitates. Then: "According to this woman," she says, "the boy she saw on the bike wasn't alone. There was a smaller child with him, too. Riding on the handlebars."

Both of Dinah's parents are looking at her. Her mother bites her lip.

Dinah hands Beagie back to her father and goes swiftly inside and up to her room.

FIFTY-FIVE

It's a different policeman this time. The other half of the Aile Quarry police force: Officer Craig, with ecru teeth. The Beaches are all in the kitchen. Dinah is standing braced against the fridge, Beagie balancing himself on her feet. *Be wary, Dinah Beach. Be wary, cagey, and alert.*

"I know you're upset, Dinah," says Officer Craig. "Everybody is. We are, your parents. Skint's mother, Ms. Dugan. K. T.'s family too. You know K. T.'s older brother, Avery, pretty well, I imagine? You all arc in the same grade?"

Dinah nods.

"All of us know the family from church," Mr. Beach tells the policeman. "Ken Vaar sings in my choir."

The policeman nods. "The older son is pretty cut up about the whole thing," he says. "Don't think I've ever seen a kid cry so hard."

The Vole? Dinah holds tight to Beagie's hands. Beagie screeches and strains forward, arching his back.

"Do you know any reason why your friend and K. T. might be together, Dinah?" asks Officer Craig. "Any reason Skint might have the boy with him?"

"You are just assuming it was Skint and K. T. on that bike!" Dinah shouts. "It could have been any old body!"

"The description sounds like him, though, don't you agree? And his bike is no longer over at Ms. Dugan's."

"So what?"

"Dinah, don't be rude," Mr. Beach admonishes her.

"His bike was only out on her porch," Dinah points out. "Somebody could have taken it. Or maybe he put it away somewhere, out of the weather!"

"Is that likely?" the policeman asks gently. "Would that be typical of Skint?"

"Yes! Skint takes excellent care of his bike."

The officer nods and says nothing.

"Skint cares about K. T.!" Dinah cries. "He would never—we think K. T.'s a wonderful kid!" *Why don't you just go out there and find them, then, if you already think*

Skint is guilty? For God's sake, why don't you start helping for once?

Mr. Beach crosses the kitchen swiftly toward Dinah, who swoops Beagie up and holds him like a shield to repel her father. Beagie roars in protest.

"Officer—" Mr. Beach begins.

"I didn't mean to upset you, Dinah," says Officer Craig. "I'm sorry if I did. In fact, I had another reason for coming by. There's some good news to tell you, too." The policeman leans against the countertop. "Ken Vaar got a call a few minutes ago from his ex. She says there was a knock at her door not long ago, and when she opened it, there was her son standing there, right as rain."

Mrs. Beach bursts into tears. "Thank God!" she cries.

Mr. Beach puts his arms around his wife, then reaches out a hand toward Dinah, who does not take it. Beagie wails.

"Why didn't you say so!" Dinah cries, sick with relief. "I told you!" Idiot policeman! He didn't tell her so he could manipulate her the whole time, try to get her to implicate Skint.

Beagie starts to cry and her mother comes and takes him from Dinah's arms.

"Skint, too?" Mr. Beach asks the policeman. "Was Skint there too?"

"No," says the officer. "He wasn't."

The kitchen is silent.

"We're still looking for him," says the officer. "We want to be sure he's safe, of course. And we'd like to ask him about this . . . this event with the younger boy."

"But why? K. T. is fine!" says Dinah. "Why do you need to question Skint?"

The policeman rubs the back of his head with his hand. "You can't just take a child without telling his parents, Dinah." He takes his hand down and looks at her. "Even if you bring him back."

"You still don't know it was Skint," says Dinah. "You don't know."

But she knows it's useless to say that. Of course they know, or they will as soon as K. T. tells them how he got to his mom's.

Her dad is clearly thinking the same thing. "What does K. T. say?" he asks.

"Well," says Officer Craig. He clears his throat. "We did ask the little boy about Skint. He says he likes him a lot. We asked him how he got to his mom's . . ." The officer rubs the back of his head. "All he'll say is, 'I flew.'"

FIFTY-SIX

Four days pass. No Skint. No news. Dinah has barely slept.

"Eat something, Dinah," her mother pleads, but Dinah can't eat, either. She can't sleep or eat or breathe. Even crocheting is impossible. Her brain is a hollow, hurting thing, overloud in her head and clanging. K. T. didn't rat out Skint, but it doesn't matter. Skint's still gone, on the run, a felon on the lam. The police are still after him, and it can only end in awful if he comes back, with courts, with trouble, with the law. She has called and texted him one hundred times, only to hear that he never even took his phone. It is still at Ms. Dugan's.

There is no Skint anywhere, no Skint at all. There is nothing left to bring him back to her. Nothing left at all.

Saturday is church-cleaning day again, but Dinah can't do it. So her father goes in and does the job, alone. That night is Mr. Beach's Evensong and the Friendly as well, but there is no way Dinah can manage those, either. The Friendly would be unbearable enough, but the church will be full of Vaars and Chathams and all manner of people for the Evensong, all of them looking sympathetic, every one of them with something to say. If not to her, then to one another, stealing glances at Dinah, and Dinah cannot bear to see Skint discussed.

"I'll stay with you," says her mother.

"No," says Dinah. "I want to be by myself. Besides, Dad will be devastated if you don't go. I'll be fine here alone."

Her mother doesn't insist. But she pokes her head in Dinah's room again as the rest of the family is getting ready to go. "Come, Dinah, please. There's no use staying here all alone."

Mr. Beach's head appears in the doorway above her mother's. "I need you!" he cries. "To witness the carnage and rub my temples when it's done."

No no no. What if tonight is the night Skint comes

back? What if he comes to see her and she's not there?

He's not coming. The thought is immediate, and Dinah knows it is true. It won't happen. Her worry is just her wish in disguise.

"Dinah, please," says her mother. "Please."

Outside it's already dark and purple, the house extra creaky and cold. The thought of being all alone is suddenly a tiny bit more horrible than not being alone.

Dinah hesitates. Then: "Fine," she says. "Fine." Feeling desiccated and thin, she gets herself dressed and goes.

She doesn't go into the church with her parents, though. She waits in the car with Beagie until she is certain all of the attendees are inside and seated. Then she totes Beagie in and settles with him in the foyer amongst the coffee urns and refreshments. The door to the nave is open a bit, so she'll be able to hear the singing when it starts.

Dinah opens Beagie's little satchel of toys and he burrows about inside.

"Do you want your horse?" asks Dinah, handing it to him.

But Beagie shakes his head and flings the horse to the ground. In the nave the choir begins to sing.

"When David heard . . ."

"Dis!" Beagie cries, and thrusts two playing cards

at her: a king of spades and a card with two quacking ducks on it from a counting game.

". . . that Absalom was slain . . . he went up to his chamber over the gate and wept . . ."

Beagie takes the cards back from her and slaps them energetically together. Dinah stands up quietly and moves toward the doors to the nave. There is her father, shoulders working, and the tiny choir, looking earnest. Dinah catches sight of Mr. Vaar and moves so that he can't see her through the space between the doors.

". . . Absalom, oh, Absalom . . ."

Inside the nave Mr. Vaar's voice rises and falls, notes trickling and shuddering like breath catching in a throat.

Dinah feels eyes on her from the back row. K. T., next to his brother, his body swiveled round to see her. They look at one another solemnly.

". . . would God I had died for thee . . ."

K. T. disappears, ducking out of sight behind the pew. But then he springs up again, clutching his blue Super Ball. He smiles at her, and waves. It's an odd, hook-fingered wave because he has to hang on to the ball. Dinah smiles back at him, blinking.

The Vole tugs at K. T. and he turns back around. Dinah steps quickly back into the foyer and picks up Beagie, who squawks in protest. She hugs him and hugs him.

FIFTY-SEVEN

School starts up again on Monday. Dinah can't not go; they'd never let her just stay home. But being in school is unbearable. All these hours of being here, all these minutes, all this alone. No Skint-studded classes with jokes and light punching. No skipping or springing him from the Pit. The teachers are all solicitous to her and extra kind, and the other kids are, too; their glances are sympathetic, and more of them say hello to her than usual. But talk about people looking, talk about being the subject of conversation. Dinah feels skinless, scraped raw.

"Sit with us, Dinah," Laley offers at lunch. But Dinah

can't. She shakes her head no and heads to her usual table in the back of the room, where she sits with her tray of lunch and stares out the window in the din.

There is a tremendous crashing of legs beside her. The Vole climbs over the bench and untangles himself down.

"Hey," he says.

He arranges four desserts in a row above his slices of pizza. "Sign of your friend?" he asks.

Dinah shakes her head no. The Vole nods and fits half of a pizza slice in his mouth. Outside the window, groups of kids are clustered, slapping and laughing around.

Dinah clears her throat. "How is K. T.?" she asks.

"Good," the Vole answers, through cheese. "He's a punk. Stuck babysitting him half the time." He chews. "Talks about your friend a lot."

Dinah looks at him warily.

The Vole looks at her back and swallows. "Says he likes him. Says he was good at playing space guy." The Vole smiles. "Eat your pizza, Dinah-won't-you-blow-me," he says. Then: "Sorry! Sorry! Excuse my mouth. Habit." He grins.

"That's okay," says Dinah.

The Vole finishes his first slice and picks up another.

Dinah crumbles an edge of her pizza. "Do you want me to watch K. T. for you sometimes?" she asks. "I could play with him and take him places for you and stuff."

"That'd be rad," says the Vole through a gulp of Coke. "You can be the one to trip over all his goddamned action figures."

Dinah nods and turns back to the window.

On her way home she passes the Rural Routes' house. Only Mr. Rural Route is out, sitting in the lady Rural Route's chair, a striped beanie on his head. Dinah waves. One hand up, bent at the elbow. Mr. Rural Route raises his hand back.

A few days later, Dinah watches from her window as her mother struggles out of the car with her arms full of bags and walks unevenly up the steps to the kitchen door. Mr. Beach meets her halfway to help. Mrs. Beach has been spending time with Ellen every day after work. She also arranged for counseling for her and listens to her a lot, too. Ms. Dugan has been helping as well. They both spend nights over there, sometimes, so Ellen won't be so alone.

Ellen. Dinah can't even think about her. She can't think about anything but Skint.

Her mother looks exhausted, even from here, hair flying every which way and her features blurred.

My mother is extremely nice, Dinah thinks suddenly. *She is.* Dinah gets up and lies down on her bed, crossways, hair hanging down.

It's too much. Too much. *Skint. My mom. People all by*

themselves and sick, or sad; people alone and gone. Dinah can't bear it.

Be better, she tells herself. *Be better be better be better.*

Her window is loose in its frame, and it rattles. Air drafts cool across her cheeks.

Dinah sits up. Then she leaps off of her bed and tears out of her room and down the stairs.

"Mrs. Beach," she cries, careering into the kitchen. "Will you take me to Augusta, please? Tomorrow?"

FIFTY-EIGHT

The entryway by the reception desk is bright and calm, not the draconian gray Dinah imagined. It's very clean.

"Room 205," the woman at the desk tells her. "Up one flight, directly over the entryway where you came in, if you can picture where that would be."

"Thank you," says Dinah.

Up, up, up.

Here it is. 205.

Mr. Gilbert is in one of the chairs drawn up by the window. Dinah is relieved to see he is in his regular clothes and not some kind of nightie.

He sees her in the doorway and smiles. "Hello, young lady," he says. "And who might you be?"

"I'm Dinah," says Dinah.

"Thomas Gilbert. Please, come in. Sit down."

Dinah crosses the room and sits carefully in the chair beside him. Together they look out the window. Heavy snow falling; already the lawn is covered.

"Skint," says Dinah, or tries to, but her voice is too thick, crushed under the weight of the word and she can't get it all the way out.

"My son," says Mr. Gilbert.

Dinah nods.

"My son," says Mr. Gilbert again. "My son." His eyes fill with tears. Dinah's cheeks chump up with not crying.

"My baby son." Mr. Gilbert's voice is splintered and full of water. "My gorgeous baby boy."

Dinah has no right to cry, but she can't help all these tears coming when Mr. Gilbert is crying, too. His reflection in the window buckles and waves.

Mr. Gilbert holds out his hand and she takes it. His hand bones are thin and hollow, like quills, like air.

"Have you seen him yet?" he weeps. "He's the most beautiful infant in the world."

Dinah's head is bowed and tears are streaming down her cheeks. She can't bear to look at Skint's dad.

"My father will never see him," Mr. Gilbert cries.

"I'm sorry, Mr. Gilbert. I'm sorry."

Skint's father is still holding her hand. Then she feels his other hand alight on her hair.

"There's a Dinah who plays in the churchyard," he says, his voice changed. "A tiny little girl with petals, flying."

Dinah looks up at him. "I'm her," she says. "That Dinah is me."

"No," Mr. Gilbert corrects her gently. "Dinah is just a little girl. She plays with my son. He loves her."

"He doesn't anymore," says Dinah. Her voice shatters, breaks. "I drove him away. It's my fault he's gone, Mr. Gilbert; I'm sorry!"

Mr. Gilbert's hand stills on her hair.

"I didn't love him back enough," Dinah sobs. "I didn't love him correctly." She weeps and weeps.

Mr. Gilbert's hand warms on her head, grows substantial, and rests. "My son is lucky," he says. "That little girl's love is in his bones."

Outside, the wind eddies up and the tree branches wave, the snow piled on them falling down. Ermine robes sloughed off, gray and stately kings.

Dinah holds on to Mr. Gilbert and sobs.

Dinah's mother is waiting in the car. It smells of old Beagie snacks and snow.

"How was it?" she asks.

Dinah nods, then sits very still. She twists her fingers

around themselves and concentrates on the cold.

Then she reaches over quickly and puts her arms around her mother's neck. "Thank you, Mrs. Beach," she says into her mother's shoulder. "I'm so sorry, Mom. I'm sorry."

FIFTY-NINE

Two Saturdays later Dinah goes back to cleaning the church. On her way over she sees that the river ice under the bridge has grown uneven and thin. It'll freeze up again, but for now it's patched gray and white, melting and cracking, black water moving underneath.

At the church she starts her cleaning in the nave, sweeping between the pews and down the aisle toward the vestry. The church is cold but not unbearable. She'll have to remember to turn up the heat.

* * *

Last week she went back to the Friendly. "I see you've brought a guest," said Bernadine.

"Yes," said Dinah. "Turn around, K. T. Let me tie this sarong around your waist."

"Not necessary, Dinah Beach. Bring the boy in as he is and find him a chair."

The motions for the pantry project and the first annual Aile Quarry Turkey Supper passed, the members turned their attention to letter-writing. Dinah had done a lot of research.

"Dear Mr. Secretary General," one of the sample letters she had provided to the group began. "The Burmese junta has long oppressed and tortured its monks and nuns . . ."

Dinah set K. T. up with a cupcake and the oversize pencil he'd been clutching when his mother dropped him off at Dinah's house before the meeting. "K. T.?" she whispered under the cover of people working.

"Yes?"

But Dinah didn't know what to ask.

K. T. held up his cupcake. "This is a spaceship for my space guy," he told her, and took a bite. "I just bit him a portal. Only I think I lost him somewhere in this church."

Under Dinah's direction, he began laboriously to write. *Dear Monks, Here are some dollars to help people with. We think you could use them for food.*

* * *

The toilets will be easy today; no choir rehearsal to contend with. Dinah sweeps the rest of the dirt from the aisles into her dustpan and empties it into the garbage bag, then drags the bag down the aisle toward the apse. She remembers Skint's forearms, dragging it outside the other week. Her eyes fill, but she blinks and moves on.

The grooved surfaces of the old wooden posts in the nave look dull, covered in dust and grit. She should clean and oil them. All the woodwork needs cleaning, really; the posts and the wainscoting and the altar trim, too. She'll have to wait until it's warm enough to keep the windows open, though, so the smell of the oil can drift out into the trees. In the meantime she'll dust, starting with the posts.

Skint came back before, when they were eleven. It stands to reason that he will come back again.

Dinah will be walking outside, along the road or under the bridge. The sky will be clear and she'll have a stone in her hand. A skinny figure will slouch down the road toward where she is. She'll know that slouch, that coatless body, those boots and that hectic hair. He will be too far away for her to see his face at first. His head will be down, and she will be waiting, standing at the side of the road in her skirt.

When he does look up and see her, his face will crinkle into smile lines. He'll come meet her by the road and she will link her arm in his.

"The Rural Routes' house is lovely," she'll say. "It would be perfect for us to live in."

"With Mr. Rural Route, of course."

"Yes. And a fire in the grate and cups of tea by the wireless."

"We'll have to practice our porch-standing and waving."

They'll stay still for a minute, until he turns to her and asks, "Where's Handcreature?"

Dinah will make Handcreature rear up and nip at his nose.

"Right here," she'll say. "She's been waiting for you. She missed you so much she can't even say."

But Dinah can't imagine about it anymore right now, because if she does, the weight of the waiting will sink her and she'll believe the opposite will be true.

Dust, dust. The church feels huge; tall; full of air. Up there is where the choir performed. Over there is where her father stood to lead them. Behind her, above, is where the choir sings on Sundays. Dinah used to go up there, too, to stand by Granny when she sang. (Pear-powder smell and an arm around Dinah. "What wondrous love is this! O my soul, o my soul!")

Today Dinah doesn't know that the rest of the school

year will pass and Skint will not return. She doesn't know he will not be back to rejoin the Friendly, or to be her co-sexton, or to help her train Beagie up to be their replacement. She doesn't know any of that. What she does know is that right now she is grateful to be by herself in the church. Because with no one else here, the church smells like music and feels like a lap, like the walls and posts themselves are made of buzzy singing.

And when from death I'm free
I'll sing and joyful be
And through eternity I'll sing on, I'll sing on,
And through eternity I'll sing on.

In her terrible, awful voice, Dinah starts to sing.

Sixty

Skint is on his bike, riding. Between Dinah and night he snuck back for his bike and even though he's sore from spending the night in some shed, the sharp pain of his muscles feels good somehow, or at least better than the no-feeling of the rest of him.

Ahead of him, alone, a tiny figure is walking. Skint stops, hands tight on the handlebars, and stares. Then he jumps back on the pedals and rides hard through the early morning light toward the child, bike gears grinding, frame solid and blue beneath him. The road is crumpled with ice and grit, but he rides steady and straight.

Skint pulls up alongside the little boy, who is puffy in his coat and mittens with the drawn-on eyes. The boy's nose is running, cheeks streaked over his scarf.

"What's up?" Skint asks him, but the boy shakes his head no. Skint can tell he doesn't want to cry again.

Skint waits. So does K.T., standing still, blinking hard.

"Here," says Skint. Straddling his bike, he plants his feet on the road. "Hop on."

"Hunh?" says K.T.

"Up here," says Skint. He lifts K. T. gently up onto the handlebars. "Can you balance okay?" he asks.

K.T. shifts cautiously in place and nods. "Yes," he says.

"Hold on, then," Skint tells him.

"Okay," says K.T. Crusty things in his eye corners, but his face is interested and clear.

"Good," says Skint. "Here we go."

He pushes off, hard. Ancient gears grinding. Air freezing around their cheeks. But Skint knows where he is going. He knows what K.T. deserves.

Winter trees are watching and Skint veers left at the Winthrop fork.

Much later, hours later, he stops in front of a house, green, with a path leading straight to its door.

"Hey!" cries K.T. "It's my mom's!"

"Yep," says Skint, and sets K.T. down on the curb. "She's home. See? Smoke's coming out of the chimney."

K. T. looks up at the roof and Skint rests his hand on K. T.'s head.

"Go on," says Skint. "She'll be happy to see you."

"She will?" asks K.T.

"Of course."

K.T. chews his mitten. He smiles, a little, and wiggles his head out from under Skint's hand.

Hands flapping, he bounces up the path to the door.

Creak crark—

Skint's looking straight ahead, standing on the pedals, pumping his legs as fast as he can. He's sweating, straining, face steaming hot and red.

Dad. Dinah.

Thank God the road is smooth here, because he's blinded, weeping; he can't see for shit.

*

ACKNOWLEDGMENTS

So many people's kindness and help made this book possible! My heartfelt thanks go to Kathi Appelt, Tami Lewis Brown, Ann Cardinal, Allen Kesten, Daphne Kalmar, Jessica Leader, Leda Schubert, and Sarah Sullivan for reading all or parts of this book at various stages of its life, and for providing wise counsel from their monstrously big brains. Extra big thanks to Joe Monti, who read the thing twice, even, each time thoughtfully and with so many helpful observations.

Thanks to Barb Fecteau for letting me borrow her

nemesis. I hope you have a less gross one to borrow next time.

Thank you so much, Jane Gilbert Keith, not only for your wonderful reading, but for thinking up the title! You are the best.

Enormous thanks to Caitlyn Dlouhy, the editor of my dreams. This book is so much better than I could ever have made it without you. I can't express my gratitude enough. Thank you for believing in this book!

More enormous thanks to Carol P., without whom this book could never, ever have been written. Your kind heart made all of it possible. Thank you. I owe you more than I can say.

And finally, thanks to my beloved Tobin, who provided eyeballs for reading and sternums for miserable face-burying at every step of this process. Thank you, thank you, thank you. This book wouldn't exist without you, either.

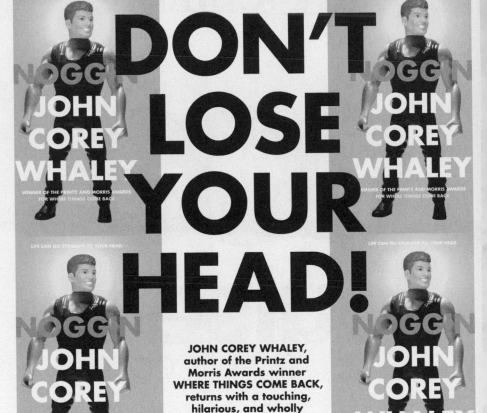

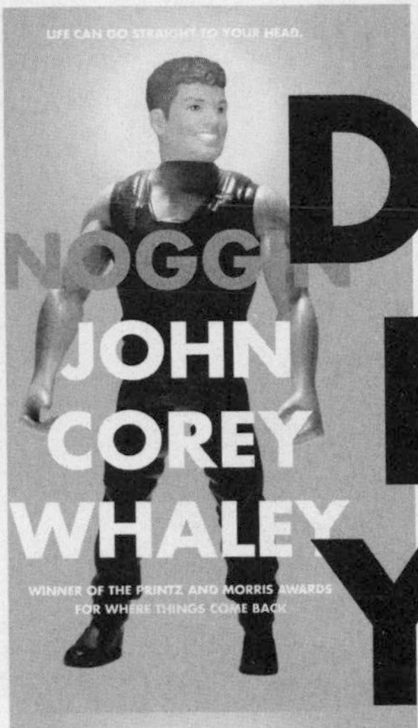

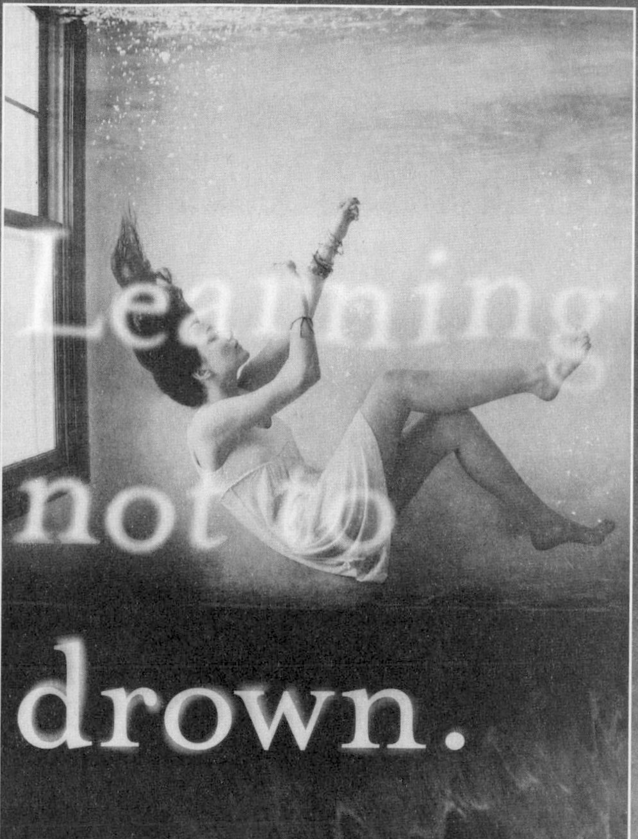
Learning
not to
drown.
A novel by Anna Shinoda.